MALIKI

GUARDIAN DEFENDER SERIES

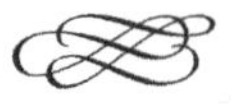

KRIS MICHAELS

❀ Created with Vellum

CHAPTER 1

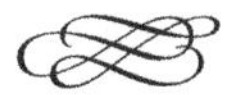

"Why am I seeing this?" Jason King, the CEO of Guardian Security, lifted his eyes to the video screen. His brothers, Jacob, Jared and Joseph, stared back at him through the monitors. He tapped another screen embedded in his desk and opened the attachment to the email his sister Jewell had sent.

"A private investigator, a damn good one, has been digging around Dr. Blue's past. From what Jewell has been able to determine, the investigator is out of Connecticut. He's former CIA and he knows his shit. She's been able to block his searches, but he's persistent and resourceful." Joseph King's voice held a tinge of respect.

"He's looking for Mal? For what purpose?"

"No, he's looking for Harrison M. Boswell, VI."

Jason narrowed his eyes and stared at the screen in front of him. "Who the fuck is that?"

"Maliki—before he walked away from his family."

Jason took off his glasses and rubbed the bridge of his nose. "Fuck, I knew that. Long hours are making me crazy. Sorry. Okay, why is this guy trying to find Harrison M. Boswell, VI?"

"We checked as far as we could without spooking the guy. He's being paid by Mal's mom and, as of now, has only been searching for his whereabouts, no other inquiries." Jared flipped a piece of paper as he spoke.

Jason leaned back and sighed. "If memory serves, he walked away from that life because of a situation at the medical practice his father owns."

"Correct." Jacob leaned forward and lifted his tablet. "According to what we have on record, his father, a surgeon of note, was operating on a patient. The procedure took a bad turn due to his negligence, and the patient died on the table. Rather than admitting his culpability, he blamed the surgeon assisting."

"Who happened to be Mal." Venom dripped

from Joseph's words. "Not an upstanding fucking father-figure if you ask me."

"I didn't ask, but I do agree. If I recall correctly, Mal was eventually cleared when several of the operating room staff came forward, but the professional damage was already done." Jason sighed and leaned forward. "Two options for Mal here, gentlemen. Option one, we tell him what the fuck is going on, let him make the determination to contact his family, or at a minimum, this investigator. Or, option two, at Mal's request, we block this guy. Shut him the fuck down. My vote is for letting Mal deal with his shit his way."

Jared's head snapped up. "What about Stratus? They tried to take him out. If he decides to go home..."

Jason placated his brother, "We're pretty damn sure he's not a target. Essentially, he was low hanging fruit. Stratus has bigger things to worry about now, *but* it is something to consider."

Jacob added, "If he decides to go home, Mal could use his old identity. Stratus isn't looking for Harrison Boswell, VI. It would add a layer of protection."

Joseph nodded. "True. I agree. He needs to know his mother is trying to find him. Let him make the call and support whatever he decides to do. It is the least we can do. That man has been through shit, first with his old team, and then with Stratus. We need to make sure we do right by him."

"We do right by all our people." Jason didn't like the insinuation that Guardian didn't.

Joseph snorted. "Not what I meant. Don't get your boxers in a wad. He's my asset, and I'm being protective. It's what you pay me to do now."

"Fuck, we're paying you?" Jacob's high-pitched question pushed needed levity into the situation. Joseph threw some colorful words in Jacob's direction.

When they'd settled down, Joseph continued, "I agree. This is Mal's life. He decides. We shield him if he doesn't want to be found, or we give him the time, and let him go home to determine what the fuck is going on." Joseph leaned back in his chair.

Jason put his glasses back on. "Concur, but only if you think Ember can handle the workload at The Rose. I don't want any further disclosure on the facility, so bringing in another medical professional is not an option."

Joseph shook his head and gave a humorless laugh. "Ember could handle the caseload in her sleep. She's worked in some of the busiest emergency rooms in the nation. Our dehydration, sprains, pains, and minor boo-boos are a cakewalk for her. Those two already do rock-paper-scissors to see who gets to treat the cases we do have."

"Do we need to consider relocating Mal?" Jacob sighed the question.

Joseph drew a breath and released it before he said, "Not until he's ready. We told him The Rose was his. We owe him."

Jacob concurred, "We do."

"True," Jared added.

"Then we have a plan. Joseph, you're on deck. You give the facts to Mal and let him decide what to do. You have the contact number for that private dick. Give it to Mal when you brief him on his options. We'll be available for assistance if he wants to go home. If he wants to shut this guy down, it will be done with emphasis." Jason waited until his brothers acknowledged and signed off before he shut down the video link.

Fuck, would Maliki Blue ever catch a fucking break? The clusterfuck of that situation with Mal's team had been unfortunate and unprecedented. Guardian had done everything right. Every precaution in place had either failed or had been disregarded when the events of that night had unfolded. That failed mission had cost the lives of three team members, and the one person Maliki had been able to bring home alive, well...

Jason shook off the lingering ghosts of his own failed mission. He'd been able, for the most part, to put his past to rest. He prayed Maliki would be able to do the same. Perhaps the man should start with the specters that had nothing to do with Guardian.

"Don't be a fucking wimp, Doc, move your ass! Hustle! Move it!" Dolan yelled at him from his position at the base of the hill.

Fucking son of a bitch. Maliki dug deep and pushed his feet through the shifting sands. Sweat and sand caked his face, hands, and arms. He dropped at the top of the obstacle and shouldered his weapon. Two exhales later, he drew a breath into his lungs and held it. His finger squeezed back. One… two… three. *Fuck, yes!* All three hit inside the ten ring. He shoved the selector back onto 'safe' and launched from his prone position. He sprinted down the man-made berm, pounded across the half mile distance to the finish line, and staggered to a stop.

Hands on his knees, he gulped lungfuls of dry, hot, air before grabbing the liter-sized bottle of water pushed in front of his face.

"Damn fine, for a pansy-ass office worker."

He rolled his eyes up and, in between pants, managed his standard response, "Fuck you."

Joseph laughed and shook his head. "Nah, the wife would get pissed."

"She would, indeed." Maliki managed to straighten, took a swig of the water, and poured half the bottle over his head. They started physical training before the sun came up, but once that bastard broke the horizon, the Arizona desert went nuclear in less time than it took to strike a match. He watched as the next Guardian crested the berm and raced to the finish line. The distant sounds of gunfire were so common since training began, they barely registered.

"Why aren't you on the course?" Mal nodded his head in the direction of the current physical training run. It wasn't like Joseph not to be running the course or manning one of the overwatch positions.

"Had a conference call with Archangel." Joseph

handed him an ice-cold cloth from the freezer by the wall of the building that marked the end of the training run. He draped it over his head. "Fuck, that feels good."

"Ain't even hot yet, Doc." Joseph leaned against the wall.

He watched as others pushed through to the finish and were greeted with water and assessed by the operatives that had finished and a small cadre of trainers. It wasn't in Joseph's character to remain once he'd said his piece, so obviously the man had something else on his mind. Mal cocked his head. "What's up?"

"Got someone looking into your background. It isn't Stratus, so put that to bed."

He froze with the water bottle halfway to his mouth. His eyes snapped to Joseph, waiting for the man to continue.

Joseph shrugged. "Your parents are looking for you."

He used the water as an excuse not to talk and took a long, hard pull from the bottle. He closed his eyes as if that would block the memories Joseph's words unleashed. His father's betrayal had left gaping wounds that still hadn't closed. Hurt had solidified into hatred and that hatred had pushed him into his new life. Even though he'd let those emotions go, the pain still echoed deep inside him.

He recapped the water bottle and swiped the towel through his hair, wiping the sand from his face, neck, arms and hands. He stepped over and placed his M4 on one of the many outdoor cleaning tables. With practiced ease, he removed the magazine, pulled the bolt to the rear—ejecting the 5.56 caliber shell—and placed the live round back into the clip. Joseph moseyed over and leaned against the wooden table, watching as he disassembled his weapon. Upper receiver and lower receiver separated, hand guards snapped off, he removed the bolt assembly group from the upper receiver and systematically took each piece apart, laying it in precise order on the table. He screwed the bore brush onto the end of a long charging handle and shoved the bastard down the barrel of the weapon with a little more force than necessary.

"We can do this one of two ways." Joseph grabbed his bolt assembly and a brush, dabbed some solvent on the tip of the bristles and started cleaning the piece of metal.

Mal glanced at his superior-slash-friend. "Yeah?

We? Interesting. How is Guardian involved with this?"

Joseph's evil chuckle spanned the space between them. "We're involved because you are one of us. Just that simple. If you want to know what the fuck is going on, we got your back. If you want this guy shut down, we'll do it—with emphasis."

"There is nothing from my past that I care to revisit." Mal switched from the bore brush and sent a patch of fabric down the barrel, collecting the loosened sediment.

"I figured." Joseph set the bolt down and picked up the firing pin, giving it the same attention. "Care for some advice?"

He put the barrel of the weapon down and picked up a cloth to wipe the inside of the hand guards. "Fucking sand gets everywhere."

"It does." Joseph reached for the lower receiver, depressed the spring-fed buffer assembly, and popped it out to wipe it off.

The intrusion of his past into his life, such as it was now, sucked. It sucked on so many levels he didn't want to try to understand how much mental damage he was pushing under a rock by not addressing it. His father was a class 'A' bastard. The motherfucker would have ruined him without a second thought. Hell, for over two months, he'd done just that. Until someone was brave enough to talk. He still wondered why that nurse and anesthesiologist decided to come forward and what his father had done to those people in retaliation, because the motherfucker would have taken them down. To top off that shitshow, his fiancée dumped his ass because she couldn't be linked to such scandal. Yeah, the superficial life he'd led was all gloss and no substance. He used what money he'd banked and the trust fund he'd been given by his grandparents to disappear. He'd grieved the loss of his family, of what had been, but he'd moved on. Why the fuck would any of them want to contact him? What could be gained? Nothing.

He watched Joseph wipe away the solvent he'd applied. "What's your advice?"

Joseph looked up at him. "When my old man died, there was shit between us that was unsaid. I'd give almost anything to have a conversation with him. Granted, I don't know your past, and I don't want to know, but think about it before you close the door. You've got time. Here's the number of the private detective looking for you. Maybe he has some answers that will allow you to make a decision." Joseph placed a small piece of paper with a telephone number on it by his weapon.

He reassembled his weapon as Joseph meandered to the next table and spoke to one of the operatives currently cleaning his M4. The guy looked damn familiar for some reason. He watched Joseph and the man he knew from... somewhere. Muscle memory put the weapon together. Lord knows his brain wasn't engaged in the action. He focused long enough to function check the damn thing prior to turning it, and the remainder of his ammo, into the operative who was acting as armorer today. They rotated the duty, and he'd filled a few shifts of issuing and retrieving the weapons. The guy he thought he knew was behind him in line. Mal stepped aside and leaned against the wall.

"Have we met before?" The man was so damn familiar...

"No, don't think so. Dan Collins." The guy extended his hand.

Mal shook it and stopped. "Has anyone ever told you that you look like–"

The guy laughed. "Yeah, I get that all the time. Would I be here covered in sand if I were?"

"Nah, I guess not." Mal shot the shit with the

guy for a few more minutes before he ambled back to the clinic. It wasn't like he was busy. Hell, even if Ember *wasn't* here, he'd be bored to tears. Thank God Joseph let him train with the men going through the advanced team prep. He understood the way Guardian was reorganizing. Teams of two. Compatible units that were in complete synchronization. Lethal and agile, a strike force that could position and act before most teams could set up. Guardian was gearing up for offensive strikes instead of the defensive positioning of the past. The organization, while massive, was adept at making changes. It wasn't encumbered by red tape or shareholders demanding a profit. Guardian answered to one person, the owner, David Xavier, and that man was a certified genius. He wanted to be part of the new structure.

Mal needed to get his ass back to his small home, because until he developed the skills he needed, he was still acting as the training site's doctor. His shoulders lifted when the siren blared signaling the range was now safe. No more live fire today. A small smile tilted the corner of his lips as a little boy ran from the clinic to the outbuildings where Joseph was making the rounds. Every morning it was the same routine, as soon as the siren rang indicating the range was safe, Blake King found his old man. He could remember idolizing his father like that. The smile and warm feelings that Blake's race across the compound elicited died with that thought.

He entered the clinic and checked the work sheets for the day. Some stitches to check and a cast to be removed, along with x-rays. Assuming no one was injured during the training runs, it was going to be slow. Again. He flipped the sheet over. Ah... Tempest was due for his physical today. The man had been making strides in his physical recovery. They were watching his blood work closely. After so much time in such deplorable conditions, his body had paid a hefty price. He'd make sure to talk to Tempest's psychiatrist via video chat today. Dr. Wheeler and he had been coordinating the man's treatment so they didn't inadvertently derail each other's efforts.

The door at the end of the hall opened, and Ember emerged from the underground facility. While there were buildings above ground, only a fraction of what existed could be seen by anyone who accessed the complex. In the barren expanses of Arizona, they were almost self-sufficient. Fruits and vegetables grew in climate-controlled buildings topside. A deep aquifer located below the facility supplied them with water. A small solar array produced abundant energy and below ground, the ventilation systems had four different failsafe measures.

"Did you see Blake?" Ember asked, exasperated.

He lifted his finger and pointed to the door. "He flew out of here the second the live-fire siren went off."

"I swear, that child..." Ember chuckled and checked the board he'd recently perused. "Wow, we're slammed today." Sarcasm filled her words.

"No doubt. I'll do Tempest's physical; you take the stitches and cast."

"Deal. No offense, but I think you should shower." She wrinkled her nose and motioned him away.

"I was heading there. I'll be back in an hour or so."

"I'll try to hold down the fort; might test my limitations." Ember flicked on her computer and sat down.

"You know where to find me if you need me." He chuckled at her grunt and made his way to the back of the hall. He slid the shelving unit to the side and stepped into the elevator, punching the only button on the damn thing. It lowered him into the cavernous belly of The Rose and the spider web of an immense training complex. The center, where he was now, opened into a common area. Here, the operatives ate, chilled, and watched television. Of course, the trainees were responsible for setting up a schedule to take turns in the mess hall feeding the people currently training at the station. To the immediate right were Joseph's offices and those of his staff. He'd declined an office down here. He didn't need one.

The next corridor over were small rooms where detailed training for the advanced operatives happened. Demolitions, archery, knife skills, hand-to-hand combat, chemicals, drone piloting, mechanical triggering, and so many more skilled instructions happened down here and above in the vastness of the desert. Every person who was brought to this facility was an expert at *something*. The students became the teacher when their expertise was on deck to be trained. Each person fed the next. The process was genius, and Joseph King ran the place flawlessly.

The trainees bunked with their new partners in the corridor past that. They were videotaped, *with* their knowledge, and the interactions between the two new partners were dissected and examined. Several pairings had been severed and realigned, and there were two men, that he was aware of, who failed to make the transition into a team. They were singular operatives before being brought to The Rose and they remained singular after being released from training, at least that is what he assumed. He didn't know anything about what happened to the people once they passed the gates of the complex.

The corridor to the left led to staff housing. He was at the end of that hall. He tapped his code into the pad, and the door clicked open. His one bedroom, living room, kitchen and a small office, was sparsely furnished and completely sufficient for his needs. The bathroom was adequate, a shower that he could turn around in, a sink and toilet. Nothing like the grandeur he'd grown up in, but then again, nothing in this life was even vaguely similar to the way he'd lived.

His shower was quick on purpose. Water in the desert was conserved. They preached it and they lived it. He padded to the kitchen wearing nothing. No one ever came to his apartment, and without the code they couldn't get in. He popped the top off his blender and glugged in some orange juice, threw in some blueberries, shoved in two handfuls of kale and a scoop of protein powder. After he pulverized that, he added a cup of ice and spun the blades again. The noise of the blender shattered the silence of his apartment but did nothing to abate the vast void that Joseph's words had opened in his mind.

Out of habit, he poured the drink into a tumbler and rinsed the blender. Staring sightlessly at the green-blue smoothie, he heard his father's baseless accusations again. He closed his eyes against the stop-action flashes of memory. The surgery, the feeling of betrayal not only from his father, but also the compounding heartache from the silence from the operating room staff, spoke volumes. His gut rolled. He set the glass down on the counter. Why were his parents looking for him? His father had severed their relationship, and his mother? Well, she'd done nothing at the time to stop his father's lies. They'd both let him walk away. Hell, they'd pushed him away. Why now? What had changed? He knew his father. There was no way the old man would apologize. An apology was considered an admission of weakness, and weakness wasn't permitted in the Boswell household. His father's strict adherence to his code of conduct had hobbled his family to the point of dysfunction. Only he hadn't realized it until he moved away. Hell, his mother was so far under his father's thumb, she wouldn't contact him and suffer the backlash of his father's anger. No, there was something brewing, something that altered the reality he remembered.

He padded back into the bedroom and fished around in the pockets of his training uniform before stuffing the filthy material into his clothes hamper. He pulled on a pair of boxers. Somehow, calling a man he didn't know while free balling it seemed... awkward. The leather on the couch was cold to his exposed skin, but he settled in and grabbed the land line phone that sat beside him. Cell phones were not authorized at The Rose. Being buried underground shit-canned reception, and the training facility was hidden for a reason.

"Outside line. Authorization code 29847." Mal spoke the words and numbers that the AI needed to hear in order to access a shielded, outside line. There were several clicks before he heard the dial tone he needed. He punched the numbers off the paper into the phone and leaned back, closing his eyes.

"Who is this?" The man's voice was calm and collected.

"Someone who wants to know why you are looking for who I used to be." Maliki wasn't about to make this guy's life easy.

"My connections have hooked me up with software that can ID any caller. At a minimum, I can identify the number you're calling from, and yet, my phone says caller unknown. I'd say Doctor Harrison M. Boswell, VI is working for the government. A very exclusive branch of the government."

Maliki chuckled. "You know what they say about assumptions."

"They make an ass of you and me, but in this case, I'm not assuming."

The confidence from this guy impressed him. Either he was damn good, or he was a cocky son of a bitch, but his parents would only hire the best, so he was hedging his bets to the “damn good” side of that coin. "Indeed. Why are you looking for me?"

"I'm being paid to do it. I must confess, you've confounded me. I've called in several favors, but you've disappeared off the face of the planet. Are you calling from lunar orbit? That's about the only way I wouldn't be able to find you."

"I will tell you that I am currently not on the face of the earth. Will that appease your wounded sense of pride?"

"Holy shit, no. Now I *have* to know where the fuck you are because, damn it, nobody has successfully hidden from me." The guy laughed at his own admission.

"Why are they looking for me? If you took the case, you know the background."

"Don't know why they are looking, and that's the God's honest truth. I was paid to find you and deliver a message."

"Well, I'm here. What do they want?"

"Hold on, I'll open the envelope. I wasn't supposed to open it unless I contacted you."

Maliki rolled his eyes. "Whatever. Rather cloak and dagger of them."

He heard the sound of the man opening an envelope.

"Fuck." The guy cleared his throat.

"Just read it."

"Okay, you asked me to, so here it goes. *Harrison, I am requesting your presence due to a matter of great concern which is causing untoward distress. Please be so kind as to return to assist me in this moment of need. I appreciate the effort this request requires. I am in residence in the Virginia summer house.* It's signed, *Mother.*"

Maliki closed his eyes. "You can tell them you contacted me and read the note to me. Thank you."

"Damn, dude, she spoke to me this way, but..."

"My parents believe in a decorum that is..."

"Archaic?"

Maliki laughed. "Basically." They should have been born in a different time. If his father hadn't tried to ruin him, he might have turned out the same way. Now? He glanced down at the scars that littered his body. Would they even recognize him? If he passed them on the street dressed in his typical jeans and a Henley, no... only because they wouldn't look at him. They wouldn't see him. But that was the thing, wasn't it? They never had actually *seen* him. He drew a breath and finished, "Thanks for the info."

"No problem. Just so you know, someday I'm going to discover where you're at."

He chuckled. "Good luck with that."

The guy spoke as he started to disconnect the call. "Are you going to come back?"

He paused before he responded, "How is that your business?"

"It isn't. I've dispatched my duties. I'm going to

get paid, but they're going to ask. Rather, *she's* going to ask. I've never actually spoken to your old man."

"You haven't missed anything. Believe me."

"I have a strong feeling you're right on that account."

Maliki opened his eyes long enough to put the receiver down and end the call before he closed them again.

His mother wanted him to come home. He recalled the words the private detective had read. *She'd* engaged the private investigator, not his father. She wanted him to come home. That bastard wasn't reaching out, his mother was. He scrubbed his face and ran his fingers through his beard. He wasn't the boy they'd raised. He no longer required his parents. His new family, Guardian, had supported him through shit his parents couldn't imagine or understand. Maybe it was time to close the door to his past, forever.

The air conditioner kicked on with an almost imperceptible hiss of air. He opened his eyes and stared at the tiny apartment he lived in. Not one picture. Not one person from his past, no happy memories, or frozen moments in time. A memory of his and Clarissa's engagement picture placed in a gold frame in his mother's sitting room flashed through his mind. No, those moments that had been saved no longer mattered.

Glancing around his small personal space, he realized he'd been transient since his father pushed him away, and somehow, even that fluid life had been put on pause. He'd felt stuck in a stasis, a holding pattern, and he'd felt that way for a long time now.

Was it time to sever his ties to the past and allow himself to build something permanent? His eyes roamed the tiny space again. Ember could hold the fort here with one hand tied behind her back. Maybe it was time to step away and gain perspective about a lot of things.

Fifteen minutes later, dressed, and firmly committed to his plan, he exited his apartment and headed to Joseph's office. Blake was at his miniature desk, which sat beside his father's larger model. The little guy worked with his head down as he wrote on a piece of paper. Joseph looked up when he stopped in the doorway and lifted a finger, halting any conversation. "Blake, recess time."

The little boy's head popped up and a wide smile split his face. "Can I go play with Liberty?"

"Ask Eve. If she says it's okay, you can, but stay where she can see both of you."

"Okay. Thanks, Daddy. Hey, Doctor Blue."

"Hi, Blake." He waited for the little guy to skip down the hall before he went into the office. "Sorry for interrupting his school time."

"He's homeschooled. He can have a break. What can I do for you?" Joseph tossed a pen onto his desk blotter and leaned back in his chair.

"I'm going to go back."

"Why?"

He blinked and then laughed. "None of your fucking business."

The corner of Joseph's mouth tugged up in an 'almost' smile. "Fair enough. I'm sure you have a year or two of vacation time built up."

"No, I used up everything after..." He let the sentence die. After that night, when his team had been decimated, he'd used all his vacation getting and staying drunk and recovering from yet another epic clusterfuck in his life.

Joseph leaned forward. "Hear my words. You are on paid vacation until you come back."

Mal leaned back and cocked his head. "You realize I don't need money, right?"

"You realize I'm not severing any connection

you have to Guardian in any way, right? We have your back on this. Period."

"So, no other choices, huh? Take paid vacation or stay here?"

"Yep." Joseph picked up his pen. "The next flight from our hanger in Phoenix is the day after tomorrow. Will that work for you, or do I need to get transport in place sooner?"

"Where is the flight going?"

"D.C."

"Close enough."

"Are you returning as Maliki or Harrison?"

"Harrison no longer exists. I'm going as myself."

"Then you need to be cognizant of your exposure. Stratus isn't considered a threat against you, but if your name hits some computer system, they could tweak to your location."

"I'm not worried about Stratus. They got the drop on me once. They won't again."

"I know they won't get the drop on you again. I've seen you fight. You're elite, but I'll call Jewell if you think there is a chance you've been exposed. She can sanitize the systems."

"Noted."

"Good."

He got up to leave, but Joseph stopped him

when he stood. "If it becomes a shitshow back there and you need help, you pick up that phone and call. This may not be an op, but damn it, we'll do whatever it takes. *I'll* do whatever it takes."

Maliki reached his hand to his brother, and they clasped palms. "As long as it takes, my friend."

CHAPTER 2

The drive from the D.C. airfield through the rolling hills in Virginia should have been pleasant. As the sun was setting, the expanses of greens that folded between the tree lined hills gave glimpses of access roads. Roads that were lined with a variety of fences. The closer he got to his parents' country home, the more elaborate the fences that lined the driveways became. He slowed his Guardian SUV as he approached the turn to his childhood home. Red brick columns supported cross hatched wooden rails, which were, as always, painted a pristine white. Gas lighting illuminated the roadway to the closed gate. Hand sculpted bronze horses, rearing ten feet tall, stood as sentinels on either side of the closed, wrought-iron gates, and they were elevated by the ten-foot-high brick platforms under them. The ornate 'HMB' that weaved through the gate's iron lace branded the home. His father's initials, and once upon a time, his.

He slowed the vehicle to a stop and stared down the blacktop drive. About two miles up that road stood over nine thousand square feet of mansion. Seven bedrooms, eleven bathrooms and a partridge in a fucking pear tree. He glanced at his watch. 8:00 p.m. He was fucking hungry, had a headache, and really didn't want to deal with the shitshow that would inevitably ensue when he punched his code into that keypad. Hell, his code might not even work anymore. He'd be reduced to calling the staff to gain access. Whatever.

Putting his foot down on the accelerator, he pointed the truck to the nearest small town, Paintville. The town had been a blip in the road when he was last here. Of course, that was because after graduating from high school, he rarely ventured past the summer residence. It had been many years since he'd driven this direction. Not surprisingly, the small town had grown. He slowed and took in the changes. A new hotel was off the road to the right. That took care of a place to stay.

He parked the SUV. Exiting, he stretched his back and rolled his shoulders before he locked his ride and entered the establishment.

"Hi, Welcome to the Paintville Inn, my name is Paul. Do you have a reservation?" The perky guy behind the counter pounced as soon as Mal opened the door.

"No, no reservation. Do you have any rooms available?"

"We have a few. How long will you be staying?" The young man started clicking on the keys of the inn's computer system. "I'll need an ID, and a form of payment, please."

"If you can arrange it, I'd like a room for the week." He wouldn't be staying with his parents, that was for damn sure. Mal retrieved his wallet and dropped his black Visa on the counter with his ID. The card was registered to a fictitious business so he wouldn't ping in any systems when he paid. He'd set that up when he joined the Air Force. The bank account attached to the card was in Grand Cayman. No one could tie it to him or to his past.

"Excellent. Thank you, Mr. Blue." The young man handed back Mal's ID then grabbed two plastic card blanks and shoved them into the key maker.

"Can you tell me if there is anything open this time of night where I can get a meal and maybe a drink?"

The guy glanced up at the clock on the wall and narrowed his eyes. "Well, there's the typical fast food. If you want a sit-down meal, there's Carmichael's, a diner down the road. Great pies. They may be closing soon. If you want a good steak and a drink, there's Shorty's. It's on the edge of town, but it's been known to get rowdy sometimes."

"Rowdy?" Mal had to ask, because there was nothing in his memory that ever disturbed the quiet of the very affluent area.

"Yes, sir. It is frequented by some of the blue-collar workers in the area."

"Is the area building up?"

"No, not really. Our community exists to support some of the estates around here. Most of the staff members for those residences live here. We have a couple construction companies that are employed year-round, what with building and upgrading and such. I'd ask if you were looking for a job, but..." The clerk lifted the black credit card from where he'd placed it and swiped it through the point of sale terminal.

"Thanks, and no, I'm not looking for a job. It was nice meeting you, Paul." He took his card and the keycard for his room and headed back to the truck. He wanted a drink, to unwind from the day, and to eat a steak the size of his head.

Mal glanced up at the sign as he parked. It appeared that Shorty's was now “orty's”. The neon pink sign had been damaged and half of it no longer worked. A mix of old trucks, older cars, and a few motorcycles filled the small gravel lot outside the pub. He parked the SUV and locked it, pocketing the key fob. He could smell the deliciousness of grilled meat as he opened the door. A massive wood bar stretched down the entire side of the building. There were pool tables, big screen TVs and dartboards scattered through the place. Several groups had formed around the tables, so he headed for the bar.

"What can I get you?" A coaster landed in front of him as soon as his ass hit the stool.

"Domestic draft. Don't care what kind. Can I look at a menu?" Mal glanced at the man behind the bar.

"Menu is up there." He pointed to a chalk board above the bottles of liquor and turned to pull him a draft. Simple enough. There were about ten options, five of which were bar food, five were steaks.

A tall, frosty glass with a perfectly poured beer landed in front of him. "See anything you like?"

"The ribeye. Medium rare."

"Good stuff. I'll let the wife know. Holler if you want that refilled."

Mal didn't respond because the man had already turned and headed to what he assumed was the kitchen. He took a sip of the beer and damn near groaned. There was no alcohol at The Rose, and that was decreed with a purpose in mind. The focus for personnel was on physical training and learning new techniques and methodology of warfare while blending two people into a cohesive team, not socializing. It had been... well, since he'd flown to D.C. last summer… since he'd had an adult beverage. That trip had had an exciting ending and brought both Thanatos and Tempest to The Rose.

He put the glass down as he heard, "... no shit, they found another dead girl."

"Fuck, no way? Who? Are they from around here?" The conversation between two men a few seats down drew and held his attention, but he kept his eyes focused on his drink.

"Dunno. That makes three in like the last year, yeah?"

"Something like that. Yeah, three. There was that first girl, the one that everyone said was an OD. She was from, like, two towns over. Someone said she was a tweaker."

"Then that college kid. Did they say how she died?"

"Not that I heard. The upper crust keeping that shit on the downlow, yah know."

"She wasn't from one of them families."

"Nah, but I heard her people work for one of 'em."

"So this one?"

"Man, I dunno."

"Fuck, she wasn't, like, mistreated, was she?"

"Like I said, I dunno. Curt didn't say."

"This used to be a safe place to live."

"Used to be. Too easy to get drugs now."

"Right? Pills. I mean, when we were growing up, man, it was weed. Nothing addictive."

Mal rolled his eyes at that comment, taking another drink of his beer.

"My cousin Masey was caught up in that stuff. She got hooked on that Oxy. Said it was easy to get."

"Damn doctors overprescribing is what is hooking people on that shit."

Mal gave a mental shrug. There might be some culpability within the medical field. He'd give the local that point.

The bartender appeared in front of him. "Haven't seen you around before. Are you new to the area?"

"Nah, grew up around here." Mal drained his glass and nodded when the bartender offered him another.

"Yeah? I've lived here for almost thirty years. Where did you go to school?" The man was probably Mal's age.

"Europe."

"Ah..." The man nodded and crossed his arms over his chest. A suspicious look crossed his face. "Slumming it?"

Surprised at the comment, the snort of laughter that emerged was honest. "Nah, I walked away from that life and joined the Air Force, pararescue."

"What's that?"

Mal thought about his response for a moment. "Pararescue airmen are the Air Force's elite. We performed rescue operations for troops that were in need of medical assistance no matter where they were located, no matter the branch of service."

"No shit? Wow. You don't usually hear that type of thing from the Royals."

"Royals?" Mal chuckled and shook his head. Yeah that was an apt description of his parents and their friends in the area.

"Meh... it's what we call them here in town. Didn't take you for one of them. You got the look of hard work around you. They usually don't. You know those office-worker types."

Joseph's constant taunt flashed through his mind, and he smiled. "I know the type."

"What brings you back?"

Mal didn't answer, instead his attention shifted as a woman brought a platter from the kitchen. His steak was the size of a hub cap, but damn he was going to do his best to finish the thing. "Thank you."

The lady smiled. "Enjoy." She lifted on her toes and the bartender gave her a quick kiss before she spun and headed back into the kitchen area.

"Damn, this looks fantastic."

"My wife, Jennie, is a good cook. I'm Daryl Cochran." The man extended his hand. "I own this place."

He reached over his food and shook the man's hand. "Maliki Blue."

Daryl tilted his head. "Blue?" He shook his head. "I know most of the families around here, don't know any Blues."

Mal cut into his steak and lifted his fork to his mouth. "When I left the life, I left the name."

"Damn, clean break, huh? Well, good on you. Seriously. I've never heard of anyone walking away from a silver spoon." Daryl used a towel and polished the bar in front of where he stood. A man down the bar lifted his glass and the bartender responded, leaving him alone. The steak was cooked to perfection. He basically ignored the baked potato and green beans and feasted on the grilled goodness.

"Another?" Daryl strolled over to him, pointing at his empty glass.

"No, two is the limit. How about some club soda?"

"Coming up." Daryl produced a large glass and filled it with ice then hit it with the soda.

"How long you plan on staying in the area?"

"I don't. In for a command performance and then back home."

"Where's home?"

Mal chuckled, the guy should be an interrogator. "Lots of places, but most recently Nevada." He wasn't going to peg his location for anyone. The Rose was off limits, so Nevada was as close as he'd acknowledge.

"Yeah? Hot there, ain't it?"

"So hot you could broil the devil's balls on the sidewalk."

Daryl barked a laugh and shook his head. "Too bad you ain't sticking around, you're all right."

Mal drank his soda water and leaned to the side reaching for his wallet. "What do I owe you?"

"With the beers, it comes to thirty-two dollars."

Mal retrieved two twenties and dropped them onto the counter. "Thanks for the food and the conversation."

"Come on back if your command performance gets extended."

"Will do." He hit the door and headed to his SUV. His boots crunched the gravel under his feet, but he pulled up short. Gooseflesh formed on his arms. What was it? A sound? What had he heard? He canted his head and listened. A low moan. Sprinting toward the sound he did an immediate assessment of the area. Fuck, he wasn't packing. He slowed his approach and scanned the area. There. A body, near the trees. Another quick scan. Fuck it. He had to go in. Keeping low he crossed the open area and kneeled down near the person.

A woman. Fuck, she'd been shot. Gut shot. The woman, hell, the girl, moaned.

"Hey, it's okay. I'm a doctor. I'm going to get us some help. You stay with me, yeah?"

He grabbed his phone and hit his emergency contact number, keying the speakerphone, which he dropped beside the shooting victim.

"Operator Two Seven Four."

Mal ripped the woman's shirt open to expose the wound, leaving her bra on to cover her. "Thorn Operative 6. I have an emergency at my location. I need ambulance and police response, gunshot wound." He lifted her shirt. Two entry wounds. Low. Whoever did this meant for the woman to suffer. She moaned again.

"Affirmative. Standby."

"Hey, can you hear me? What's your name?" No answer. There was no compromise to the woman's airway, and she was still breathing. Assessing circulation, Mal tore off his Henley and wrapped it as tight as he could around the woman's wounds. Although there wasn't a lot of blood loss, the swelling of the woman's abdomen wasn't a good sign. Probable internal bleed.

She wasn't coherent. He found a pulse point. Damn it... thready and weak.

"First responders are en route to your location, Thorn Operative. Is there need for sanitation?" The operator's voice was steady, and given the stress of the volatile situation, he appreciated the professionalism.

"There will be law enforcement involvement. I found the victim when leaving a local establishment. Advise Thorn Operative One. He'll ensure protocols are followed."

"Affirmative. Your responders are two minutes away," the woman informed him as the shrill wail of a siren pierced the silence. "I hear them. Make that call."

"I have already sent notification to Thorn Operative One. I'll stay on the line until you have emergency responders on scene, or you clear me."

"Roger that." He checked for a pulse. "Fuck. Guardian, I have no pulse. Initiating CPR."

"Affirmative. Time now is 21:23."

A mental count started. Thirty compressions, at least two inches in depth and two breaths. Thirty compressions, two breaths. Thirty compressions, two breaths. Mal wasn't aware of responding personnel making their way to him until he saw the paramedic kit drop beside his victim. A face appeared across from him. "How long have you been doing compressions?"

"Guardian, time!"

"23:24. CPR time elapsed two minutes, one second." The operator responded.

"Can you continue while we prep to take over?"

"I've got it." Mal continued counting and breathing for the girl, checking for a pulse when he performed the rescue breathing.

"Ready to transfer, sir, on the next breath."

Mal nodded, sweat dripped from his brow as he pushed in that one-hundred compression per minute beat that he'd learned so fucking well. He counted out loud, and at thirty, he moved and the medics took over.

"Excuse me, sir. We'll need to talk with you when you..." The female voice behind him irritated him.

Without looking at who he spoke to, he snarled, "Fuck off." Turning to the medics he stated, "I'm a doctor. I'll relieve you if you need it."

The paramedic doing the compressions acknowledged him before he stopped, and the other gave two rescue breaths and felt for a pulse. He held up a hand. "We have a pulse. It's weak, but it's there. We need to move. Now. Doc, pull up that gurney, will yah?"

He assisted the crew in getting the woman onto the gurney and followed them as they loaded her up. "Shauna? Is that Shauna? God, no! Please, No!"

Mal spun as Daryl Cochran pushed through the crowd. A uniformed officer stopped Daryl and asked, "Do you know her, sir?"

"That's my daughter! Oh God, that's my girl. Sam! Get Jennie, someone go get Jennie and take her to the hospital." Daryl jumped into the ambulance before the back doors slammed shut. Mal stood and watched as the ambulance tore from the parking lot.

He turned and looked at the litter the ambulance crew had left behind and leaned down to grab his phone. He thumbed the face and took it off speaker, putting it to his ear. "You still there?"

"Affirmative."

"Thank you for the assist."

"Whatever it takes, Thorn Operative Six."

"As long as it takes and seriously, thank you."

He hit the disconnect button and pocketed his phone.

"Sir, we still need to talk to you."

Maliki rolled his shoulders. *Fuck, the local yokels.* He turned around and came face to face with a woman wearing blue jeans and a badge. She had a nine-mil holstered on her hip and her long red hair gathered into a ponytail. She was tall and strikingly pretty.

"Can you tell me what happened here?"

He put his phone in his back pocket. He'd say what he'd done was pretty rudimentary, but he answered the question, "I performed emergency medical assistance on a person who had sustained two gunshot wounds to the abdomen. She went into cardiac arrest and I initiated CPR. You saw the rest."

"Right, and we appreciate you taking care of her, but I'm going to need a few more details." She smiled, but it didn't reach those big blue eyes. She gave him a slow, assessing, once over, and he did the same.

"Such as?"

"May I see some identification?" The woman extended her hand.

"Sure." Mal retrieved his wallet and handed her his driver's license.

She glanced down at his ID and flicked her

flashlight over the face. "Care to sit down while we do this, Dr... Blue?"

She nodded toward an SUV parked about fifty feet away. He shrugged, and she held onto his license as they walked to the SUV. The driver's door was open so he couldn't see what department she was with, city or county, but the blue laser light bar on the top and the cream and brown colors were indicative of a county cop. Mal walked around the vehicle and approached the other door. Yep. Nailed it. County Sheriff.

She flipped a switch which illuminated the cab of the vehicle and positioned her computer closer to her using the extendable mount on the center counsel. "So, Dr. Blue, would you please tell me what transpired tonight, pertaining to your involvement in the situation behind Shorty's?"

"I exited the establishment after having dinner at approximately 21:20 this evening. On my way to my vehicle I heard... something. I'm not sure what it was, but I stopped and listened. That is when I heard what I believed to be a person in distress. I approached the scene, determined a safe avenue to the downed person, assessed the threats to the best of my ability, and made the decision to move forward. At that point I made contact with a young female with two GSWs to the lower abdomen. I called my office and had them contact first responders as I provided emergency aid. When the victim stopped breathing and had no pulse, I initiated one person CPR until first responders relieved me of the responsibility."

The woman blinked and tipped her head. Her high cheekbones and light dusting of freckles were accentuated by the interior light. A furrow buried itself between her light blue eyes. "You're a *doctor*?"

Maliki nodded, giving her nothing more.

"Right... okay. But help me with this if you would. You stated you were going to your *vehicle, you determined an avenue to the downed person,* and what did you say... *you assessed the threats*? That is not common doctor speak, sir."

"Where I work, it is."

"And where exactly do you work, sir?"

"I'm employed by Guardian Security."

"As?"

"I'm sorry, I don't understand the question." Maliki liked how sharp the woman's mind was, but he wasn't volunteering anything.

"Are you employed as a doctor with Guardian or do you do other work?"

"I'm a doctor."

She lifted her brows. "That's not what I asked you, either."

"Then let me be specific. I'm employed as a doctor with Guardian Security." Which he was. The fact that he was also training with the hopes of becoming an operative had no bearing. None whatsoever, especially since he hadn't informed Joseph of his intent to be part of the program once his skills were where they needed to be.

"Right. Then let's get your statement down. Are you staying in the local area?" She started typing as she talked.

"I'm at the Paintville Inn." He told her the room number.

"What is the purpose of your visit to Paintville, sir?"

"Why?"

She blinked and looked over at him. Her long dark red hair slipped from her back falling over her shoulder. "You were involved in an incident tonight. A violent crime. I will ask any question I find germane to determining what happened. Now, what is the purpose of your visit to Paintville, sir?"

Maliki smiled. Oh, he liked the spunk in this one. She reminded him a bit of Ember. But where

Ember was curves and curls, this woman had an athletic build and her hair was straight and thick, but that fire that burned inside… that was almost exactly like Ember.

"The reason for my visit is not germane to the investigation, in any form, unless you suspect that I was somehow involved in the shooting, which I was not. The girl's father served me dinner, and I visited with him most of the evening. So, my whereabouts from about 20:15 to the time I found his daughter, shot and bleeding, are not in dispute. Considering the severity of the GSWs and the criticality of the victim due to internal bleeding, I would suspect the shooting occurred several minutes prior to me exiting the establishment, and no, neither I nor anyone else heard anything unusual, because if anyone had, I would have responded with assistance sooner. Therefore, based on how quickly everyone inside responded when they heard your sirens, I would assume the assailant used a suppressor of some kind. Now, if you'd like, I will allow a swab of my hands for GSR to confirm I did not fire a weapon." He lifted his hands and shook his head. "Of course, the woman's blood will compromise any swab of my hands. You could test my shirt, which is on the way to the emergency room as a bandage. Or perhaps you'd like my t-shirt?"

Her eyes lowered and traveled over his chest. He flexed his pecs and biceps on purpose, to mess with the cop. He'd bulked like crazy during the last year's physical training. The woman's eyes snapped away, and she shook her head. Damn, it was all he could do not to laugh.

She cleared her throat, "You have some pat answers, Doctor Blue."

"I have the truth, Deputy..."

She lifted her eyebrows. "Senior Deputy Campbell."

Maliki nodded. "Senior Deputy Campbell, if you don't mind, I'm going to go back to my hotel room and clean up. Then I plan on calling the hospital to check on Daryl's girl. Shauna, right?"

"Yeah, Shauna."

"How old is she?"

She sighed and shook her head. “Early twenties."

"So... close to your age." He nodded, pigeon-holing the deputy sheriff firmly in her late twenties.

Her explosion of laughter snapped his attention back to her. "Okay, so you're not as smart as I was starting to believe." When he blinked at her in confusion, she added, "I'm almost thirty-six, Doctor." She waved at the lighting. "I need to invest in vehicle dome lighting, obviously it subtracts years from one's appearance. Before I release you, let's get your statement down. You can swing by the office tomorrow and sign it, and I'll need your contact information, cell phone, office phone, the usual information—"

The radio crackled, "Unit Four, this is County."

Deputy Campbell picked up the mic. "Unit Four."

"Roger, we have a fire alarm at the Ogden estate."

"Roll Hannaford. Tell Granger to stay with the GSW."

"Hannaford is at a major vehicle accident on the other side of the county."

"Fuck." The deputy glanced at him before she lifted the mic again. "En route." She yelled at another deputy who was working the crime scene. "Dobson, I'll be back, caught a fire at the Ogden estate."

The deputy lifted a hand in acknowledgement. Mal exited as the blue lights switched on. She lifted his license. "I'll give this back to you when I see you tomorrow."

Mal chuckled and shook his head as the woman tore from the lot, sending rocks flying over the asphalt when she merged onto the blacktop.

"You need any help?" Mal ambled up to where the deputy was standing, taking photographs of the area where he'd found Shauna.

"No, we got this. Thanks." The man's flashlight strafed the area. He stopped and laid a small yellow triangle with a number on it by a spatter of blood in the rocks beyond the spot Mal had treated the kid. "Make sure you walk that way, okay?" The man pointed back behind him.

"You got it." He made it to his SUV before his phone chirped. He lifted the phone to his ear. "Well that took you longer than anticipated."

"Fuck you, man, I was in the middle of the evening training run." Joseph's voice floated back to him. "Seriously, you're gone not even twenty-four hours, and you're in trouble?"

"Not like that. Stumbled upon a kid that was gut shot."

"Where the fuck was that?"

"Outside a roadhouse tavern where I stopped for dinner in Paintville, Virginia. The kid was the owner's girl. Anyway, the cops now have my name. No doubt they'll eventually run me through the system."

"No doubt. I've called it in. Cyber already has your name tagged as crimson. Anyone trying to find anything about you will run into a brick wall a hundred feet thick."

"Thanks. Sorry to be a pain in the ass already. I'll talk to you later." He lifted himself into the confines of the SUV.

"No worries. Hey, Mal?"

"Yeah?"

"Did the kid make it?"

"I performed CPR on her before first responders arrived. She had a heartbeat when she left."

"I'll get us a status on her. What's her name?"

"Shauna Cochran."

"Roger that. I'll have updates sent to your phone."

"Appreciate it."

"No worries, take it easy up there, doesn't sound like a very safe environment."

Mal turned on the vehicle and leaned back into the bucket seat. "See, that's the thing. This should be nothing more than a bedroom community. Things are... off here."

"What do you mean?"

"Fuck man, I don't know. I've been gone for years, and I never really haunted this place, so... I'm probably tired."

"Then go get some sleep, my man."

"Will do. Give Ember a hug for me."

"Fuck you, I'll hug her for myself." Joseph disconnected the call.

He chuckled and put his phone on the center console before edging out of the parking lot. He needed a shower and eight hours of sleep.

CHAPTER 3

"Hey, Poet? Got a second?"

Deputy Sheriff Poet Campbell stopped two feet away from the break room door. She drew a breath, plastered a smile on her very tired face and turned around. "Yeah, whatcha got?"

"Just an update. Shauna Cochran made it out of surgery early this morning. She's in critical condition, but she's hanging on. Granger has the bullet, and it's been secured as evidence." Faye Burnside, the midnight-shift dispatcher, leaned over the counter as she spoke. The county seat was here in Paintville and their people worked the county's 911 system for fire and police emergencies. They also dispatched for the local ambulance company, which brought in more money and allowed the deputies and dispatchers to be trained in Charlottesville when new classes became available. The Sheriff's Department provided court security, too, but that was work for the junior deputies. She'd done her time on courthouse duty and thankfully only had to enter those boring hallowed halls when she was testifying or getting a warrant. Thank God they didn't have a county jail. She'd heard horror stories from her friends about that detail.

The demographics of Pleasant County showcased the haves and have nots with very few people residing in between the two classes. Pleasant County was the home of citizens who were affluent beyond imagination and the private security employed by the owners of the estates in this county alone could form a small army. Pleasant County was exactly that… pleasant… usually. Unfortunately, something had shifted in the county and the petty crimes they were used to handling had escalated to kids getting capped in the parking lot of their parents' business.

"The sheriff been in yet?"

"Oh, yeah. He isn't a happy camper."

"That's why I'm here. Figured he'd want

answers. We need to talk to Shauna as soon as she regains consciousness."

"Granger said he told the docs and the nurses. He said Daryl and Jennie are holding up as well as can be expected. Anyway, Granger told me to tell you the sheriff is at home now getting some sleep. Said he'd be in about noon."

"Good. I'm expecting a witness to come in this morning. Dr. Maliki Blue. When he shows up, give me a call, please?"

"I'm off shift as of six, but Sharon is on duty. I'll let her know."

Poet glanced at the clock. She'd managed four hours of sleep last night and needed coffee. She opened the break room door, hit the brew button on the coffee pot, and opened the blinds to let in the morning sun. She sauntered back to the coffee pot and poured a cup from the carafe while holding it precariously under the stream of coffee the machine was spitting out.

Drawing a deep breath of the wonderful aroma, she wandered back to the window to look at traffic on the street. Movement to her right caught her attention. A runner. She watched as the man pounded down the highway that split the town in two. Damn, what fantastic form. His strides were even, fluid and fast. She loved to run and admired great form. This guy had it. In spades. His pace was eating up the distance. Fuck, his build was superb. She took a sip of her coffee and admired the man as he came closer. *Dear heavens... look at those legs. Oh, hell, the shoulders. Mmmm hmmm.* If there was a god, that runner was single. *Single and straight. Single, straight and liked redheads.* Wowzers, he was delicious. She blinked as the man came close enough for her to distinguish his facial features. *Well, hello...* That blond hair and full, darker, red-blond beard was one she recognized. Dr. Maliki Blue. *Dayummm.* Yum being the operative word. He was gorgeous. He flew past the office, his form still impeccable, and his pace blistering fast. She shifted as he ran and tracked him as far as she could see. He didn't slow down, so the fly by wasn't for effect. The man was stunning. If she said he wasn't, she'd be lying. He exuded masculinity and confidence. The very things that attracted her to a man and, *that man…* well, he was extremely attractive, even if he had been evasive last night. Why couldn't she find someone like that around here? *Because men like him don't exist in podunk towns like this.*

She chuckled at her wayward thoughts, headed

to the office area, and dropped into her chair. She took a drink of coffee and glanced out the window again. That man could *run*. It had been over fifteen years since she'd separated from the Air Force, but she'd kept up her physical training. Not that the Air Force was as stringent as the other services, but she'd always worked out and the Air Force had cemented the habit. Hell, her Security Forces training had given her a Basic Law Enforcement Officer Standards and Training certificate and she used that to launch into her career as Deputy Sheriff. For her, the service had been a starting point, not a career. This, what she did now, was what she was made to do. She loved dealing with people, working the issues and, yes, even the challenges of the darker side of her business, including three deaths, two of which were still open due to suspicious circumstances, and now a shooting.

Something disturbing was brewing in the county. She could feel it, but she couldn't put her finger on what was going on, and the inability to provide concrete evidence for her belief had caused problems for her at work. She'd tried everything she could to get the sheriff to bring in the big guns from the state crime lab, but because she had no evidence, nothing to go on, he'd denied her requests. Repeatedly. Damn it.

She grabbed her laptop from her bag and docked it at her desk. She had reports to finish, for both the fire she'd responded to and the shooting last night. As senior deputy, she responded to serious calls even when she wasn't on duty, particularly when they happened in her backyard. Taking one more bracing sip of caffeine, she called up the forms she needed and started typing.

"What are your thoughts about the shooting?"

Poet jumped. "Shit, Sheriff, I didn't hear you come in." She drew a calming breath and hit save on her computer.

Sheriff James Watson made a sound somewhere between acknowledgement and disgruntlement. The man was tall, dark, handsome, and single. A much sought-after commodity in the county from what she'd heard, but she didn't find him attractive. His arrogance and superior attitude nudged any physical attributes into the 'nil' column.

He lowered into the chair beside her desk and sipped his coffee. "Your thoughts?"

Poet grabbed her own coffee and drank the ice-cold liquid, scrunching her nose in distaste. "We've had contact with Shauna in the past, nothing major. When she was underage, she attended keggers that we've busted. She's had a couple speeding tickets, but basically, she's not one of the youth we worry about."

"Typical kid shit. What happened? How did she end up behind her dad's place fighting for her life?"

"I don't know. I keep going back to the fact that she was gut shot. *Gut shot* and if I had to guess, I'd say whoever did it meant for the girl to suffer. This was a vicious attack. We need to talk to Shauna. Granger has the bullets the surgeon was able to retrieve and has informed the hospital staff of our desire to speak with her. I was going through the photos of the crime scene and the notes that Dobson has in the system. It looks like Shauna stumbled forward about ten feet after she was shot. The gravel obscured any footprints, but we have a blood trail. There were tire tracks right beside her blood trail, but again, because of the thick gravel, there was nothing we could distinguish other than an approximate width of the tire. Shorty's doesn't have a surveillance system. We have some cameras we can access. The bank's ATM, the security feed outside this building and the ones outside the courthouse. Even if we did see vehicles moving at that time, there is absolutely no way we can tie the vehicles on the road to the shooting. As soon as Dobson comes in for his shift at three, I'll work through the crime scene with him again. Granger and I will do the same about noon when he comes in."

"How did Granger happen to be there? Wasn't he supposed to be off?"

"Housman needed the night off so he traded with Granger." It wasn't unusual for the deputies to work out any scheduling conflicts between themselves.

The sheriff grunted in acknowledgement. "The initial report indicated a Good Samaritan on scene?"

"Yeah, Doctor Blue. He's probably the reason Shauna's still alive. He had dinner at Shorty's and when he was leaving, he heard her. He called us and provided emergency assistance. He's coming in today to sign his statement. I couldn't get it done because of the fire at the Ogden estate." She flipped through her briefcase and tossed the man's driver's license to her boss. Big Jim lifted the piece of laminate and did a double take and frowned. "It can't be..."

"What?"

"I know this guy, but not as Maliki Blue. This is Boswell's kid."

"Boswell as in Harrison Boswell, the owner of half the county?"

"Close to it, but yeah. We're about the same age. He's a couple years younger, I think. I went to public school. He was at boarding school, but I'd see him every summer. He was okay, for a royal. Never pulled any of that entitled shit, even though his old man owned about everything in those days. I haven't seen him in... fuck, over ten or fifteen years, maybe longer."

"Maybe Doctor Blue is this guy's doppelganger?"

"No... Mal... shit... I think that's what his friends used to call him. Short for Maliki, maybe?"

"So, you think Doctor Blue is actually a Boswell?"

"Don't know. Did he say why he was in town?"

She slowly shook her head from side to side. "As a matter of fact, he was pretty evasive on that point. But he did say he currently works for Guardian Security."

His coffee cup froze halfway to his mouth. "Guardian?" He shifted his eyes to her.

"Yeah. I had to ask him if he was employed as

something other than a doctor. He spoke like a cop. A highly trained one."

"But he's a doctor?"

"That's what he said."

"Get his statement and cut him loose."

"That's the plan." She extended her hand for the license, but Jim held it, staring at it intently. Finally, he stood up and dropped the driver's license back on the desk.

She picked up the license as she said, "I'll up-channel the reports to the BCI as soon as we get them completed."

"No. Let's keep this in house."

"We have the bullet in evidence. I can send it to the state crime lab to see if they have any other crimes with matching ballistics. We've got limited resources and experience; they could do this better than we could. Are you sure–"

"Do I need to repeat myself, Deputy Campbell? Do *not* contact the Bureau of Criminal Investigations."

She blinked, taken aback at the sharpness in his voice. "Ah, yes sir."

"In house, Poet. Everything stays in *this* house."

"Yes, sir. I understand." She didn't, though, not in the slightest. Jim was usually a pretty easy-going boss, even though he was an arrogant ass. He was only ten years or so older than her, one of the youngest sheriffs in county history. He was connected to the families in Paintville and had an excellent rapport with the affluent population in the area. Why he wouldn't let any of the major crimes go up the chain was baffling, and quite frankly, concerning.

She drew a breath and decided to tread where angels feared to go. "Jim, have you heard anything back from the state about the links to the films we found?" The pay-by-the-minute phone they'd found at one of the death scenes was beaten to hell, but she and another deputy were able to get it to activate for a few minutes. There were no calls, no pictures, no texts, no contacts list, on the smart-phone, but the internet browser had several links saved. Poet managed to take a picture of the links before the phone died. Four links. All to snuff films. Horrible, unbelievable, and unquestionably real footage of young women being killed.

"I forwarded the links to them. That is out of our hands, and we'll probably never know. We have enough to worry about without that shit. Drop it." Jim dropped his head back and stared at the ceiling. "Damn... Look, I'm sorry for that. I didn't get much sleep last night. Just don't call BCI. I don't want them up the department's ass. Did you see the disaster over in Pope County when the BCI took over a simple assault case? No, you wouldn't have because it's being kept on the down low." He sighed and rubbed his face. "Let's see if we can take care of our own problems first. Okay?"

"Sure." She nodded her head north and south even though her brain was doing the 'what the actual fuck' audio loop in her head. The BCI was made for *exactly* these types of situations. They provided expertise, resources, and oversight for major crimes. All they had to do was *request* the assistance. She had no idea there was an investigation or a mess in Pope County, but that wasn't unusual. What was unusual was the sheriff's reluctance to ask for help. *Again.* This case should be an automatic call to the BCI. It fit every parameter.

"What about the fire at the Ogden estate?" Jim shoved his hands in his pockets.

"Really strange. One of his classic cars was engulfed in flames in the garage. The caretaker was baffled, but Ogden's private security had it extinguished and called off the fire department right before I got there. I've got the report almost done. I got statements from the caretaker and the security guard with the extinguisher before I went back to help Dobson at the scene of the shooting. It was a long night."

"Yeah, well, that's why we get paid the big bucks, right?"

Poet snorted; the extra seven hundred and fifty dollars a month was not why she worked her ass off. She loved what she did. Period. "Yeah, right. If you say so. I'll let you know if we come up with anything else on that one. I'm sure the insurance company will be looking for our report."

"Thanks. I'll be heading over to the hospital as soon as we get word Shauna is awake."

Again, she sent him a confused look. "What? You?" He *never* performed actual police work.

"Why not? I know Daryl and Jennie. I'll handle the interview with Shauna. This is personal, and last time I checked, I still wore the sheriff's badge in this office. I think I can handle a victim interview."

"Damn, sorry, I didn't mean to..." They weren't sure what happened to Shauna in that parking lot, and she could be involved in something shady, but Poet backpedaled because he probably *could* do the interview without assistance, and he was her boss.

He lifted his coffee cup in a salute. "Save it.

Maybe it's time I get my ass from behind my desk a little more if my deputies are questioning my abilities. Check in with me after you talk to Dobson and Granger. Let me know where we stand."

"Roger that, sir." Poet watched him leave. Well, damn. Why did she feel like Alice after a tumble down a rabbit hole? Since he'd been elected, Jim had done nothing but the politically correct hand shaking, luncheons, and meetings with the county officials. She'd seen him at maybe three callouts, and all of them were photo ops. She narrowed her eyes and stared down the hall where Jim had disappeared. How was he going to use this to advance his career? That *had* to be why he was inserting himself and not calling in the state.

She leaned back in her chair and returned her attention to her laptop. How many brick walls was she going to run into before Jim allowed her to ask for help? She minimized the report she was working on and clicked on the folder icon at the bottom left. Three dead women over the course of a year. The first one was an apparent drug overdose and had been closed, but Poet still had the case file on her computer. She didn't buy it. The young woman attended junior college, part time, two counties over, but lived in Pleasant county. By all accounts, she wasn't the type to do drugs. Studious, serious and not a partier, according to their initial interviews. But the fact that she'd been missing for over a week and had numerous track marks in between her toes and enough H in her system to kill an elephant put a cover on the file as far as the medical examiner was concerned. It also seemed to appease the sheriff and all other entities involved. She didn't like it. She kept mentally tripping over those damn films, but lacking any evidence linking the women's deaths to each other, much less the films, there was little she could do. One in particular tugged at her. The rock formation in the background, seen only for a few seconds, seemed so familiar, but she couldn't place it.

She glanced at her watch and clicked on the second and then third folder. Until Granger or Dr. Blue showed up, she would fall back into the cases and try to find something she'd overlooked.

Mal stopped the SUV at the gates of his parents' summer home. He sat staring at the ornate iron entrance. Memories of his childhood and teenage years, of summers spent in this place rolled forward. He'd loved coming home. He and his mother lived here during the summers. His father would visit, but his busy practice demanded he be available and close by, so he usually stayed on Long Island. A bird flew by the windshield, jolting him back into the present. He drew a breath. Time to ask what his mother needed. Depressing the tab, he lowered the window and keyed in his code to the gate. It activated immediately, sliding the heavy barriers apart.

He put the truck into gear and drove up the long winding drive. The shaded, tree lined roadway twisted over the hills until he crested and saw the house. Almost ten thousand square feet of pristine palace living. The house itself was made of limestone. The three-story high colonnade formed arches that were mimicked by the windows and doors. The vast expanse of greenspace was manicured by a dedicated staff. Pulling up to the front of the manse, he parked the vehicle in the visitor's area. He wasn't here as family.

He dropped the keys into the pocket of his worn blue jeans and stomped his busted ass combat boots on the concrete to drop the cuff that had caught on the boot top. The fifteen steps up to the front door seemed like a fucking mountain. He didn't want to be here, but he reached over and punched the doorbell. He could hear the echoes of the Westminster chimes. Through the etched glass of the front door he could see a person walking down the arched hallway that stretched from the front door to the back fountains. He stepped back from the door, clasped his hands into fists a couple times and waited for the door to open.

"Yes?" A small woman peered up at him.

"I was summoned here by my mother." His tone was clipped but civil. Barely.

She frowned and angled her head. "Who is your mother?"

"Catherine Boswell."

"You're her son... the doctor?" He could see she didn't believe him. The way her eyes traveled from his full beard, down his old Henley and worn jeans before landing on his combat boots told him she wasn't impressed. Like he cared?

He lifted his brow in challenge. "I am. You can either let me in, or I can leave. Your choice." He lifted his wrist and glanced at his watch. If he played his cards right, he could be back at Dulles and catch a commercial plane going anywhere but here by dinner time.

"Please come in. You can wait in the drawing room while I inform Mrs. Boswell you're here."

"Is she in her rooms?" Maliki walked into his childhood home and scanned what he could see. Nothing was different. Strange that he thought the interior of the home would have changed as much as *his* interior had altered.

"I'll go–"

"No need. I know where I'm going." He strode down the hall with the little woman hustling to catch up with him.

"Sir, I'm sorry, but I'll have to ask you to wait."

"You can ask all you want." He turned right and hit the stairs, taking them two at a time. The first door on the right was his mother's sitting room, and it was open. Mal knocked on the oak frame and entered.

"Harrison?" His mother stood from the chair where she'd been reading. "Oh, dear. You've grown a beard." The disapproval in her voice sounded loud and clear. He'd heard it before. Strange how he'd thought that would change, too.

Maliki's eyes scanned the woman in front of him. There were slight differences in her appearance. Her hair was shorter, a different style, and there were deeper crinkles around her eyes and parentheses around her mouth that hadn't been there when he'd left. Age could be fought, but not denied. Even the best plastic surgeons couldn't stop the march of time.

He crossed his arms over his chest and greeted her. "Mother. You look well."

"I tried to make him wait, Ms. Catherine."

He put his hands on his hips when the little lady who'd been tagging behind him spoke in a breathless pant.

"Thank you, Lucinda, my son is welcome anywhere in this house at any time. Please see to your duties." The smaller woman nodded and did an odd curtsey like dip thing before she exited the room.

He was ready to leave, and he hadn't been here two minutes. It was almost as if he'd been caught in a time-warp. "What did you need so badly that you hired a private investigator to find me?"

His mom took a step forward and lifted her arm, only to hesitate and drop it. "Ah... Harrison, could you sit with me for a moment? Please?"

"I've changed my name, legally. Please don't address me by *his* name." They both knew exactly to whom he referred.

"Oh. Well, that would explain why the detective

had a hard time reaching you. What do you wish to be called?" She motioned to a chair across from the one she'd been standing next to when he knocked a mere minute ago.

"Maliki."

"Your middle name." She nodded as if approving of his choice. "Very well. Would you please?" She once again motioned to the chair and gracefully sank down into hers.

Mal sat down and crossed his leg, ankle over his knee, before he leveled a stare on her. "Well?"

"There are several things that need to be addressed, Harri... Maliki." She gave him a momentary smile.

"The floor is yours. I'll listen." And he would. He loved his mother, although theirs had always been a distant relationship. Not a bit of the fun and warmth of the families he knew now, but there was a certain type of love. He'd acknowledge that.

She cleared her throat and dropped her eyes to her fingers that were rolling a lace handkerchief. "First, I know that I can never redeem myself for my lack of support during the… incident."

Mal snorted. "The incident? Is that what you call it?"

She swallowed hard and nodded. "I've never

been allowed to question your father. My life has been devoted to supporting him, his practice, the family name."

"At the cost of your only son." He wanted her to hear the price from his own lips.

"So it would seem." Her words were faint yet verbalized. "I was wrong. I regretted it when it happened, but I knew no other way." She snapped her head up and leveled a determined stare at him. "That isn't an excuse. My past is mine to shoulder, and I cannot change what I did. But I can control my future. I am sorry I hurt you. You'll never know how much I've grieved my lack of support... but this *isn't* about me, and I don't want to make it so. I have hurt you. I am sorry. If you allow me back into your life, I will do better. I can't promise I won't make mistakes, but I no longer want or need to be the woman I was."

He dropped his foot to the floor and leaned forward, placing his elbows on his knees. "What's changed? Why now?"

"About three years ago, a colleague of your father's, one of the partners in his practice, brought to my attention he was making mistakes, forgetting things like names of employees that had worked in the business for years. I hadn't noticed.

I've stayed in residence here year-round since you left, only leaving when social engagements absolutely required my attendance. Together, the partners and I were able to manipulate your father into a physical examination. He believed it was for a new insurance program. We discovered your father was suffering from a form of vascular dementia. While there were, and still are, periods of absolute lucidity, it was obvious to everyone, but him, that he was ill. After two years of legal maneuvering, the partners, with my assistance, were able to remove your father from the practice."

Mal stared at her. She drew her shoulders back and looked straight at him as if daring him to find fault with her actions. He couldn't do that until he actually understood what the hell was going on. He dipped his head and narrowed his eyes. "Explain to me what you mean by you gave the partners your assistance."

"I allowed his partners access to conversations your father would have with me. Conversations that showed without a shadow of a doubt that he was incapable of continuing as managing partner for the practice. They put him over a legal barrel he couldn't fight."

"And how did he handle that?"

"Not well. He served me with divorce papers. I fought his lawyers with mine. A year ago, his lawyers withdrew the petition."

"What happened to make them withdraw?"

"They couldn't deny what we all knew. He wasn't well."

"What did you do then?"

"I had him declared legally incompetent."

Mal's head snapped back. "What?"

She lifted her chin. "It was necessary. As I said, he isn't well."

Mal leaned back in the chair and shifted his gaze to the window, although he wasn't seeing any of the grandeur beyond the glass.

"Where is he now?"

"Here, in his rooms."

"Vascular dementia..." Maliki racked his brain trying to remember what he knew about the progressive disease. "Strokes?"

"When I took over his care, there were none that we knew of, but we had a CT done. The doctors tested and retested and they believe he had several mini-strokes."

Mal nodded. "Transient ischemic attacks."

His mom's smile was brief. "Yes, I believe that was the term."

"His behavior changed at that point?"

"Yes."

"Has it gotten worse?"

She drew a breath and shook her head. "Since I've been able to direct his healthcare, the disease has not progressed as quickly. He had undiagnosed and uncontrolled high blood pressure. We have that under control now. However, six months ago, he had a stroke. He didn't have full time nursing. I had arranged to have someone on the premises at night because if he became confused he could wander. That was the only thing we were concerned with at the time. So the drugs to combat the effects of the stroke were delayed. The damage was permanent."

Mal swallowed. He wanted nothing to do with his father, but he never would wish this demise on the man. "How bad is he now?"

"On good days, we can visit without him becoming too confused. His left side was affected by the stroke. He has some facial paralysis, and his left arm is very weak. His speech is slow and delib- erate. He gets upset when he is forced to make a decision, so I plan his days for him. Keep him to a schedule. It helps a bit, although he forgets more and more." His mom's eyes filled with tears.

"I'm sorry." He blinked at his comment. Was he honestly sorry? Yes, damn it, yes, he was sorry his mother was going through this alone, and he was sorry for his father. Dementia was an undiscriminating, fucking, thief.

"Thank you." She gave him a sad smile. "We've talked more in the last six months than we have our entire marriage, which is... a statement to our dysfunction."

Mal kept his mouth shut. What else could he say? I'm sorry? He'd already given her that. Instead he waited. There had to be a reason she'd sent a private investigator looking for him.

"So, the reason I called you is that I want you to come home, to be a part of this family again and... he'd like to see you." She sniffed and delicately blew her nose.

Mal blinked at her. "I'm not inclined to grant either of those requests." Years ago, he'd have loved to have had this conversation. Before he forged a life that had nothing to do with his parents.

"Why?" She dabbed at her eyes.

"I'm not the man you think I am. I'm not the person you knew."

She stared at him before she acknowledged, "I can see that, but I'm willing to accept the man you've become. Please Har... Maliki, give me the opportunity to know the man you are now."

He stood and wandered over to the window. A gardener was tending to the flowers that circled one of the many fountains that were erected in the back acreage. He didn't fit into this life any longer and he didn't want to be a part of it.

He felt her come to stand beside him. She barely reached his shoulder.

"I know I don't have the right to ask you to give me a second chance."

"You don't." He agreed.

Her head dropped and she nodded.

"But I can stay for a few days."

She tipped her head up. Joy flashed across her face. "I'll have Lucinda put fresh linens–"

"No, thank you. I have a hotel room in Paintville. I'll stay there."

She blinked rapidly at the rebuff but gave him a careful smile. "Of course. Perhaps we can start with lunch today?" She glanced down at the diamond encrusted watch on her wrist. "Cook will be ready to serve, soon."

"Perhaps tomorrow. I have an appointment in town, and I'll need to check in with my employers." Guardian wasn't an issue, but right now he sure as fuck was going to use them as an excuse. He needed to wrap his head around the massive, double-clutching shift he'd just experienced.

She put her hand around his arm, and he bent it, placing a hand on hers before walking with her toward the front door. "I long to hear what has happened in your life."

"It isn't the life I was raised to have, but I believe I've made a difference."

"A difference?" His mom looked up at him. "In what?"

"In this world. I've made a positive impact."

"Do you do charity work? Doctors Without Borders?"

Maliki dropped his head back and laughed. "No, I don't work for that organization but borders never really bothered my employer."

His mom gave him a baffled, confused smile. "I don't understand."

"I work for Guardian Security." He slowed his pace as they approached the grand stairway he'd flown up earlier.

"You're not practicing? Is that why you've changed so much, physically? Because of this job?" She stopped at the top of the stairs.

"No, I started bodybuilding when I was in the

Air Force." He took a step down, but she remained on the landing.

"You served in the military?"

He nodded. "Six years. Pararescue."

"You jumped from planes?" Her eyes widened, and she fanned her free hand over her chest.

"And so much more."

She snapped her mouth shut and blinked rapidly. "You've lived." The awe in her voice was palpable.

"I have, and I've lived well." He'd launched from this place and became a man he could be proud of, and that was of utmost importance to him. "I'll be back tomorrow, Mother. Until then." He leaned down, even though she was a stair above him, and kissed her cheek before he turned and trotted down the stairs and out the door.

The fresh, warm air that greeted him smelled of newly cut grass. He shut the door behind him and took a deep breath. His mother's words and actions were a balm for a wound he knew he had but until today had no way of healing. He glanced up at the sky, brilliant blue with a few tufts of white fluff hanging to accent the splendor of the noon sun. Perhaps this trip back could begin to heal those old injuries. Perhaps.

CHAPTER 4

Mal drove into the parking lot, found a vacant slot and cut the motor. As he dialed his phone, he glanced around the lot, noting several SUVs with similar markings to the one Senior Deputy Campbell had driven.

"I talk to you more than I talk to my wife," Joseph growled.

"Bullshit. I'm going to stay for a week or so."

"Everything okay?"

"No. Not really. The old man is sick. Mom is offering an olive branch."

"Grab onto that motherfucker."

"Plan on it, that's why I'm taking a week or so." Mal chuckled at the grunt he got in reply. "Is there any problem from the incident last night?"

"Not on our end. I checked with Jewell first thing this morning. She's got you boxed in, cut off, and sanitized. You're golden."

"You okay with me being gone?"

There was a pause before Joseph sighed into the phone. "Keep up with your physical training. The skills classes you've been attending aren't going to wait for you, so I'll insert you in different ones when you come back. I can't guarantee Jason is going to approve you going down this road, though."

Well, damn, Joseph noticed more than he let on. "I don't know if I want to pursue it or if it is a pipe dream."

"Having the option open is smart. You have the background, minus medical school. Not everyone can be a wimpy ass office worker, right?"

"Medical school, residency and internship." Plus, countless hours of continuing education to hold his accreditation, but hey... who was counting.

"Yeah, yeah. I get it. You're smart."

"I'm fucking badass," Mal countered.

"For an office worker," Joseph shot back at him. "Seriously. Keep up with the physical conditioning.

Stopping will only make getting back into the groove harder."

"I am. I ran six miles this morning. Going to look for a gym after I deal with the County Mounty who wants a statement about last night." His parents had a personal gym, but he'd be surprised if it had anything more than dust in it.

"Only six miles? Lightweight."

"Ran, not jogged, asshole."

"Whatever. This county cop going to be a problem?"

"Nah. She's in the trenches of the paperwork war." According to some of the former law enforcement types who came through training, death by papercuts was a very real form of torture for a cop.

"Got intel that the girl is expected to make it."

"I got that, too. Thanks."

"You know, her still being alive... that's down to you."

"I was in the right place at the right time, at least for her." He was glad he'd listened to his instincts and stopped.

"So it would seem. You got anything else, or are we going to keep gossiping like a bunch of silver-haired hens?"

"Has anyone ever told you that you're an asshole?"

"So many times. So many ways." Joseph laughed; evil laced the edges of the sound.

"It was a rhetorical question. I'll call if anything else happens."

"Definitely call. We'll chat. I can peck at the gravel with you if you need me to do that. You know that old saying... Whatever it takes."

Laughter burst from him. "Fuck you, asshole, as long as it takes."

"See, I keep telling you, Ember would object."

Mal shook his head and cut the connection. "Fucking idiot."

He made his way into the building and stopped at a counter in front of what appeared to be a dispatch center. The woman held up a finger and finished talking on the base station radio before she ambled over to the bulletproof glass that encased the small nerve center. "What can I do for you?"

"I'm here to see Deputy Campbell."

"Your name?"

"Maliki Blue."

"One sec." The woman turned, picked up a phone, and hit a button. He couldn't distinguish what the woman said, but the conversation took less than five seconds.

"She'll be right up. You can take a seat." She pointed to the bank of plastic chairs that were connected by aluminum rods. It looked like it was made for kindergarteners. Yeah, not happening. He smiled and meandered over to the glass double doors he'd entered through. The little town was bustling and had grown up, which was surprising. When he was in high school, the town had been dead. A single screen movie theater was the height of attractions, but for him and a few of his friends who summered in the local area, it had been enough.

"Dr. Blue?"

Senior Deputy Campbell's dark brown uniform highlighted her pale complexion and freckles. Those big blue eyes were sharp, intelligent.

"Senior Deputy." He nodded.

"You can come back." She held the door open and waited for him to pass her before she shut the door behind them. "I was beginning to wonder if you were going to come in."

Maliki stopped and turned. She was looking down and nearly ran into him but skittered to a stop before she did.

"Why? Did we set a time?" He knew they hadn't.

"Ah... no we didn't, but it is after noon, and most people would have been down here first thing. Highly emotional events and requests from law enforcement tend to have people spring loaded."

"Indeed, however last night wasn't a highly emotional event, at least not for me. I was, however, pleased I was able to help the young woman." He spoke to her back as she walked past him. And yes, he dropped his eyes and noticed that pert ass and those toned thighs. She made polyester look damn good. He noticed. Sue him.

"Life at Guardian must be extremely interesting, then?" His eyes returned to her face when she turned her head.

"Actually, lately, I'm bored to the point of tears." Which was the truth.

The deputy pointed to a chair beside a desk. There were four other desks in the area, but only one other was occupied. "Sorry to hear that."

Maliki mentally rolled his eyes. It was pretty damn obvious the woman wasn't, but hey, she was being polite. She had a way about her, too. Small things tweaked him to the fact she was probably prior military. The way she carried herself, the precise way she talked—small things that only another who'd served would probably notice.

"I'd like to get your statement down on paper, and I have several questions."

Maliki handed her a thumb drive. "My statement." He took a seat.

She blinked and took the small silver capsule from him. He'd completed his statement last night while the event was fresh in his mind.

"Oh. Thank you." She uncapped the cylinder and slid it into a USB port.

Maliki leaned back in his chair. There is no way he would have done that. The jump drive could have contained a virus or malware. Damn good thing he was honest.

It took several minutes for her to open the doc, read it and then print it. She handed him his statement. "Normally we require statements to be on our forms, but we'll consider this a professional courtesy. Sign and date please."

He complied and handed her the pen back. "You said you had questions?"

She slid the statement back toward her and opened her desk drawer, retrieving his driver's license. "Yep. Several. Why can't I find any information about Dr. Maliki Blue?"

Mal shrugged. "What type of information are you looking for?"

"Oh, you know, simple things. Driver's record, criminal record. Things that my background checks always provide." She leaned back in her chair with his driver's license firmly in her hand.

"I'm sure you know the answer to that question."

"As a matter of fact, I do. Not one minute after I ran your name in our system, it crashed. Hard. As in, went offline, and then not five minutes after that my boss received a call from the State's Attorney General's Office. That episode was a particularly unpleasant point in my morning. You have powerful employers, Dr. Blue."

Mal tilted his head and lifted an eyebrow. "I'm sorry, I don't think I caught a question in any of that."

"Why is your identity so closely guarded?"

He leaned forward and whispered conspiratorially, "They are trying to make sure the bad people who are looking for me don't find me."

"Bad people?" The deputy leaned forward, lowering her voice.

He nodded and added, "Very bad people." He

leaned back, already bored with the sixth degree. "Are we done here?"

"Not quite. My sheriff said he may have recognized you." She lifted his driver's license. "Said he thought your last name was Boswell."

He hadn't expected that. His summers here were more than a few years ago. "Did he?"

"He did."

"Who is your sheriff?"

"James Watson."

"Sorry, doesn't ring any bells." James Watson. Nope. Not a name he recognized.

"Too bad. He seemed to recognize you right off the bat. Anyway, I got interested in why someone would want to change their name. So, I did a search on Harrison Boswell, VI."

Maliki officially lost all humor and patience. He stared at the woman. She might be beautiful, but right now she was a boil on his ass—one he wanted to lance, purge and forget.

"Seems he dropped off the face of the earth."

"Is that a crime?"

"No. Not a crime, but a curiosity." She handed him his driver's license. "How long are you staying in town, Doctor?"

"I'm not sure. Maybe a week or so." He took the

laminated card and stood, pulling his wallet from his back pocket.

"Damn, too bad."

"Yeah, why's that?"

"Well, I was thinking..."

"Thinking? Odd habit for a cop."

"Hmmm... funny, but I figured that a person who worked for Guardian would have... resources. That system crash and a call from the AG made me think that perhaps a concerned citizen could get some... assistance without a lot of fanfare."

"Did you?"

She nodded; the long ponytail moved with her head, drawing his eyes to her dark auburn hair. "Why would a concerned citizen need that type of assistance?"

She glanced past him, and when her eyes landed back on him, she was deadly serious. "Have dinner with me tonight, Dr. Blue, and I'll explain," she murmured. She leaned forward, picking up a piece of paper and lowered her voice even more, "I'd prefer to talk to you in private."

"Poet, do you have that report on the fire at the Ogden estate done? I have an insurance company representative claiming he's being stalled."

Maliki turned to stare at the man who'd shouted the question. The name tag said Watson and the badge touted the title "Sheriff". A tickle of recognition tugged at him, but he couldn't place the sheriff's face.

"I submitted them right after we spoke this morning." The deputy didn't offer to introduce them, but the sheriff didn't seem to mind.

He narrowed his eyes at Maliki. "The Attorney General called to personally ensure you're not hindered in any way." His eyes slid to Deputy Campbell. "You're not hindering the good doctor, are you?"

"Nope. We are done here. Doctor Blue will never have to see me professionally again."

His eyes bounced to her and then back to the sheriff.

"Good. We appreciate your assistance with Shauna." The sheriff extended his hand. The grip was crushing but Maliki had been in pissing contests before. He bore down and watched the sheriff's eyes narrow even further before they released their grip by mutual accord. Watson spun and stomped from the office.

"Normal behavior for your boss?"

"Lately? Yeah; before that... not really."

"You have my number, Deputy. Send me an address and a time." He turned on his heel and left.

The drive to Carmichael's diner took less than five minutes. The booth he sat in faced the street, providing only rare glimpses of vehicles driving past. He ordered and drew a deep, revitalizing breath. Fuck, what a morning. His father was sick. Several TIAs, strokes, caused in part by the uncontrolled blood pressure his father wouldn't address. Mortality meet pride, the conclusion was always the same. Mortality won every time.

The waitress brought him his water and left. He took a deep drink of the ice water and leaned back into the booth. The changes to his mother, well, they were drastic. Not her appearance, rather it was the way she owned the fact that she'd fucked up. She didn't place blame; didn't tell him he should have done something differently. A sincere apology. God, he didn't realize how much he'd needed that.

He was halfway through his sandwich when Sheriff Watson entered the diner. The man waved to the waitress and made a direct line to his booth. He slid into the seat opposite and folded his hands in front of him on the table.

"Do we have business?" Maliki asked with his

mouth half full. He'd dropped any pretense of giving a fuck about this guy about point three seconds after the motherfucker had started that bullshit posturing handshake.

Watson glanced around before a smarmy smile split his face. "Why the fuck is Guardian in my county?"

He shrugged and took another bite of his sandwich. He spoke around his food because he was fucking hungry. "Guardian isn't. I am. You look familiar. Do I know you?"

"You work for Guardian, and we didn't run in the same crowd growing up."

"Is that so?" He didn't doubt that. He'd grown up with the privileged in the area. He sighed and put his food down. He wiped his hands carefully. "Is it illegal to be on vacation in Pleasant County?"

"Depends on the person and the reason."

"I'm curious, Sheriff. What did I do that got your dander up?" Maliki picked up his ice water.

"I don't appreciate the state's Attorney General calling my office and directing me to... extend every professional courtesy."

Mal laughed so hard several heads turned their way. "Is *that* what you're doing?"

"No, I'm trying to understand why Guardian is in my county."

He threw his napkin on his plate. The asshole across from him ruined what was a damn good sandwich. "I'm not here in an official capacity."

Watson pushed a finger at him and jabbed the air. "If that changes, I'm the first person you tell."

He leaned forward and smiled evilly, channeling every mannerism he'd ever seen Joseph use. "If Guardian ever decides to muck about in your precious little piece of overpriced farmland, I'm sure you'll be the first person they contact." He stood and the waitress was there a second later with his ticket. He took it from her and dropped it in front of the sheriff. "My good friend is buying my lunch today. Thank you for extending the professional courtesy." He turned and flipped Watson a middle finger salute, and headed out.

He made it to his truck and turned it on before he keyed the numbers on his phone.

"I'm not joking. I think I *do* talk to you more than Ember."

Maliki watched from his seat in his SUV as the sheriff left the diner. His eyes tracked the man to the decked-out patrol car. "You know every class

I've ever sat in on, the person leading it always says, trust your gut."

"Yeah. What do you got?"

"An achy gut."

Joseph sighed. "Hold on." Joseph's voice muddled, but he heard his boss say, "Blake, take your homework and work with Mommy, okay?" He heard Blake's voice and then Joseph's laughter before the man came back on the line. "Lay it out for me."

He described the encounter with the sheriff. "The fucker sends up warning flags. He's ringing bells. Something irritating around the edges of my memory. I don't know why, but when you add it to the fact that the deputy wants to meet me for dinner, it's lighting me up."

"Whoa... what?"

"The deputy I gave my statement to wants to meet me away from the Sheriff's Department to talk. Privately. I have no idea what type of drama is going on."

"Sounds like a regular little *Peyton Place*. Follow your nose on this, Mal. If you smell something rotten, you dig, but if you're going to do that, I'll need to make a few calls, and you'll need to arm up."

"Arm up? Where the fuck am I going to get a gun?"

"You have a Guardian SUV, right?"

"Yeah." He glanced around.

"There are two keys on that ring. One for the engine. One opens the armory."

He palmed the key ring and looked at the keys. "Get the fuck out of here."

"Dude, seriously how many times have you driven one of our vehicles?"

"Ah... never?"

"No fucking way."

"Seriously, I have my own money. I've always rented a car, taken a taxi, or Ubered it." Mal looked over his shoulder. "Where's the armory?"

"Open the back hatch."

He followed Joseph's instructions and flipped up the carpet as Joseph detailed the process. He inserted the key and opened the latch. "Holy fuck."

"Armory."

He whistled. "Son of a bitch. I'm impressed."

"You should be, and you should be briefed better. Damn, Jason is going to have my ass if you shoot off your fucking foot."

He slammed the door of the armory and locked it as he said, "I'm an expert marksman. The only foot I'm going to shoot off is yours if you keep being a dick." He climbed back into the front of the SUV. "Wait, why are you calling Archangel?"

"Follow the bouncing ball, Mal. You can't be tracking down shit without a way to defend yourself and credentials that cover your ass. You can't use the weapons unless you have a permit to carry. You can't get a permit to carry without Guardian's blessings. You are not an operative. You don't have creds and need them. Tell me how I'm going to get all of that without briefing Jason?"

He dropped his head back against the headrest. "Shit."

"Eloquently said for an office worker."

"Fuck you."

"Again, not interested. You'll need a concealed carry permit and Guardian credentials. Yeah, fuck. Okay, I'm going to put together a folder on you. Every class you've taken, the scores on your physical evals and training runs. Can you keep your ass out of trouble long enough for me to make you legal?"

"God, I sure as fuck hope so." Sheriff Watson's car passed by his SUV and the man stared at him. He lifted his hand and waggled his fingers at the guy before he flipped him off again. Probably not smart, but if the bastard was going to come after him, he wanted him good and pissed off. Mad people made mistakes.

"Get somewhere and hole up until tomorrow. I'll give you a call when we've got this shit sorted."

"Roger that," he acknowledged and cleared the line. His phone vibrated and he checked the text.

> 1900hrs. 4894 Lincoln Avenue. Park across the street. Apartment 5C.

He read the text again before he fired up the SUV. Well, he could honestly say he was no longer bored.

CHAPTER 5

Stupid. She was absolutely stupid... or paranoid. Yep. Paranoid and maybe delusional. Poet stared at the computer files and shook her head. There was absolutely nothing connecting these women. Nothing. One died of an overdose, although to anyone's recollection she wasn't a junkie. That case was closed. The second woman had no cause of death other than the fact she stopped breathing. The medical examiner couldn't find any other reason. No needle marks, no bruises, no wounds, nothing except she'd… died. They'd found her behind the wheel of her car. Rigor had broken, so there was no telling how long she'd been sitting in her vehicle. She was a local woman who'd moved back to town recently. The third woman, when she was found in her own vomit, reeked of alcohol. They were waiting for the bloodwork to come back, but discussion with the medical examiner suggested the death resulted from acute alcohol poisoning, however the cause of death was asphyxiation of a foreign substance, i.e., her own vomit. But why would a woman drive to the middle of nowhere and pound a fifth? Her coworkers and everyone else interviewed said she was a careful, social, drinker.

She stared at the documents depicting the three women and added a mental picture of Shauna. They were all young, beautiful and petite. Was she grasping for straws? Probably, and it was very likely she'd have dropped any concern if the BCI had been called in. But they weren't and she couldn't drop it. The cases were under her skin.

Add in the snuff film links that they found, which had absolutely nothing in common with the deaths, and she was a mess. Because damn it, her gut told her they were related. She just didn't have any proof.

Poet glanced at her watch and groaned. If the sheriff ever discovered why she'd invited Dr. Blue to her apartment, there would be hell to pay. Yes, she was so going to pay for jumping over the line he'd pissed in the sand. Lord, she could imagine that display, especially after the Attorney General *ordered* the sheriff not to inconvenience Dr. Blue.

However, she'd found a loophole. Granted, not a big one, but one nonetheless. Jim said no BCI. He didn't say she couldn't ask other organizations. Right? Well, for Shauna's case, he had demanded the investigation stay in house. The others, no BCI. So, maybe she'd skirt Shauna's case, because it wasn't a murder—yet. It wasn't like the others, the deaths of perfectly healthy women with no history of drugs, poor health or alcoholism. Damn. Even when she racked the cases together in her own mind, making any leap from one case to the other was impossible. She shook her head. Still, there was something off. Those films, the women's deaths, the unrelenting feeling that she was missing a link. Those concerns kept her awake at night and kept her going back to the cases. If this backfired, she'd lose her job. God, she hoped Maliki Blue was able to help.

She flopped onto the couch and dropped her head back. She had great instincts about people.

Usually. Those instincts were telling her Dr. Blue wasn't a mere doctor. *Ha.* She chuckled and then groaned. The man was gorgeous. That blond hair and golden red beard. She'd never had a thing for beards, but on that man... damn, the facial hair really did it for her. The good doctor was bulked up, and when she saw him run past the office this morning, she knew he wasn't a casual runner. That man had pushed himself hard, and if he started from the Paintville Inn, he'd have run three miles when he passed her office. Why would a doctor train in that way? He didn't fit the physical features for a long-distance runner. He was too big, too much muscle. A curiosity, indeed. Then there were his eyes. Those sky-blue eyes were hard, intelligent, and saw everything.

He'd pegged Jim's testosterone-laced cowboy act fast this morning and had zero problems handling the macho bullshit Jim had whipped out. Talk about a dick measuring contest. The doctor had won, hands down.

She stopped and thought about that for a moment. She bet the man was proportional. *Whoa, pull the reins in girl.* Doctor Blue hadn't been anything less than professional. So, no drooling on or fantasizing about proportions of strangers. Well, he wasn't exactly a stranger. She'd met him twice. She knew who he worked for. She'd invited him to her home, so they were basically on their third meeting. *Wow, reaching for straws much, girl?*

Still, she was happy she'd gone with her instincts and reached out to the doctor. For most of the day, she'd been okay with that effort. Now, however, she was struggling to recount the reasons asking him to take a look at the murders was a good thing.

She closed her eyes and held up her index finger. First, his background had been vetted by the best. He worked for Guardian. The massive security company put the FBI and CIA to shame, and every law enforcement agency in the world would kill to have a liaison available for an assist. That was a huge mark in his favor. Second, it meant he had access to resources she couldn't touch. Third, she added another finger in the air; she *knew* he had experience as some type of law enforcement. There was no way he didn't. He radiated that knowledge whether or not he'd admit to it. Hell, his witness statement was a textbook example of law enforcement report writing.

Fourth, she dropped her hand. He had an objective perspective. She needed that. Having been wrapped up in these cases, every day, for almost a year now, an outside perspective was absolutely necessary.

Now, however, she was second-guessing her gut. If the good doctor turned out to be an asshole who made waves for her, she'd be thoroughly screwed.

She rolled her head and looked at her laptop. It was a risk she was going to take. She needed someone to have outside eyes on these cases. If he thought it was nothing, then she'd shut up and color inside the lines. Maybe.

The timer on her oven chirped and she glanced at the wall clock. Okay, Dr. Blue, anytime. She pushed herself off the couch and headed into the kitchen. Her small apartment had been her home for the last eleven years. Her mementos of her assignments were scattered throughout, including several plaques for winning Airman and NCO of the Year. She should probably put those in storage, but every time she looked at them, it gave her a sense of accomplishment.

She checked on dinner, took the ham out and

put it on a platter to rest before she covered it with foil and turned the oven off. The knock at her door exactly on time prompted her to open it without checking who was on the opposite side. She froze, gaping at the man who leaned against the door jamb.

Oh shit. "What are you doing here?"

Jim Watson sneered at her. "That's a hell of a greeting, Poet. How about asking me in?"

"Ah, yeah, sure... come in." She let him pass before she popped her head into the hall and scanned the vacant hallway. *Fuck. Fuck. Fuck.*

"Am I interrupting something?" He motioned to the kitchen table which was prepared for dinner and had two place settings.

"Ah, I have someone coming over."

"Okay, then I'll get to the point. I want you to steer clear of Dr. Boswell or Blue or whatever he's calling himself now. I don't know if you are aware, but his past involved a man dying. He left in disgrace. I'll be going to the Boswell estate tomorrow to talk with Old Man Boswell and make sure he doesn't need assistance in removing the guy."

Poet sat down on the arm of the couch. "I did

some research on him today. He was cleared of those charges."

Jim looked at her. "Yeah, I can see I was right to come over here tonight. Don't you know money makes shit go away? My source tells me the old man took the rap for this guy. His reputation could absorb it. The kid left in a huff and basically stole money from some trust fund when he bounced." Jim stood with his hands behind his back and stared at her plaques on the wall.

"Who is your source?"

"Someone who was around when that shit went down. I didn't know you were in the Air Force."

"Yeah." She narrowed her eyes and glared at the back of her boss. "Why are you here?"

He glanced over his shoulder at her. "I told you."

She shook her head as he turned around. "It isn't like you to spread rumors and speculation." Or at least she didn't think it was. "What about Dr. Blue has you worried?"

"I'm not worried. I don't want him here stirring up problems for Boswell."

"Yeah... no. I'm not buying it." She stood and crossed her arms. "If you had anything legitimate to base your speculation on, you'd take action or have one of us do it for you. So, this little end run here? What do you possibly think you could gain by this?"

"Keep away from him, Poet. You've always been a reliable deputy. I'd hate to think you're no longer trustworthy."

She recoiled in surprise. "Did you threaten my job?" She glared at him and watched the vein on his forehead throb under the deep red stain of the anger that spread over his face. He was pissed and that was fine because she was right there with him.

"You don't want to test me on this. You won't win." Jim pushed past her and slammed out of the apartment.

Poet followed him to the door and thumbed the deadbolt. She combed her hands through her hair. Moving away from the door she turned and looked at it. "I've fallen through the looking glass."

She jumped at a soft knock at her door. This time she checked the peep hole. "Fuck." She threw the deadbolt, reached out, grabbed Maliki, and yanked him into the apartment. She slammed and locked the door behind him.

"Whoa. Relax. He took the elevator. I saw him

coming up when I parked across the street. I used the stairs. I listened at the door, knew he was in here, and waited in the stairwell until he left. I take it he was an unexpected guest?"

She dropped back against the door, her heart pounding against her ribs. "The first and only time in eleven years that he's been here."

"Strange. Why did he show up?" The man strolled into her front room.

"I think it was to threaten me."

He turned; his blue eyes examined her from head to toe. "Did he hurt you?"

She snorted. "Fuck no. I'm not a wilting flower. If he'd touched me, there would have been blood. His."

"The threat?"

"To stay away from you, I think."

"Figures. He followed me to the diner this afternoon and used intimidation tactics on me as well." The doctor shoved his hands into his front jean pockets and nodded to the wall. "Senior Airman and then Staff Sergeant Poet Campbell. You were Air Force."

Poet blinked, catching up with the topic change. "Six years."

A wide smile split his face. "Me too. What AFSC?"

"Security Forces. You?"

"PJ."

"Pararescue? Damn. Impressive. Wait... did you enlist before or after you obtained your medical degree?"

The man shrugged his big shoulders. "After. That was a difficult point in my life. I walked away from medicine for a short time."

She moved away from the door. "What caused you to do that?"

He shrugged again. "Long story. There was a reason you wanted me to meet you tonight?"

"Yeah. It is going to take some explanation. I've made dinner. I figure it was the least I could do since I'm probably chasing ghosts and wasting your time." She headed into the kitchen and put on two oven mitts.

"Dinner sounds good. Hell, it smells good. What ghosts are haunting you?" He leaned against the door jamb and watched as she put the dish of homemade mac and cheese on the table along with the ham.

"Hit start on the microwave, will you?" She

nodded to the other side of the small kitchen. The machine chirped, starting to warm the green beans as she cut slices of ham from the bone. "The ghosts are recent deaths that have happened in the county."

"Three, right? All women?"

Poet spun with a huge carving knife in one hand, a serving fork in the other. "How did you know that?"

"You plan on using that on me?" He nodded to the knife.

She blinked down at the implements she was wielding and shook her head. "No, but how did you know we had three deaths?"

"It was the talk of the bar, or at least the portion of the bar where I was sitting last night. According to local gossip, one was a tweaker. The next one who died, well the royals were accused of keeping that one quiet because her folks worked for one of the estates. They didn't know much about the third one."

"Yeah, three murders—at least I consider them murders—in the last eleven months. Please, take a seat." She placed two large slices of ham on his plate. "Help yourself to the mac and cheese. I'll get the beans." She sat down with the veggies and noticed he'd placed a slice of ham on her plate along with a large scoop of pasta. "Ah, thank you."

"No problem. So, what has you bothered? Do you think they're linked?"

"That's just it." She picked up her knife and fork. "Honestly there is nothing tying them together other than the fact that none of them should be dead." She sighed; her shoulders dropped. "It isn't just the deaths. At the first scene we found a phone. The screen had been smashed and the battery was dead, so Granger and I found a charge cord that worked and powered it up before we turned it on. There were no calls made on the phone, at least in the phone log, but the web browser had four websites listed. I took a picture of the screen before the phone gave up the ship. The websites were of snuff films. Horrific, unbelievably graphic depictions that couldn't have been anything but real.

He put down his fork and stared at her. "You took that to the FBI, right?"

"No. I took it to Sheriff Watson. He said he'd up-channel it to the BCI."

"But..." He encouraged her to continue and took a bite of the food. "This is… good."

"Thanks. The 'but' is... well, it's that my instinct

is telling me that although nothing is connecting the murders and the websites, they are related."

"Why is that?" He sliced into his ham as he asked.

"A myriad of reasons. The first woman wasn't a known drug user. She was actually a health nut. She ran, had close friends, and none of them had any clue she was using. We both know someone who is a chronic user will show signs."

"True. I take it the lab and toxicology supported an OD determination?" He speared a couple green beans on his fork.

She lifted a mouthful of pasta and nodded before she took a bite and spoke around her food. "She had track marks between her toes, and she'd gone missing for three weeks prior to us finding her body. The medical examiner listed drugs as the cause of death."

"No one dug deeper?"

"No. We were told it was a closed case, and the department wasn't going to expend assets to prove what was already known. She died of an overdose."

"I can see the sense in that directive..."

Her eyes narrowed on him.

"If all other questions had been answered. From what you told me; they weren't."

"It was closed so fast. As soon as those toxicology reports came in, the case was pulled from us."

"What about the girl's family? Are they pursuing it?"

"She doesn't have much family. Her parents are dead. She has an elderly aunt who is devastated but isn't asking any questions.

"But you are?"

"She wasn't a drug user."

"So, you think what, someone killed her?" He took another bite of his meal.

"Yeah. I think she was kidnapped. That would account for her being missing for three weeks, and I think she was killed."

"Was she sexually assaulted?"

She shook her head. "According to the report there was no foreign DNA on her."

“But were there signs of assault?”

“I don’t know. The ME didn’t indicate it, and since it didn’t appear to be a suspicious death…”

“They didn’t look.”

“Right.”

He leaned back and patted his mouth with a napkin. Damn, he'd finished his food, and she'd only picked at hers. "More?"

He nodded. "Thank you, it's very good. What about victim number two?"

She took another bite and answered after she'd swallowed. "Stopped breathing."

He caught her eyes, suspending a large spoonful of pasta halfway between the casserole and his plate. "That usually happens when a person dies."

She gave him a sad smile. "The cause of death is unknown. The medical examiner concluded the woman just stopped… living. No heart issues. No trauma. No ligature marks, no indication of strangulation and toxicology came back negative. She was a healthy woman who just... stopped living."

"What did the Bureau of Criminal Investigations say?"

"They weren't called in. The death wasn't labeled as suspicious. The medical examiner said he had nothing to go on. She just… died."

"Family?"

"She had a grandmother who worked at one of the estates. She died shortly after her granddaughter was found."

"How did the grandmother die?"

"Massive heart attack."

"But her death isn't linked to the others?"

"No. There were witnesses. She was serving lunch when she died."

He took another slice of ham. "Had the granddaughter gone missing like the first?"

"I don't know. She lived alone, worked from home as a freelance photographer. The grandmother hadn't spoken to her in a month, but that wasn't unusual."

"And you learned this prior to the grandmother dying?"

"I have it in her statement. Yes."

He sliced a portion off his ham and studied the plate. "The third?"

"Missing for over two weeks. Found in her car. Aspirated on her vomit according to the Medical Examiner."

He nodded. "It happens."

"When a person is sitting up?"

That got his attention. "She was in a seated position?"

"We found her behind the wheel of her car. Seated with her head lolled forward. Cause of death was aspiration and asphyxiation."

He pushed away his dinner plate and leaned forward. "It can happen. If she'd passed out..."

"But you have to admit, it is unusual."

He leaned forward. "There isn't enough if you take each case individually."

"And then there's Shauna."

Maliki turned his head and a single eyebrow lifted. "Why would you assume her case belongs with the others?"

"The easy answer would be, she's a young, pretty woman."

"But Shauna has family, people who know what she's doing and when."

She shook her head. "Shauna doesn't live with Daryl and Jennie. We discovered that she lives near Charlottesville. She'd enrolled in a cosmetology certification course. According to what Granger discovered when talking to Daryl and Jennie while Shauna was in surgery, they hadn't seen her in months."

She picked up her plate and took it to the sink. "I know there isn't anything tying the cases together except for the fact they are young women. But three dead and one fighting for her life, all in this small county? All within the last year? And how did they die out there in the middle of nowhere? Add all of that to the snuff films..."

"Why do you keep returning to the films?"

She sighed and angled her head away from his

gaze. "There was one film. The woman died in the woods. I've hiked through this state, but most of my experience is in this county. The background... I could swear she was killed somewhere in these hills. I'm not a botanist or geologist, but the trees, underbrush, those damn rocks... it was just so familiar."

He stood and brought her his dishes, setting them next to hers in the sink. "And what do you want from me?"

She turned and leaned against the counter, and he followed suit. Their arms brushed together when she looked over and up at him. "I don't think you're just a doctor. I think, based on what I've heard and seen, you're, maybe, an agent."

"Agent?" He chuckled. "Guardian employs personal security officers, investigators, and operatives. We leave the agent banner for the government types."

"I thought Guardian was government."

"Federally recognized, privately owned and funded."

"But you're more than just a doctor, aren't you?" She held his gaze and watched him closely.

Finally, he lifted his shoulder and tipped his head. "What do you need from Guardian?"

"Can you run the girls through your systems? Determine if there is a link between them? I need a thread of connection, something, hell anything, to go over the sheriff's head and take these deaths to the BCI."

He drew a deep breath and dropped his eyes to the floor. "Say, hypothetically, I'm able to pull in a few favors and there's nothing we can find. What are you going to do then?"

She let a low humorous laugh fall. "I'll be looking for a new job. I don't know what's going on with Jim, but he's acting weird. He's changed over the last year, maybe year and a half. The little scene here tonight? Never going to happen again. I'll find someplace to land."

"And if Guardian *is* able to find a connection?"

"I go over Jim's head to the BCI, and *then* I'll start sending my resume, hopefully landing a job before he can fire me. Probably move out of state." She chuckled. "I'm pretty sure if I don't leave willingly, he'll find a way to make me leave. I'd rather go without disciplinary measures in my employment jacket."

They leaned against the counter for a moment in silence, arms touching although they both could easily have avoided the touch. She closed her eyes and drew in a deep breath. The intoxicating cologne he wore filled her senses, and she let it settle around her.

"All right."

She shifted and snapped her eyes to him. "All right what?"

"All right Senior Deputy Campbell, I'll take this to my leadership and see what they have to say. I'm not sure what I can do, but I will run it up the flagpole."

"My name's Poet." She extended her hand.

"I know. Plaques, remember? I'm Maliki." His hand grasped hers and engulfed it.

"I know. Shooting, remember?"

He laughed for a second before he stilled. "I'm going to need everything you have on these cases."

"I took a gamble that you would. Hold on." She darted from the kitchen and headed to her laptop. She grabbed the little silver thumb drive he'd given her this morning from the USB port and closed the attached cap over the top.

She turned to find him standing next to her. "You forgot this today. I'm returning it to you." A smile spread across her face.

"I don't know how long it will take. I'm not

sure if my superiors will approve this, or what resources I'll have at my disposal."

"Anything you can do." She wrapped her arms around herself. "Those girls deserve the effort." She motioned to the couch. "I'm really a crappy hostess. Have a seat. Can I get you an after dinner drink?" She motioned toward a small bar she'd bought in Korea when she did her unaccompanied tour.

He smiled and glanced at her bar. "Is that Sake?"

"It is. The good stuff. I found a small liquor store in Alexandria that stocks it. I can't find the brand we used to buy when I was stationed in Okinawa, but this one is smooth. It probably should be served chilled a bit, but with the air conditioner blasting in this room, I think it is sufficient." She poured two small cups and handed him one.

"Thank you. How long were you at Kadena Air Force Base?" He took a sip and smiled. "This is very good."

"Man, it is so cool to talk to someone who knows where Air Force bases are." She took a sip and motioned to the couch. "I was there eighteen months. It was my overseas short assignment. I should have been there for twenty-four months, but I was reassigned to Kunsan, Korea. They gave me my short tour ribbon for Kadena and remote credit for Kunsan, so I was happy. I spent eighteen months in Japan, a year in Korea, and then I was stationed stateside. Tyndall Air Force Base."

"We have a lot in common. I was stationed at Kunsan for two years and I finished my enlistment at AFSOC before I separated."

"Air Force Special Operations Command." She nodded her head. "Why did you punch?"

He took another sip of his sake before he spoke. "When I joined the Air Force, I left behind a life and my medical career. I wanted to incorporate that career and knowledge with my new skills and independence. I was approached by Guardian about six months before my end of enlistment. They'd done their homework. They knew everything about me and told me they could get my medical license transferred to my new name. They wanted me to work on a team overseas."

"Did you?"

"I did. Now, however, I'm a facility physician." He lowered his eyes and took another sip.

She cringed. The poor guy. "God, no way. That has to be killing you."

He flicked his eyes to her. "Why would you say that?"

"Why?" She snorted inelegantly. "You're an adrenaline junkie."

He angled his head. "Do tell."

She rolled her eyes at his expressionless demeanor. "Oh please." She scooted back into the corner of the couch and lifted her feet onto the sofa.

"No, I'd like to hear why you think I'm an adrenaline junkie."

"First, you were a PJ for six years. Isn't your training for that, like, over a year?"

"Two years."

"And while in training you went through survival school and jump school, right?"

"And dive school."

She tapped her nose with her finger. "Bingo. You moved from being a PJ to Guardian and were placed on an ops team." She made air quotes around the word team. "I'm assuming these teams were utilized for overseas deployments?"

He shrugged and set the empty cup on the coffee table before he rested an arm on top of the back of the couch. She watched as his shirt seams screamed for relief. The man's body was sculpted.

Chiseled. She would be lying if she said she didn't notice. She did. Boy, howdy, she noticed him. She'd bet a month's pay that man knew his way around the bedroom, too.

She lowered her eyelids and her voice, hoping like hell the look was enticing. "I watched you while you worked on Shauna. Last night you were in your element. You performed like a madman and yet... you told me that you had no emotional investment in the situation." When he started to speak, she lifted a hand and rushed, "I'm not criticizing. I get it. You meant it. What you did last night wasn't that big of a deal for you. But let me tell you, what happened last night was a *major* event for every other person that responded. You've done that, responded to emergencies, dealt with gunshot wounds, coordinated medical care, so many times that it was… routine." She finished her sake and tipped her head. "Tell me I'm wrong."

Well, he sure as hell couldn't tell her that. He stared at the woman across from him. He liked her. She picked up on a lot in a short amount of time. Sharp, intelligent and sexy, but also brave. She was putting her career on the line to make sure her victims received justice. Instinct told him Sheriff Watson was, at a minimum, a pompous asswipe—at the maximum, a dirty cop trying to hide something. Whatever Watson didn't want the BCI to find if they came to his county was irrelevant. The cases Poet had told him about were easy to explain away, but Poet's instinct was telling her something was off. He didn't feel the connection in the cases. All could be easily explained and had been, but she'd grabbed onto something, something she was willing to lose her career over. He wouldn't dismiss her concerns out of hand.

"You're staring at me, but you're not telling me I'm wrong." Those big blue eyes sparkled.

"I may tend to gravitate toward activities from which others would walk away."

"I knew it." She slapped her leg. "This deserves another drink."

"Aren't you on call?"

"Nope, I didn't know how tonight would go down, so I asked Carter Hopson to take my calls. Normally, we are a very quiet county." She lifted off the couch, and he watched her pull down her shirt, covering the creamy expanse of skin that had been temporarily exposed. When she strode over to the small bar, he watched her go. Those long, sexy, jean-clad, legs and phenomenal ass were damn near impossible to miss. Her hair spilled down her back and shifted when she stooped over the bar, exposing her trim waist and the swell of her breasts.

She straightened and eventually, his eyes wandered back up to her face. She tilted her head, adding a sexy as fuck smile. "Want another drink… or maybe you'd be interested in something else? A diversion of another nature?"

His gaze slowly rose to meet hers. "That depends. What exactly are you offering?"

She leaned against the wall by the bar, and stared at him, looking at him in a way that made plain what she was offering. She licked her lips, and he followed the glistening tip of her tongue. Finally, she broke the tension between them. "Sex, between two consenting, willing adults. A night, maybe two."

His eyebrows shot up. Damn, she wasn't playing any games.

"I can see you think I'm being forward." She shrugged. "I'm not shy. When I see something I like, I go for it, but I'm not looking for a head trip filled with emotional baggage." She lifted her sake cup to her mouth and drank it, not taking her eyes from him. He extended his other arm along the back of the couch and dropped his knees open. His cock, which had been half interested since he walked through the door, was now paying close attention to the conversation.

"I checked my emotional baggage all the way through to the final destination so there's no need to worry about any luggage issues from my end." Hell, it had been a hot minute since he'd been intimate with anything but his right hand. He didn't want the emotional encumbrance either. Unfortunately, this woman had other issues besides emotions to deal with. "I'm staying for a week or so, but I believe you were warned to stay away from me?"

She gave an inelegant snort before she added, "As if *he* is in charge of my life outside the office. Besides... do you really want to talk about him?" She walked over and dropped to her knees in front of him. "I want to feel this." She reached up and ran her fingers through his beard, tugging it lightly. Her eyes held his for a moment before they dropped to his lips or perhaps his beard. "Oh yes, I want to feel this... everywhere." Leaning forward she pressed her body closer. He let his hand cup the side of her waist above her hip. She moved forward, collapsing the small space between them.

Her warm sake-scented breath caressed his lips before her skin touched his. He moved back before they could kiss, even though it killed him. "We need to talk about protection." He didn't have a fucking condom, and he'd never gone without protection, not even years ago when he was engaged.

"I have us covered." She moved from the floor and climbed into his lap. Her long legs folded and resting on either side of him.

He leaned back when she dipped down to catch his mouth. "I don't have sex without protection."

She cupped his face in her hands and smiled. "Don't trust easily do you, Doctor?" She leaned forward and nibbled on the lobe of his ear.

The action sent a shiver of desire through him–one he didn't try to disguise. "I don't trust anyone with my health, and you shouldn't either."

She slid her lips up the curve of his ear, her hot breath skimming the sensitive skin. Fuck… it was killing him to say no. His dick was begging him to shut his brain down and take what was being offered.

"I'm on the pill and I have a box of condoms in

my bedroom. I don't take chances; I take responsibility. My body, my choice, my responsibility. Now, is there anything else you need to address before you shut up and kiss me?"

"Only this." He grabbed her ass and heaved her over to the side and onto the couch, following her as she fell on her back, his body positioned between her legs.

"Damn. That's sexy as fuck. I like that you're that strong." Poet linked her fingers behind his neck and tugged him down to her. This time he went. The kiss surpassed eager and lapped needy before it slammed into desperate. He was fucking starving, and this woman was his feast. He pushed up her t-shirt. She got the hint and squirmed from it as he unfastened her jeans. He stood and slid the denim down and off her long, sexy legs. Not giving him a moment to enjoy the view, she bounced off the couch and pushed at his shirt. He whipped it over his head as her hands trailed quickly down his chest and found his waistband. It took seconds for her to open his jeans. She yanked on the denim, pulling his boxers down in the process. His cock bounced, heavy, full and straining.

"You're a big boy. Please tell me you know how

to use that." Poet grabbed his shaft with one hand and tried to remove his jeans with the other.

"Fucking boots." He tried to pull them through the material, finding her mouth as they tried to get him out of his jeans. Finally, she pushed him backward. He laughed as he bounced on the cushions.

"Lift your foot."

She grabbed his calf and helped him. He'd been with more than his share of women, but he'd never been with someone *this* bossy. She grabbed the leather and loosened the laces, tugged the boots off and tossed them over her shoulder. "Fucking combat boots, and of course you ladder laced the sons of bitches."

As she mumbled and worked, he drank in the sight before him. Her ivory skin was sprinkled with freckles over the shoulders and on her chest. Her breasts, full and high, moved behind a white lace bra that matched her thong. Fuck him standing, she was waxed. He licked his lips. He loved women who waxed. He thought it was fucking sexy.

"Ha! There! Finally!" She jerked the jeans from his feet. Free of the encumbrance of his jeans she dropped down between his legs and took his cock into her mouth. No warning, no preamble, just hard, hot suction.

He grabbed her hair, and when she moaned around him, he tightened his grip. She moaned again and continued her assault. Holy crap, she was as hungry for sex as he was. "Fuck, that's it. Suck me."

She lifted onto her knees and started bobbing her head up and down his shaft. Her hand grasped him and pumped up, meeting her lips while the other one cupped his balls and squeezed lightly.

"Stop. Close." He pushed his hips up, sending his cock into her throat. She gagged around him but didn't stop. "Poet, stop." He grabbed her shoulder and barred her forward movement.

She groaned and popped off him. "Why?" She wiped her lips with the back of her hand.

Because he was over forty and unlimited trips to the orgasm buffet wasn't a guarantee anymore. He'd damn well get what he wanted on the first pass through. "Where are the condoms?"

She stood up and extended her hand. She braced and helped him up. Fuck, she was fit. Beautiful, healthy and fucking sexy. She lifted his hand, licked down the palm and lowered it to his shaft where she cupped his hand around his cock and together, they stroked his shaft. His eyes nearly rolled back into his brain. She was fucking killing him. "Keep that hard and follow me."

Follow her? Hell yeah. He followed that firm ass to the bedroom and watched as she retrieved a box of condoms from her bedside table. She grabbed some and dropped them on the bed before she unclasped her bra, releasing her full breasts. Her dark, dusty-rose nipples were taut and as fucking enticing as a hit of H to an addict. She slid her fingers under the elastic of her thong, and with a small wiggle of her hips, it dropped to the floor. Flicking her fall of dark auburn hair to her back she extended her arms. "Like what you see, Doctor?"

"God, yes." He moved around the bed and snagged an arm around her waist. He intended to lower the flame on the heat between them, to enjoy the evening, but the second they kissed his intentions went to shit. Flame, meet isopropyl alcohol. The combustion was immediate and incendiary.

Her hands ran up his arms and grabbed his biceps, her firm, lithe body molded against his. "I don't want sweet. I want to be fucked, hard. I want to know you were here when I wake up tomorrow morning." She slid her hands up and tangled them in his beard, pulling him forward. "Show me you can use that cock. Fuck me like you mean it."

He growled as he consumed her. She battled for control of the kiss. He shifted his grip and bent her backward until she had to grab onto his shoulders for balance. That's when she stopped trying to drive the train and got on board. He explored the depths of her mouth until breathing became the priority. Slowly he lifted her up, kissing the column of her neck as they both panted, desperately gathering air in their lungs. He pushed forward, holding her, placing them both on the bed. Her soft, firm breasts pushed against his chest as he manhandled her to the middle of the bed. His teeth scraped her collarbone before he found the top of her breast and then her nipple.

Her hands speared through his hair. She gasped when he tongued her nipple, stopping to suck and nip at the apex of her sensitive skin. Her legs parted for him. He rubbed his beard over her skin using the scrape to sensitize and then used his tongue and lips to entice. After feasting on her breasts, he lowered his assault, inch by glorious inch. Her body arched under him. He moved her legs over his shoulders and opened her. Fuck, she was gorgeous. He loved the taste of her.

Oh my God... Poet angled her hips, pressing into Maliki's mouth. It had been forever since anyone had gone down on her. Fuck that, it had been forever since any man had ignited more than a passing interest. She wanted that shaft inside her. She wanted this man to send her into oblivion and then maybe she wanted to do it again. He sucked her clit into his mouth and flicked it with his tongue. "Fuck, yes, fuck..." Heat pooled low and her legs trembled. She stretched and tightened, her body seizing hard. "Oh God... yes!" She bucked against his face as she climaxed.

Her world flipped, and she was being pushed chest first into the bedding. Maliki lifted her hips while pushing down her shoulder. She felt him lean over and snag a condom. Her core still tightened rhythmically, the phantom echoes of one hell of an orgasm.

Thick, strong fingers wrapped around her hips and held her as his thick, long, cock speared into her, faster and harder than she'd anticipated. She gasped, and he stilled immediately. "Good, so good." She panted the words knowing he needed her to acknowledge she was okay. He pulled out and pushed forward again, and again, gaining speed with each thrust. The friction of their bodies moving together, the intense pressure of his body as he slammed into her, and the rasp of his dick inside her, transformed her into an exposed nerve ending. Everything was intense and overwhelming. Heat and pleasure built, surpassing any sex she'd had in the last fifteen years. His thrusts were hard, sharp, and fast. She pushed back against him, meeting his thrusts with her own. She snaked a hand down and rubbed her clit.

"Fuck, yeah. I can feel you touching yourself." His words came in fast bursts. "Bring yourself off. I'm going to lose it."

She had no problem doing that. Her fingers flew over that tight nub and not more than fifteen seconds later she crashed. Flashes of white behind her eyelids exploded the same time she did. Mal continued his hard, relentless pace until he finished. His hips stuttered, his breath caught, and he thrust through his orgasm, finally, gasping for air.

Liquefied she oozed bonelessly down onto the

bed. Somehow, she moved her arms from underneath her and flopped them to her sides, where Maliki promptly landed on one when he moved off her. He shifted his weight, and she reeled her arm from under him. "Damn."

Maliki snorted and took off the condom. She watched that rock hard, chiseled butt as he headed into the bathroom to dispose of it. Fuck, he was probably the best-looking man she'd ever been with, and he fucking knew how to deliver an orgasm—or two. When he returned, he slid into the sheets beside her. He lay on his stomach and turned to face her. "Damn is not a ringing endorsement."

She rolled toward him. "Oh, I'll give you one hell of a review. Five Stars."

A deep rumble of laughter vibrated the mattress below her. "Yeah? And where would you post said review?"

"Ah..." she popped up on her elbow. "Awesome sex dot com? Best bang for your buck dot net? Hung Well-Tongued Well dot org?" He laughed and snaked an arm, pulling her onto his muscled chest. She ran her fingers through the hair that lightly covered his pecs. "Oh, I know! International Orgasm Rating dot net. Hell, I'll wax poetic over all the platforms. You'll be in demand when you go back to..." She frowned, trying to recall if she knew where he'd come from, but nothing came to mind. "Where do you live?"

"Working for Guardian, I live where they send me. Currently I'm working in Nevada."

"As a doctor."

"Correct."

"Is there a huge need for a doctor in this Nevada location?"

"Not really, and we have two, which is why I can be here."

"You're visiting who?"

He chuckled and pushed her hair away from her face. "You are definitely a cop. Questions, questions, questions."

"What can I say? I'm naturally curious."

"And a risk taker." He leaned up and kissed her.

"You know us adrenaline junkies, we need to stick together, but for future edification, I enjoy jumping out of planes. I love rock climbing. I'm all about living, but I don't do snakes or spiders. A girl has to draw the line somewhere." She dropped her head onto his chest. God, it felt good to be held by someone this strong.

"And your line in the sand is snakes and spiders?" His voice rumbled under her ear.

"As of this moment, yes, but I reserve the right to change my mind." She lifted her head and rested her chin on her hands as she looked up at him. "You didn't answer my question. You're really good at diverting."

He smiled. "Thank you."

"You're welcome, and you still didn't answer." She lifted her eyebrows up and down.

"Yes, I'm here to visit my parents."

"The Boswells?"

"Yes."

"For a week."

"Or so. My mother needs some support dealing with a few issues."

She popped up on her elbows. "Oh. Just FYI, Jim said something about going to see your father to make sure you weren't here causing problems."

Maliki followed suit and pushed up on to his elbows, lifting them both easily. "Excuse me?"

"Yep. Is that going to cause problems for you or your mom?"

Maliki shook his head, but the carefree easiness that had surrounded them after the great sex disappeared quickly. "Shouldn't." He glanced at the clock and then back at her. "What time do you have to be at work in the morning?"

"I'm usually there by six. Why?"

He wrapped his arm around her and flipped her onto her back. "Wouldn't want to wear you out." His lips found her neck and she shivered against him.

She ran her hands up his strong arms and arched her back as his lips traveled lower. Her voice caught when his tongue traced her nipple. "Who the hell needs sleep?"

CHAPTER 6

Mal stood outside Poet's apartment complex. He'd used the side entrance to leave, the one without a working exterior light so it was easier to let his eyes adjust to the darkness. At four in the morning, he didn't expect to see anyone, but he was covering his bases so Poet didn't have to engage in any battles before he'd be able to talk with Joseph. He carefully scanned the area and walked slowly along the dark brick.

After several minutes and no discernable movement, he made his way to his vehicle and back to his hotel room. He showered and fell into the bed. The sex had been fantastic. The woman was intriguing, and with the promise of more nights like tonight, he'd left her bed this morning feeling pretty damn good.

He smiled and closed his eyes. Well, at least one good thing had come from the trip. He chuckled at his own pun and rolled onto his side. With the practiced ease of a man who'd learned to sleep when there was an opportunity, he fell into an exhausted slumber.

Damn it. He slapped the nightstand until he found his phone. Without looking at the screen he swiped his thumb and face planted the phone. "What."

"Thorn Operative Six, Standby."

"Roger that." His eyes opened into narrow slits. The alarm clock's blue face came into focus. 8:30 a.m. Fuck him, sleeping that hard wasn't a trait with him, but then again, neither was multiple episodes of outstanding sex.

"Fury online."

"Alpha online."

"Archangel online."

"I want a fucking code name."

Mal burst into laughter at Jade's comment. That woman was as crazy as they came.

Joseph's comeback was immediate. "We

checked. The Wicked Witch of the West was taken."

"Fuck you. I want a code name."

"How about Pretty Woman?" Mal offered and heard the groans of her brothers.

"See, Mal gets it. But seriously, I need a code name."

"Jade, this call isn't for that purpose. Where's Jared?" Archangel's voice grated the question.

"He's sitting right here–laughing." Mal heard someone whack something and Jared's laughter boomed over the line.

"Enough!" Jason's voice cut through the antics and silenced everything. "Maliki, I have in front of me your training jacket which Joseph has forwarded to me."

"Yes, sir." What else was he supposed to say?

"In addition, there is a request for a concealed carry permit and a request for permission to work as an investigative entity with credentials."

"Yes, sir." Mal rubbed his face and sat up, throwing a couple pillows behind him, propping himself up.

"Your training is impressive. I see your time at The Rose hasn't been wasted, but before I decide on this case, I want to hear from you exactly what is going on down there."

He drew a deep breath and started at the beginning. He finished several minutes later. His little story was met with nothing but silence.

"So, you have three death scenes and a shooting that don't seem to be tied together and a dipshit county sheriff that is, for all intents and purposes, an asshole." Jared tied up his concerns in a tight little bow.

"Pretty much. Sheriff Watson also said he was going to go to my parents' estate to ascertain whether or not I was a 'problem'."

The line was quiet for several seconds before Jason asked, "What's he hoping to gain from the end run?"

"Since he told Poet about it, I don't think it's an end run. He's pulling a power play. I don't know what this guy knows about what happened years ago, but if he was around at that time, he could have gotten a whiff of the discord between my old man and me. Maybe he's hoping dear old dad will give him the ammunition to send me packing."

"Will he?" That was Alpha talking.

"No, sir. He can't. My father has been diagnosed with vascular dementia. He's had a stroke, and my mother has had him declared incompetent. She's the one who asked me to come home, so I can't see an issue."

"Damn, I'm sorry to hear that." Jade whispered, but they all heard her.

"It is what it is. Look, I haven't been in this place for years, but what I'm getting is that the association with Guardian has the sheriff skittering like a cat in a room full of hungry dogs. His deputy has been muzzled, and he isn't allowing her to call in any help with these deaths."

"What do you recommend as a way forward?" Jared's question hung for a second.

Maliki leaned forward. "If I were directing this investigation, I'd start with an exhumation of the first two bodies, and Guardian should take jurisdiction of the third body, doing a complete postmortem without the influence of local authorities."

"That's a good start." Jared replied. "What else?"

Mal smiled. He understood. He was being tested. "Interviews with the deceased's next of kin, friends, people who worked or went to school with them. I'd look for inconsistencies, pieces of the puzzle that don't mesh or have been manufactured. Get ahold of their electronic trail for at least three months and try to determine if they are connected in any way."

Jared prompted, "Go on."

"Then if I found any substantial information, I'd start looking into why the sheriff wanted these cases closed and put away without BCI involvement."

"Why would you wait to look into the sheriff?" Jacob asked, his confusion clearly detectable.

"Because if you start looking into the locally elected good ol' boy without probable cause, it would be seen as a witch hunt, and it wouldn't be a credible investigation. One piece of the puzzle at a time. If James Watson is dirty, he's going to stay dirty," Maliki finished and waited for further questions.

Jared sighed. "Doc, I know you realize exhuming the bodies probably won't yield a slew of new information."

Mal agreed, "I do. As a matter of fact, it will reveal little to nothing, but it may make any culpable entities pushing a mandated closure of these cases squirm and maybe make a mistake or even flush them out of the woodwork."

Archangel interjected, "While we're federally recognized, we can't go into a county and start an investigation without someone requesting our assistance."

"Senior Deputy Campbell has requested our assistance, however, she is fearful of repercussions should the sheriff discover she's gone around him. You could use me. My family lives in the county. I could be the requesting party." Poet had every right to feel uneasy, that was for damn sure. Using him as the client took that onus off her.

"Can we contact any federal judges in Virginia? Get permission to go in?" Jade's voice came over the connection.

Jared answered, "I'd prefer the Attorney General inviting us in, and I can see some ruffled feathers if we don't go that route. They have their own system for inhouse investigations."

He closed his eyes. It was going to suck to go back to Poet and tell her they couldn't help, but he hadn't made any promises.

"Then we contact the AG, and we explain we have a man on the ground already. One who is visiting family and can work a low-key examination. Get the AG to exhume the two bodies and give us jurisdiction on the third without announcing it to the public. Promise to give him the credit if there is anything found and relieve him of the financial burden since, in our opinion, there really isn't anything to go on anyway, but we are going to appease the very connected person who requested we look into it."

His eyes popped open. That could work, if the AG was willing to play ball.

"I'll call Robert. We've got a pretty good working relationship," Archangel concurred, but added, "In the meantime, get Maliki's creds and concealed carry established. I'll need a courier dispatched to his location the second the documents are done. Mal, if we get the AG to play ball what else do you need?"

"I'll need backgrounds on all these women, oh and the list of websites that were turned into the BCI."

"Websites?" Jared interjected his question.

"Senior Deputy Campbell stated a badly damaged phone was found at the first death scene. The deputies were able to activate it and although it had no calls in the call log it had four websites listed in the browser. She took a picture of the sites and turned that and the phone over as evidence to the sheriff to be forwarded to BCI. She said the sites held videos. Snuff videos. Each portraying the death of a woman."

"Holy fuck. Well, at least that case was handed over to the BCI. They'll undoubtedly hand it over to the FBI. Does this deputy feel there is a connection?"

Mal sighed. "There is no evidence of a connection, but..."

Jason's voice filled the void his trailing words left. "If I get buy in from the AG, we can authorize looking into the deaths, but it won't be a priority on any level. We'll leave the websites to the FBI, their sexual crimes unit would have more opportunity for success than we would. That being said, we have too much shit going on to bump this situation ahead of another case. Jared, what is the backlog for backgrounds without priority?"

"Three to six weeks. Jewell's team is working 24/7. Unless we put this as a priority, they are going to languish and may get bumped back based on our caseload."

"Maliki, are you good staying in Virginia longer?"

He drew a deep breath and nodded, then cleared his throat before he spoke. "I'm good with it. Ember has the facility; she doesn't need my help. I'll need a POC to contact with requests."

"That would be me." Joseph interjected.

"No, that should be me." Jared countered.

"He's one of mine," Joseph reiterated. "Granted he isn't in a duet, yet, but we'll match him eventually. He calls in to me until he's released from the program. It's protocol. Once the teams are released, they answer to either you or Alpha, as dictated by mission. He hasn't been released. He's my responsibility. I'll coordinate any assistance through either you, Alpha, Cyber, or Archangel."

"That is the most I've heard him say in like... three years." Jade chuckled. "He's getting to be chatty, isn't he?"

"I agree, Mal reports to Joseph until he's either officially entered *and* completed the training program or decided against following through, in which case we'll look at reassigning him somewhere his talents won't go to waste. So, credentials and a concealed carry permit are being drawn up. You can't be given investigator status; you don't have the classroom certifications or the experience. Let the deputy run the show. You're assisting and coordinating our efforts, if they are needed. Consider yourself a liaison. Anything else?"

He volunteered a request, "I could use a shoulder holster and one for my belt."

"Easy." Alpha chimed in, "What type of weapon?"

"The forty-five that is in the SUV will suffice." Mal liked the weight of the handgun when he'd handled it yesterday.

"Mal, if shit gets harsh, you call for backup. We can roll the state police in a heartbeat. No playing on this. You and the deputy interview the witnesses and re-examine the crime scenes without stirring the waters. We'll get the bodies exhumed and processed, but you know any additional lab tests from them will take weeks, if not months to finalize. Keep this quiet. Do not rock the boat, and make sure you don't end up dead. I'd be all kinds of pissed. Archangel out." An audible click sounded.

Jade laughed, "Well, that went well."

"Why the hell are you on this call?" Alpha chuckled as he asked.

"I was in Jared's office, and he said Mal was going to be on the line." Her voice morphed into a sing-song affair and she asked, "Hi Mal! How you doing?"

He laughed and shook his head. The woman's audacity was mind-altering. "I'm fine, Jade. How's married life?"

"Dude, you know, it ain't half bad. Actually, it is more than half good. Regular sex. Stupendous sex. *All* the time. You should try it. I highly recommend it. But seriously, I heard you were home and wanted to check and see if everything is okay. I'm sorry about your dad, even though I know you're not on the best terms. Dementia sucks."

"It does and I'm fine. I haven't decided whether or not I'm actually going to try to talk to him."

"Talk to him."

"Do it."

"Don't let this pass you up."

"For fuck's sakes, talk to him."

The sibling's comments tumbled over each other.

Mal chuckled humorlessly and shoved his palm into his face, scrubbing hard. "Whoa, so I take it you all think I should talk to my father."

"We didn't get a chance to say goodbye. Don't waste this opportunity, Mal. It may be the only chance you get." Jade's voice, for once, wasn't flip or caustic, rather sincere and sad.

"I get that. Thanks for the advice."

"Joseph, you have Mal's current address?" Thankfully Alpha switched the conversation.

"I do. Sending it to you now."

"Mal, be safe. I honestly don't think there is jack shit you're going to find." Jared popped into the conversation.

"Except maybe a paranoid blowhard sheriff." Jade laughed at her own joke.

"Except that. Take care. Get Joseph the info so we can put the background investigations into the queue. Jade and I are out." The line clicked.

"Mal, stay sharp and be careful. The holsters, creds and badge will be sent to you, today. Alpha out." The line clicked again.

"How many favors did you have to pull in from your brother to even look at my request?" He spoke to the only person left on the line, Joseph.

"Jason owes me a thousand or so. Pulling one is a non-factor. Listen up, though. This case remains below Watson's radar. Keep it quiet. As far as anyone knows you are there to reconnect with your family. By the way, you do that. You plug in, and you get straight with your old man, even if that is telling him to fuck off, but you get that closed. You don't want the hole in your soul not having that closure brings. Trust me on this."

"I get it. It's just..."

"And I get your position. I want daily updates, but do me a favor and fucking email them. Ember is starting to get jealous. I don't get a status report by the end of my nightly training run I'll send in the Marines. Understand?"

"Roger. I got it. Daily updates via email. Stay under the radar."

"Keep your shit tight. Consider this a test drive. Do well and we'll finish your course of instruction and match you with your counterpart."

"And if I don't do well?"

"Well, hell. There's always that office job. Fury out."

He dropped his cell phone on his chest and closed his eyes. Moving forward with his father was going to suck. Anger, hurt and damn it, even disappointment, clung around his past like sentinels. He'd learned not to look in that direction, but the past was there and looming larger every fucking moment. He scrubbed his face with his hands. One step at a time. He picked up his phone to text Poet... No, she'd be at work and if her phone displayed texts on the home screen it could complicate things for her. He'd call after duty hours.

He pushed the covers off and stood and stretched. His muscles moved with each movement. He glanced at the clock again and drew a deep breath. "Exercise, shower, and then head to Mom's. Deal with Poet afterward. One step at a time." His stay extended and his purpose altered, he adjusted his mental compass, shot an azimuth and determined a way to his objective. Damn, finally having a purpose was liberating and fucking empowering.

The housekeeper opened the front door before he could reach it. "Doctor Boswell, your mother is in the garden."

He paused, rolled his shoulders and drew a sustaining breath. "My name is Maliki Blue, please address me properly."

The little woman blinked, her mouth agape. She snapped her mouth shut and nodded. "Of course, sir." She stepped back and opened the door wider.

Mal headed down the elaborately designed marquetry hallway. The expansive concourse naturally drew the eye from the front of the house to the extravagant gardens at the rear of the residence. The living spaces were divided in half by the intricate, detailed, architectural bay.

Mal stepped onto the massive loggia and scanned the area for his mother. He found her immediately. She stood when she saw him. His father lifted his head and turned to look in his direction. His father. Damn, he wasn't the man he remembered. No, the man sitting in the wheelchair wasn't the larger than life, egotistical tyrant he recalled. Life, or perhaps the specter of death, had taken its toll on Harrison M. Boswell V. Even from this distance, Mal could see the frailness in his father's frame.

The deterioration of his physical health was more marked than he'd anticipated and it… startled him, even though it shouldn't. As a doctor, he knew the progressions of diseases and how they affected physical systems. The step by step failures that moved a healthy body into a slow transition toward death were unique to each person, but the overall progression was predictable and inevitable. The only thing guaranteed after birth was death. Watching death approach was difficult when one observed the lonely trial of patients. The loss became arduous and grueling when the person passing was a friend, and it was absolutely debilitating to witness the demise of those who were part of your family.

Maliki shoved his hands into his jean pockets. Damn it, he wanted to pigeonhole his father in another category, but he couldn't. He'd idolized his father for so many years, seeing him, like this... hurt. A tsunami of emotion plunged him into the depths he'd fought for years. Yet escaping this moment was impossible.

His mother patted his father's shoulder and said something before she placed a kiss on the man's temple. He focused on the small act of tenderness. He'd never seen any physical kindness between his parents. The reserved and distant relationship they shared didn't perpetuate a loving connection, or at least it hadn't.

"I'm so glad you came today," his mother said as she approached.

"I told you I would." His eyes remained locked on the man across the patio.

"You did." She stopped in front of him and glanced back. "I didn't mean to do this. It's such a lovely morning, and your father is having a good day. We normally sit outside for a while every day. He's been asking for you."

"Has he?"

"He wants to talk to you, when you're ready."

"I'm not sure that would be a pleasant experience for either of us."

"He knows he failed you. Failed us. Would talking to him cost you more than ignoring him will? His time is waning. His good moments are fewer." She drew a shaky breath and rubbed her arms.

"I'm not sure I can forgive him."

"I know." She blinked back moisture and a sad smile appeared for a fraction of a second.

Mal swung his attention back to his father. He drew a breath and let it go slowly. It was time to deal with his past. The first step wasn't intentional. The second step across those travertine tiles brought realization, the third footfall bolstered his resolve and the fourth... hell, that step drug a small sliver of hope into the light. Hope that he fully expected to be extinguished and buried at the first minute at his father's side, but he couldn't help feeling the tiny shard of emotion.

He sat down in the chair his mother had vacated and glanced at his father. The left side of his face hung, limp, the muscles no longer working. He tore his attention away and leaned forward, put his elbows on his knees, and steepled his fingers. His eyes scanned the vast, manicured gardens and rolling hills.

"Thank you."

He closed his eyes at his father's slurred words. "For what?" He waited, the answer would be slow as his father battled the ravages of the stroke and perhaps the dementia.

"Coming."

Mal leaned back in his chair. Thousands of angry words formed and dissolved. A decade of hatred, hurt, and questions condensed into one word. "Why?" he whispered, and turned his eyes slowly to meet the eyes of the man he loved and hated in equal measure.

A tear formed and fell from his father's eye, and then another followed the first. "Pride. Vanity. Fear." The words were slurred and slow, but clear enough for him to understand.

He drew a sharp breath and turned away again. So, his old man's reputation had been more important to him than his son. Well, hell, what had he expected? He stared at the hedgerow in the distance. After a moment he shrugged, because hell, he'd come to that realization years ago. "All right."

He stood and slammed his hands in his pockets again. His father lifted his right arm toward him. "So... damn... sorry."

He dropped his chin to his chest. For years, those words would have been redemptive, enticing and appreciated. Now? Perhaps it was too little, too late. Trite, but... yet... "Thank you for the apology. Unfortunately, it is about a decade too late. Your actions ruined me. My loving fiancé waited five days before she dumped me. Maybe I should thank you for that. She seemed to love my status and title more than she loved me." A humorless chuff fell between them.

"Guardian... now?"

He snorted. "Yes, they recruited me after I spent six years in the Air Force as an enlisted pararescue specialist." Well, fuck him. He was having a conversation with a man he swore he'd never speak to again. He shook his head in disbelief. His damn empathic tendencies sucked balls.

"Doctor... still?"

Mal snorted. "Yeah." He glanced at his father. "Thanks to whoever it was that was brave enough to dispute your claim. How did you make it go away? Did you pay off the family?"

"Settled."

Of course. Money. His father's answer to everything. "Look, I should probably go." Truth be told, he needed to go find a punching bag or run again. His emotions were twisted, knotted, and bunched tight under his skin, and he needed to work through... everything. But escape didn't look plausible at the moment.

"Come back. Please." His father's slurred plea hit his bruised psyche and exposed nerves.

"What purpose would it serve?" He didn't ask to be an ass. He really wanted to know why his father wanted this conversation.

"Penance."

Mal barked a laugh. "Mine or yours?"

"Me. Need to... ask... forgive me."

Mal blinked back his surprise. "I've attempted to forgive you. I needed to move forward, to become the man I am now."

"Are you happy?" The words came slowly, but with more confidence.

He considered the question for a moment. "Content, to a degree. I work for an organization that focuses on the greater good. I'm part of a team. Well, actually we're more than a team. We're brothers and sisters in arms. That bond is special and unique. I'm a better man because of them, and hopefully they are lifted by my efforts." He swung his attention to the doors where his mother stood.

She leaned against the wall and stared in their direction.

"A wife or family?"

"Ah, that would be a no." He'd dodged a bullet when Clarissa Prentiss tossed him aside, and he didn't date as much as have sex. Like with Poet last night. No strings, no attachments. He'd attempted the 'wine and dine' thing a couple times. Most were flaming disasters. Some ended up in friendships. Jasmine and Jade came to mind.

"Do you… know... where I am?"

He snapped his head toward his father. His heart sank. Fucking dementia. "Yes. You're at your home in the country."

His father nodded. "I... need to go to the office."

"Not today."

"No?"

"No, no work today."

Mal stared as his father's eyes slowly blinked closed. He waited for several minutes before he left the side of his sleeping father. A woman in scrubs walked toward him as he walked away. "He's sleeping."

The nurse paused and smiled at him. "I'll sit with him until he wakes and then take him upstairs and get him comfortable again."

He watched her go.

"Were you able to talk?" His mother was at his side.

"Some. He seemed to forget where he was." His mother took his arm, and he turned to escort her back into the house.

"Since we've got him on a regimen for his blood pressure, it appears the progression has stalled. The doctors tell me if he has another stroke, it could worsen. But breaking down complex tasks into simple steps and reminding him where he is helps his fear and confusion."

"It must be hard for you." He escorted her to the small sunroom where a table for two had been prepared. He slid her chair away from the table and waited for her to take a seat.

She sank into the chair and sighed, "It is difficult, but I ask myself what it must be like for him. He was stripped of his practice, his pride, and his independence. He couldn't manage his accounts; he'd get lost going from his apartment to the clinic or the hospital. He's confided in me that he's terrified. I try to keep that fear from being magnified." She placed her damask linen napkin in her lap.

He copied her actions and within seconds a servant placed a smoked salmon and charred asparagus salad in front of his mother and then him. The food was exceptional, as always. The silence, punctuated by the polite soft sounds of silverware, bordered on oppressive. He finished his salad. "You've lived here since I left?"

His mother placed her fork on the plate and smiled. "I have friends here. Some more special than others."

If his eyebrows could have hit the ceiling, they would have. He leaned forward and whispered. "Did you just admit to having a lover?"

His mother's face went crimson. She cleared her throat and glanced around, probably to make sure there wasn't any staff around to hear her. "Harrison… excuse me, Maliki, I'm old. I'm not dead. Your father and I haven't had marital relations in almost twenty years. I do have a gentleman with whom I am affectionate. I love your father. I'm not in love with him. Your father was... active, but discrete, and I learned from his example. I decided after the incident that forced you from us I was going to become a woman who stood up for herself. What about you? Do you have someone special?"

He leaned back as the servant entered the sunroom to remove the salad plates. "No. After

Clarissa there wasn't anyone, for a long time, and now there is no one special." Poet's smiling face flashed in his mind. He immediately pushed that vision away.

"That's such a shame. I'm sure she regretted her haste after the truth was discovered, but we'll never know."

"Well I'm sure as hell not going to call her." A plate of spiced lamb, baby potatoes and roasted vegetables was placed in front of him after his mother's smaller portion was served.

"You don't know?"

He sliced a tender piece of lamb. "Know what?"

"Clarissa Prentiss died in a car accident the summer after you left. It was a few days after her mother passed. Richard was beside himself with grief. He left the country for years, only recently returning."

"What happened?"

"A hit and run, I believe."

"Did they find the person responsible?"

"No, not to my knowledge. A horrible loss."

The news was surprising, but there was no rush of emotion tied to the announcement. Clarissa and he had never been in love, but they'd been intimate. Grieving her passing wasn't necessary since he already buried her, at least metaphorically. "That is a shame." With careful movements, he placed his utensils down. "How did Dorothy Prentiss die?"

"Oh... a massive heart attack. We'd played tennis two weeks before. Such a tragedy. Richard buried them both on the same day. It was a private ceremony. Family only."

"Where did Richard go?"

"His villa in Spain, I think. He travels but comes back to check on me. His last trip was to Thailand."

He picked up his fork and parroted, "Thailand? Really?"

"Yes, evidently the country is absolutely beautiful. Richard said he immersed himself in the history and learned the culture of the nation. He is unbelievably intelligent."

He took a bite of food and eyed his mother as a faint hue of rose tinged her cheeks. "So, you and Richard?"

Her eyes popped wide and met his. "Well... yes."

"How long?"

"On and off for years, more so since he returned. But lately, I've been deeply involved in gaining control of your father's business and managing his medical intervention. Richard is a godsend. We visit for hours, and he's comforting. We've gone to Charlottesville to dinner on several occasions and visited New York for the weekend. We're very careful not to upset your father."

He watched his mother for a moment and returned to his lunch, which now resembled saw dust in his mouth. His mother was seeing another man. The father of his ex-fiancée.

"I know this isn't my business, but I'm going to ask anyway. Do you and Richard have plans?"

"Plans? As in?" His mother lifted a tiny bite of lamb to her lips.

"Marriage."

She laughed and shook her head. "No. Richard has speculated that someday we may join forces, but your father's disease is one that can linger. Hopefully, he'll have many years of comfortable, quality life ahead of him. I'll be at his side until the end. I have no desire to marry again. Ever." She ate a bite of her food and tipped her head, studying him.

He ate another bite of the impeccably prepared, and one hundred percent, tasteless, meal. He glanced at his mother who was studying him. "What?"

"Are you worried about losing your inheritance?"

"What? Hell no! I don't want a fucking dime of his money. I took the trust fund your mother gave me because it had nothing to do with him."

She leaned forward and placed a hand on his arm. "Honey, you are the sole benefactor of your father's estate, with the exception of this house, if you'll allow it. He and I both agreed everything he's amassed should go to you. When I pass, you will receive everything that remains. Besides, I have my own family money, and I have no elaborate needs except for this house and staff to maintain it. My coffers are more than adequate to take care of my needs and have a multitude left for you. Our wills are locked in the safe in your father's office. It doesn't matter if you want the money, it will go to you. After all that has happened... it is the least we can do."

He pushed his plate away from him and leaned in. "Mother, I don't need or want his or your money. I'm very well paid. I want for nothing; I've established a wonderful life, and I have most of my trust fund available should I need it. It is more than I'll spend in this lifetime."

"I know, sweet boy. But someday you will have

children, pass it on to them."

"Mom, my chance at a family has come to an end." When he was finished dealing with Poet and his father, he was almost positive he was going to request formal entry into the program at The Rose.

"Don't ever discount love. It will find you whether you're looking for it or not." Her blush rose again.

"Do you love Richard?"

"I believe I'm in love with the *idea* of being in love with Richard. Everyone should have that one person who simply takes their breath away. Richard isn't that person, but he's lovely. More than I've had in the past."

"I'm sorry your life has been..." He shrugged. How did he verbalize regretting she'd had a life of opulence instead of one brimming with love? He'd witnessed both sides of that coin. He'd pick true love, family and friends any day of the week and twice on Sunday.

"Half-lived? I signed up for this life with my eyes wide open. What I didn't realize was I was dooming you to the same type of loneliness. I know you didn't love Clarissa, but she would have made a proper wife for you."

He couldn't dispute her statement. They would have been successful and utterly hollow. The plates were cleared before two individual tart dishes with two exquisitely, decadent strawberry gateau were presented and placed in front of them. "Your favorite. I had the chef make it for you." His mother smiled and gestured to the delicacy.

He hadn't had a gateau since... Well since the last time he'd been here. The Air Force dining facilities weren't horrible, but they didn't provide haute cuisine—unless you asked the Army. The Army would definitely say the Air Force catered to its people. His time in Guardian had been a three-way divide between MREs, take out, and solitary meals. He tested a small bite and closed his eyes as the flavor burst onto his taste buds. "Absolute perfection."

His mother laughed happily. "Thank you for coming back, and thank you for trying. I know this is hard for you. I also know you don't have to be here, that you could walk away."

Except he couldn't. Not now. Not after Poet's plea for assistance and not after the few words he shared with his father. "I've decided to stay for a while. A month or so, perhaps."

Her fork clattered to her plate. "Will you stay with us?"

He smiled sadly and shook his head. "I'll stay in town. I'm trying. Give me time. This isn't easy for me."

"No, no, of course not. You were hurt by people you trusted. Wounded by our actions. I was rash to ask, but I won't lie, I'm so grateful you came, that you're willing to try." She lifted her napkin and dabbed at her eyes. "It is more than we deserve."

He smiled sadly. More than anything he wanted to bridge the canyon of pain, isolation, and anger that had split him from his mother and his father. He'd try to move forward, at his pace, in his way, so he could minimize the damage walking through that minefield could cause, both to his parents and to himself. Today was a tenuous start to a harrowing journey. However, one thing he'd learned since he'd left this life was the art of survival. Life had knocked the shit out of him twice, but he'd gotten back up. If this situation imploded, he'd find an outcropping and prop himself up until he was ready to fight again. He wasn't who his family once knew, he was more. He was a Guardian, a warrior, and yes, a healer.

CHAPTER 7

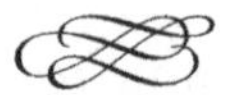

Poet chuckled at her best friend, Tillie, who flopped into the luncheon booth across from her. Tillie shoved her purse against the wall, swiped her mass of curls away from her face and flagged the waitress as she passed. "Hey, Marie, the usual please?"

"Pink or yellow today?" Marie asked as she kept on walking.

"Pink!" Tillie raised her voice and Marie lifted a hand acknowledging her. She flopped back in the booth and sighed. "Sorry I'm late. I had a teleconference about next quarter's budget, and not only did they kill that topic, they resurrected it and killed it again. On and on and on. Thank goodness it was a teleconference. If it had been a video conference, they would have watched me load my fingers, put them to my brain and pull the trigger. It was painful."

She chuckled at her friend's harried appearance. But that was Tillie, an F5 tornado on her calm days. The woman was her own energy turbine, but she was also fun, and the best friend Poet had ever had. When Poet moved into her apartment, Tillie, her next door neighbor, promptly introduced herself and the rest was, as they say, history.

"I doubt they would have enjoyed the visual." She wrinkled her nose at the idea of budgetary meetings. At least the sheriff handled all that crap. Moving up the food chain any farther would require her to delve into the muck of finances for the department. No thank you. "I couldn't do your job."

"Pfft... Money doesn't affect my creatives. I build them and give them to the people who put them online. They worry about the budget; I don't give a crap unless they stop paying me."

Marie did a drive-by with two large glasses in hand. One with pink lemonade and one with a refill of her iced tea. "You ladies ready to order?"

"I want the chef salad. Extra ranch dressing on

the side and a slice of strawberry pie." Tillie tossed her order to Marie and then looked at her.

"BLT, fries, mayo on the side and I'll pass on dessert."

Marie nodded and turned away not even bothering to write down the order. In all the years they'd been meeting for their weekly lunch date, she'd never seen the woman write down an order, and she'd never had the order wrong. Unless they carved some time to meet, their crazy schedules, lives, and Tillie's classes kept them apart. Poet smiled and asked, "So what's new with you?"

"Same stuff, different day. Oh! Lyle finally asked me to go to dinner with him. I'm thinking, no."

Wait, what? "I thought you wanted the man to ask you out. Hell, you've been an outrageous flirt with him since he started teaching graphic arts with you!"

Tillie sighed, "Well, yeah, I did, like six months ago. He took his sweet time. I don't like the idea maybe I'm his second or third choice, you know? Like, it took him six months to ask me out." Tillie flopped back in the booth, bouncing her knees.

"Okay, stop. From what you tell me, Lyle is a nice guy. Did you ever think that maybe you intimidate him, and he had to build up the courage to ask you? You're kinda intense, yah know."

Tillie stopped moving. "I am?"

"Hell, yes. Give the guy a break. Go out to dinner with him. Don't kill any chance of a good time before you know for sure you won't have fun."

"Maybe."

"Not maybe. Sex is not overrated." She stared at Tillie and lifted an eyebrow.

Tillie's eyes narrowed and she leaned forward. "How the hell can you have black circles under your eyes and still look so... serene?" Tillie's eyebrows shot up. "You got laid!"

"Shhh!" She glanced around and smiled at Mrs. Jensen. The woman smiled sweetly and went back to pretending she wasn't listening to the conversation. She leaned forward and whisper hissed, "You're an ass. Why would you shout that?"

Tillie leaned forward and hissed back, "I'm sorry! Who? Hannaford or Granger?"

"No! I don't shit where I eat."

"Gross!"

She waved a dismissive hand. "You know what I mean." She'd never date the men in the department. That would be disastrous. But she enjoyed men and yes, sex. The tiny town limited her potential partners. They leaned back as Marie approached with their meal.

Tillie bounced in her seat until the platters were deposited, and then as one, they leaned forward again. "Who?"

"You don't know him."

Tillie's head snapped back. "I don't know him? I call bullshit. This is a small town!"

"Shhh..."

"Okay, okay, but dish, will you?" Tillie grabbed her fork and stabbed her salad.

"No. Suffice to say he's not from around here." She wasn't going to compromise Maliki by telling anyone anything.

Tillie dropped her fork. "We share. We always share. What's up with this guy? Why are you acting different? Oh fuck, do you like have *feelings* for him?"

She picked up her sandwich and narrowed her eyes at her friend. "You don't have sex with people you don't have feelings for, even if it's just lust."

Tillie nodded and talked around a mouth full of lettuce, "Okay, let me rephrase, is this scratching an itch, or is this a rash, or maybe a permanent skin condition?"

She thought about that for a hot minute.

"Scratching an itch. Not going to lie though, if he lived around here, I wouldn't mind a rash." Hell, the way the man had worked her body last night, she might entertain a permanent condition, but that wasn't going to happen.

"Was it good?" Tillie dipped her already dressed salad into a huge cup of ranch dressing.

A smile she didn't care to stop spread across her face. "Fan-fucking-tastic."

Tillie squealed and then laughed, her mouth full of food.

"Damn it, Til, will you please act semi-normal?"

Around her full mouth of food she smiled. "Hello, do you know me? Are you going to see him again?" Tillie shoved another forkful of salad into her mouth and waggled her eyebrows as she munched.

She grabbed several fries and dredged them through the mayo. "Maybe. I don't know. Last night could have been a one and done. I'm not sure." She popped them into her mouth and glanced up as the door opened. *Fuck.*

"What?" Tillie's eyes widened at her sudden change of mood. Her head snapped around and then sighed. "He is so damn good looking. Too bad he's your boss."

She picked up her sandwich and grumbled under her breath, "Looks only get you so far."

Tillie waved at Jim. He lifted a hand and strolled in their direction. Tillie scooted over and patted the bench seat. "Hi! Long time no see. How's life been treating you?"

"Tillie." Jim acknowledged her but didn't sit down. "Poet, I need to speak with you. Sorry for cutting your lunch short." He glanced at Tillie and smiled briefly.

"That's okay. Maybe I'll catch you tonight, Poet. We can finish this conversation then." Tillie laughed and shoved more lettuce into the ranch dressing.

She nailed her boss with a pissed off look and waited. Jim held her stare for a moment before he dipped his chin. *Damn it.* "I'll be right there." He nodded again and smiled at Tillie before he left.

She took a bite of her sandwich and wiped her hands.

"Whoa, what happened there?" Tillie stared wide-eyed.

"Nothing."

"That wasn't nothing. That... was a whole lot of pissed off." Tillie moved her finger between her and the space where Jim had stood.

"That was a whole lot of my boss overstepping his authority, but we'll fix it."

"Well, damn, I hope so. I don't like drama."

"Bullshit. You live for drama."

Tillie laughed. "Yeah, I do. Get the hell out of here. I'll get the check."

She slid from the booth and adjusted the weight of her gun belt. "Talk to you later." She headed to the door.

"Tonight. We are talking tonight." Tillie raised her voice. As if she wouldn't hear her. *Sheesh*. She lifted her hand in acknowledgement. She pushed the door open and found Jim waiting for her on the sidewalk.

"Walk with me." Jim turned and stepped off.

Grinding her teeth together she bit back her attitude and fell into step with him. "I don't believe we have anything to talk about."

Jim stopped and drew a deep breath. "Nah, we need to clear the air. I was out of line last night. Look, I don't let people know about the pressure I'm under, but there are a few issues that have affected me lately. I acted out, against Dr. Blue or Boswell, or whoever he is. The idea that Guardian was in my county was the straw that broke my back. I overreacted."

"Then you aren't going to the Boswell estate?" She stared down the street and watched traffic at the four way stop.

"No, I'm going. I want to make sure the guy isn't stirring up shit for those folks. The Boswells are good people."

"And Dr. Blue isn't? That is rather presumptuous, isn't it?"

Jim shrugged; his leather gun belt creaked when he moved. "Perhaps. You seem to be enamored with him."

She swung her attention back to her boss and lifted her brows. "Meaning?"

"Aw, hell. Meaning nothing. It's just... something about that guy. He gets under my skin. I don't know what it is, call it a gut feeling. There is something there, and my instincts are screaming that he's dangerous."

"Really? I don't get that at all, and I've spent more time with him than anyone." Boy had she, and damn, she'd really like to spend even more time with him.

Jim jumped slightly and reached into his pocket. He grabbed his cell. "Watson." His eyes snapped to her. "Perfect. I'm on my way."

"Shauna is coming around. I'm heading over to the hospital."

Thank goodness. "Want company?"

"No, I've got this." He started to leave but stopped and turned back before he asked, "Are we okay?" The worry on her boss' face lined his brow, making him look older than his years.

She nodded slowly. "Yeah. We're okay." Not really, but she'd let him believe they were. She valued her job. She liked working in the small department. What she started last night was putting her employment in jeopardy. Thank goodness she had resources beyond the job. That safety net gave her the ability and the nerve to beg for forgiveness rather than ask for permission... again.

"What are you doing for the rest of the afternoon?" He walked backward as he spoke. "Earning your keep?" A smirk she hadn't seen in a while crossed his face.

"I'll set up for traffic enforcement. It's quiet, for once."

"Thank God for small favors." Jim quipped as he spun and headed to his vehicle. She waited until he got in, made an illegal U-Turn and headed toward the hospital.

Forty minutes later, she'd taken up residence in her favorite turnout on the main road through the county. After calibrating her radar, she rolled down the windows and allowed the breeze to circulate through the SUV. *This* was the county she'd fallen in love with. Slow days, small crimes, and friendly patrolling. She tugged her cell phone from the holder at her hip and pushed the speed dial.

"Are you trying to write tickets again?" Her mother teased.

"I'm trying to relax, so yes, I'm set up and not looking too hard. What's up with you?" She glanced down the road seeing nothing but blacktop.

"Not much. We are going to dinner tonight with the Blacks. Your father has decided to try his hand at golf again."

"Oh no. How long before he throws out his back this time?" Poet chuckled at her father's expense. He'd injured his back on the front nine of the golf course they'd retired to in Florida. He'd fussed and fumed about putting the condo up for sale and never golfing again.

"Well, hopefully he won't any time soon. I signed him up for lessons with the Golf Pro on staff. Did you know learning proper form was a thing?"

"No, I didn't."

"Neither did your father. He was miffed that I paid money for the lessons, but I told him it was nonrefundable, so he's going."

"Is it nonrefundable?"

"Goodness, no, but we aren't telling him that."

"Mom, you're devious."

"Is this a surprise?"

"No, not really. I knew it when you tricked me into eating my green beans."

"I had to do something. You wouldn't eat a vegetable. But enough about us old farts. What's new with you?" Her mom's voice lilted. Ever hopeful.

"Well, let's see. There was an incident behind the roadside tavern two nights ago. A young woman was shot--"

Her mom gasped, "Oh my! Is she all right?"

"Should be. The sheriff was notified she was coming around earlier today."

"Did they find the person who shot her?"

"No, *we* haven't been able to find any leads. The sheriff is heading over to interview her and see if she can identify the person who shot her."

"This quiet county of yours isn't really all that quiet, is it?"

She drew a long breath and let it go. "Usually it's calm, boring even. There are always things happening, like everywhere else, there are people who think they can take what isn't there's. Vehicle accidents, small time drugs, petty shit."

"Language."

"Sorry, petty crimes."

"That does sound boring." Her mother chuckled humorlessly.

"Yeah, *Mayberry RFD*." Which was boring, but the pace was okay for her.

"With shootings behind bars."

"With that."

"Have you met anyone?"

A standard question that her mother played like a trump card. She stared sightlessly out the windshield for a moment. Visions of the gorgeous man with blond hair, blue eyes and a red beard flashed through her mind. "No one I'll be able to bring home and introduce to the parents."

There was silence. "Hello? Mom? Did I lose you?"

Her mother cleared her throat. "Ah, no, but you stunned me."

She laughed, "Yeah, how so?"

"The man you're seeing... you wouldn't bring him home to meet us?"

"No. He's only here for a short time. It isn't serious." And it's just sex, but hey what Momma didn't know wasn't going to come back to haunt her.

"I fell in love with your father the moment I saw him."

She smiled at the breathless comment. Damn, she wanted that someday. "He says the same thing."

"It's the truth. When you know, you know."

"And when I know, I'll tell you."

"Fair enough. What does this gentleman do for a living?"

"He's a doctor." No harm in telling her mother that.

"*Really?*"

"Yes, really. He's here visiting family. We met and hit it off." *With lots and lots of orgasms.*

"So, he could come back?"

"Sure, I guess, but it isn't like we're dating."

"Then what are you doing?"

Relieving stress and having great sex. "Having fun. What's up with Paul? I haven't heard from him in a while." A change of subject was absolutely required. Paul was her go to off ramp of any conversation. Her older brother was assigned to a submarine and was currently on sea duty.

"I got an email a couple days ago. He seems content, of course he doesn't tell me much."

"Probably can't, Mom. You don't exactly have a security clearance."

"Well, there is that. When are you going to be able to come down for a visit?"

"Don't know. I've volunteered to take on a project. Could be several months before I can get some time off. How about I try for a week around Labor Day?"

"That would be nice, but make sure you save enough vacation time to come home for Christmas. Paul should be back on shore by that time. What kind of project did you volunteer for?"

"Just something for the county, clearing up and closing old cases. Basic, boring, dull admin and gopher work, but it needs to be done so I raised my hand. I should have Christmas off. I worked it last year."

"Good. Now tell me about this man you're having fun with."

"Well would you look at that, Mom. I see a car going well over the speed limit." The old car that came over the hill was rusted and was rattling by at forty miles an hour. Max.

"Oh, did I step over the line, dear?"

"Yes, Mother."

"Fine, but don't hang up. I have gossip to tell you. Did you know Noreen's son was arrested for--"

Poet eased back into her seat and smiled as her mother detailed the gossip of the small retirement community.

A large black SUV crested the hill. She watched as the vehicle slowed and then turned on its signal indicating it was turning into the turnout where she'd parked. "Hey, Mom, I hate to interrupt, but I really have to go. Love you."

"Okay. Love you--"

Poet disconnected the call and reached for her weapon, keeping her hand on the grip, finger outside of the trigger. The SUV parked beside her and the dark, tinted window wound down. Blond hair, those baby blue eyes and sexy as fuck beard were slowly revealed. He gave her a once over.

A smile spread across her face. "Well, well. Dr. Blue. How are you today?"

"Deputy Campbell. I'm very relaxed and slightly tired. You?"

Poet smiled and lifted her eyebrows several times. "About the same. Been to see your family?" She nodded down the roadway that led to several of the larger estates, the Boswells' included.

"I was. May I interest you in dinner tonight? I have some information we need to go over."

"You could, but I'm thinking being seen together would still ruffle feathers. Unless you want to go to another town away from this county? Charlottesville? It's not a huge city, but big enough that we can get lost. Or, you could come over to mine again."

"Let's stick to your apartment, but I'll bring things for dinner and cook."

"That is a deal. What time?"

"Seven?"

"Perfect. You know where to park."

"I'll text before I come in to make sure you don't have any uninvited guests."

She shook her head. "That was surreal. He cornered me today on my lunch break. He apologized. Tried to explain that he's under pressure and that you set off his radar."

Maliki blinked in surprise and then chuckled. "Me?"

"Yup, said you gave off a dangerous vibe. Are you dangerous, Doc?" She smiled at him.

"Nah. I'm connected to dangerous people, but as far as I know none of those Guardian types are in the area."

That was interesting. "I've heard Guardian teams are made up of mercenaries. Is that true?"

He shrugged. "I've never met a mercenary, so I'm going to say no. The people who work for Guardian are screened at every stage of employment, vetted to a standard few can pass, highly trained, and tested continuously. They're the preeminent select of the elite, and they are extremely proficient at doing exactly what Guardian, and the country, requires of them. They are patriots and defenders who receive no credit for missions they perform. Not that any of them want recognition. The job doesn't lend itself to glory, only sacrifice."

Damn. Talk about passion. Maliki's fervent and earnest response figuratively sat her on her ass. He advocated for the company he worked for and that eloquent response was heartfelt. He appeared to believe every word he'd said. "Wow. Okay, so we'll chalk that up to rumor."

He chuckled. "Sorry. Guardian has saved my ass on more than one occasion. I'm a fan."

"Yeah? Maybe we should talk about that when we discuss that information tonight."

He shrugged. "I'm an open book."

"Really?"

"Sure, ask me anything."

"Is this a new leaf we've turned over? I seem to remember you being decidedly evasive when we first met." She laughed when he rolled his eyes and stroked his beard.

"Admittedly, I *was* fucking around *and* being evasive."

"Why?"

He laughed. "Because I could?"

"Shame on you, Doctor Blue. We'll have to do some remedial training. Complete cooperation with the local authorities is mandatory."

He placed his elbow on the driver's side window ledge and leaned toward her. "I thought we were in complete cooperation last night. Several times last night, if I remember correctly."

She lifted her hand and wobbled it back and forth. "Meh, I think there is room for improvement."

He barked a hearty laugh. "Is that so?"

She tried desperately to keep a stern face and nodded as she groused, "Absolutely."

"Well then, after we eat and talk, perhaps we'll explore some remedial training."

She sighed dramatically, "If I must..."

He laughed again and put his SUV into reverse. "You must!" He laughed as he backed out of the turnout and waved when he put the vehicle into gear and headed back into town.

A smile lingered on her face as she watched the vehicle leave. It had been years since a man had captured her attention. Years since she'd enjoyed the banter and the friendship that went with good sex. But he wasn't here to stay, and she wasn't going to get attached to the handsome doctor. Nope. Not going to happen. That was her plan, and she was damn well sticking to it. Maybe.

CHAPTER 8

Sheriff James Watson sat in his car outside the hospital, bracing himself against what had to be done. He sent a quick glance at the face of his phone. The sight of the damn thing sent his blood pressure through the roof. His gut clenched and every fiber of his body screamed for him not to listen, but he... couldn't ignore… what was required of him.

"Have you fixed the problem?" The same disturbing, altered voice that first spoke to him almost a year and a half ago split the silence of his mind.

He sighed and looked out at the parking lot. "No. I just arrived at the hospital. She's coming around now."

"Fix this before it becomes difficult."

Anger spiked and he hissed, "I'm getting really tired of cleaning up these messes."

A low rolling chuckle was the only answer he received.

He looked through the windshield at the white stone exterior of the hospital. "This is the last time."

"You'll do it, or people will find out the truth about what happened that night."

"The truth is that it was an accident!"

"Is that what you've convinced yourself of? You killed her. You have nothing; no defense. And if you tell anyone what you've done, you'll be the only one with blood on your hands and you know it. Fix this."

"It is too risky. There's a Guardian agent in the county." His hand shook as he massaged his brow. If only he could go back to that night. Do things differently.

"Leave him alone. Avoid any further contact."

"Stop killing women. Please."

Silence fell for a moment. *"That won't happen. We both know why."*

"If we have another dead woman show up, the state will be impossible to keep at arm's length. I've run out of ways to stage their deaths to dissuade suspicion."

"You're going to go to jail for life anyway. Maybe death row. No one cares about you. No one."

Jim shook his head. "I matter..."

"You're wrong. You don't. You enjoy what happens. Kill the girl. You've killed before. Your future depends on you fixing this. We have work to do." His tormentor's words ended as suddenly as they had started.

He took a deep breath and stared at the odometer of his vehicle. He'd cleaned up the women, and he'd kept his people from investigating. Shauna had found the connection between the three women. That damn dating app. Shauna knew each of the victims, from the app. She'd come to him, because he was a friend of her parents. He told her she was imagining everything. He gaslighted her into believing the connection wasn't valid. She'd left his office doubting herself. He'd told his fucking puppet master about Shauna's conclusions. The fucker said to handle it. He had. He used an old weapon of his father's and he'd shot the girl. Twice. Shauna didn't deserve this, but if she survived and remembered...

A tap on his driver's side window jolted him from his thoughts. Daryl and Jennie Cochran stood beside his vehicle. He hit the tab and rolled down the window. "Daryl, everything okay?"

Jennie smiled. "Better than okay. Shauna woke up."

"That's awesome. Did she say anything about the incident?"

"No. She's still under a lot of meds. She didn't know why she was in the hospital. Right now, she doesn't remember anything, but when we asked her, she got real upset." Jennie rubbed her arms and Daryl wrapped a big arm around her and held her close.

"I'm still going to have to talk with her. I was heading in."

"Sure, sure. We understand. The doctor said her memories may never come back to her. You might want to wait, though, they gave her something to help her sleep." Daryl kissed Jennie's temple.

"I'll sit with her a little bit, until she wakes up at least."

"Thank you, Jim. For everything. I hope you don't hate me for this, but I pray she never remembers. It had to have been horrible." Jennie added.

He ground his teeth. Jennie was thanking him, and he was heading in to kill their only child. He cleared his throat. "Are you two heading home?"

"Yeah, we haven't been home or caught a shower since that night. The doctor said she was almost out of the woods, barring any unforeseen complications."

"That's great, Daryl. Jennie, I'm really happy she's going to be okay." His eyes teared up despite everything, and he tried to stop the physical reaction.

"Jim, I know you're a damn good cop. Please, please, find who did this to our baby."

"We'll do everything in our power, Daryl. There wasn't much evidence at that scene, and if Shauna can't tell us anything, it will be tough, but I'm not letting this go. I have my best people on it."

"Thank you." Daryl sniffed back his emotion. "Come on, honey. Let's get cleaned up so we can get back."

"Right. Thank you, Jim. We know you're doing everything you can." Jennie wiped at her tears and leaned harder into Daryl's side.

"You two get cleaned up and maybe try to grab some rest. I'll see you later." Daryl lifted a hand, and they shuffled toward their old SUV. They were salt of the earth type people. He'd been raised with them, and went to school with them, although he was a few years younger than Daryl.

He dropped his head back and stared at the hospital. Shauna didn't remember anything. A flickering of hope extinguished before it took flame. It didn't matter. *He* wouldn't allow her to live and now, fuck, now he was responsible for silencing the girl, for good. He hated himself. Hated his cowardness. He scrubbed both hands through his hair and then punched the steering wheel. "Fuck!"

He grabbed a small leather packet from the glove box and exited his car. The pack went into his front pocket. He leaned back into the car and retrieved his leather gloves, tucking the open ends into his belt, he locked the car and headed into the hospital.

The small hospital was modern and well equipped. That was due to the landowners in the area. They supported businesses that benefited them. The hospital was one such entity. He turned right making his way to the post-surgical ward. He offered a wave or a nod as people spoke or recognized him.

He stopped at the nurses' station. "Shauna Cochran's room?"

"Oh, hi, Sheriff. She's in room 332, but the Doc ordered a pretty heavy sedative for her." A small nurse smiled up at him after pointing toward Shauna's room.

"I'm not going to wake her up. Just saw her folks. I thought I'd sit with her until they got back."

"That's so sweet! We had to pry them from her room. They haven't left her side. Has anyone determined what happened yet?"

"That's an on-going investigation, sorry." One that he'd killed, cutting his deputies off at the knees.

"Oh, yeah, right. Sorry. It is so insane. We've had hunting accidents, and that one domestic, but not a straight up shooting like this. Makes a girl afraid to walk to her car in the dark."

"Don't worry yourself about that. We'll catch whoever did this." The words sounded sincere, at least to his ears.

"I surely hope so. You can go in if you want."

He touched his finger to his forehead and gave her a salute as he sauntered down the hall and entered Shauna's room.

He stood inside the door and let his eyes adjust to the dimness of the room. The blinds were shut, and the lights were off except for a low wattage LED light up by the bed that illuminated the machines attached to the slender woman sleeping in the bed.

He reached for his gloves and put them on as he

silently walked to her bedside. He opened the small locker and rummaged through the plastic bag that held her personal items. He snagged her phone and shoved it in his shirt as he pushed the bag back into the locker and shut the door. He buttoned his shirt and arranged the phone at his side so it wasn't obvious. From his front pocket he withdrew a syringe, removed the cap and inserted it into the IV port. He didn't look at her. He couldn't. He depressed the plunger, withdrew the needle and recapped it, putting it back in his pocket. He opened the valve on the line until the drugs emptied into the tubing and then returned it to the position it had been in. He removed the gloves, reattached them to his belt and then sat down on the chair that had been sitting beside the bed. He lowered his head to his hands and waited.

The drug wouldn't take long to do its job. One of the women killed had been shot up with the stuff. He'd positioned the young woman, cleaned the scene of all evidence and left her, an empty syringe beside her. The track marks told the story of what had been done to her. When he'd disposed of her body, he'd kept the kit with the drugs.

The heartbeat from the monitor stuttered, then skipped. He glanced at the IV port and back at the monitor. Another stutter and then an alarm sounded. He lifted and jogged to the door. "Hey, Nurse! There's something wrong here!"

He held the door open as two nurses dashed into the room. The heart monitor flatlined. He stood in the corner, out of the way, as the nurses called a code and more people flooded into the room. The nurses lowered the bed and they worked on Shauna. The doctor who flew in the room shouted orders, she was intubated, CPR initiated, and the crash cart was activated. In what seemed like hours but was probably only ten minutes later, the room stilled. The doctor glanced up at the clock. "We're calling it. Time of death, 1:43 p.m. Where are her parents?"

"They went home." One of the nurses pushed Shauna's hair back in a motherly gesture.

"Fuck." The doctor hung his head and propped his hands on his hips.

"I'll head over there and tell them." He volunteered the information. "What... what happened?"

The doctor shook his head. "I don't know. We'll do a clinical autopsy of course, to determine the actual cause of death. She's suffered some pretty grievous injuries as a result of that gunshot wound. It could be a myriad of things."

"Doc, she's part of an investigation, which is now a murder. The county ME will take this one."

"You'll have to talk to the administration, not my call to make."

"That's right, it's mine." He reached for his phone and hit speed dial as he left the hospital room. He hit the steps and headed to the first floor.

"Giles."

"Doc, we have a case that needs your immediate and special attention."

There was a sigh on the other end. "Another one? I wasn't aware we had one scheduled?"

"Yeah. Shauna Cochran. She's at the hospital. Just passed."

"I'll get someone over there."

He stopped at the bottom of the stairs and looked up the vacant stairwell making sure he was alone before he asked, "What exactly do you get from this, doc?"

"I'll put down my cards if you show me yours first." The ME whispered.

"It's getting messy."

A humorless chuckle sounded at the other end of the connection. "Nothing we can't handle. You going to stop?"

He placed his palm against the cold steel of the fire door. The beige of the door was a perfect screen for the images of Shauna's death to play. He closed his eyes tightly and admitted, "No."

"Neither am I. I'll have my people pick her up." The line went dead.

He strode to his car, got in, and drove to the Cochrans' house. Jennie's deafening scream of anguish replayed over and over. Her absolute despair fed the frenzied howls inside his head.

Jason King pressed down the intercom to his assistant's desk. "Sonya, would you please get Robert Cavanagh, the AG of Virginia, on the line for me."

"Absolutely."

She buzzed back several minutes later. "As a reminder, the afternoon briefing is being moved an hour earlier so you can make it to Reece's school play."

He chuckled. "Is that Sonya talk for I'll call, but don't talk too long?"

"That's Sonya talk for you need to watch your kid because your wife has called three times today to make sure there hasn't been a sudden emergency--hold on."

Jason smiled and closed his eyes. Sonya was a godsend. If she ever retired, he was punching his ticket, too. She clicked back on the line. "As I was saying, this is important. Reece has a big part."

"I know. We've been practicing lines for the last two weeks." He and Reece spent hours going over his lines while Faith fed, bathed and put Royce to sleep. That little guy had his days and nights sorted, for the most part, which meant both he and Faith were starting to remember how it felt to sleep more than three hours at a time.

"Take videos. I want to see his performance and the AG is on line two." The line clicked and she was gone.

Jason accessed the line. "Robert, thank you for taking my call."

"Well, when the CEO of Guardian calls, you drop whatever you're doing and pray that shit in your state isn't about to be decimated."

"No, nothing like that. Actually, I have a favor to ask."

"Really? What can a lowly public servant like me do for Guardian?"

Jason leaned forward and tapped the embedded

screen in his desktop so the documents he needed were at his fingertips. "I have a client who currently resides in Pleasant County…"

"Not surprising, some fancy estates in that county."

Jason crafted his words carefully to ensure his words were correct. "My client is asking if Guardian can take a look at a certain set of instances they believe may be connected. I honestly don't know if there is any merit to my client's allegations, but I happen to have a man in that area who is on extended leave due to a family issue. He's available to take a look at the situation. The good news for you is we'll do this gratis and if there is anything there, you get credit for directing the investigation and snagging any bad guys."

"Uh huh. What crimes?"

"My client believes three recent deaths that occurred within the last year are interconnected."

He heard keys tapping as Robert commented, "I'm not sure I follow. The only deaths I have on file are completely unrelated and none of them are marked as homicide."

"Which is why we will do almost everything below the radar. I want to make my client happy without disturbing the local watering holes." Jason had him on the hook. He could feel the man's interest.

"What do you mean almost everything?"

"We believe the ME still has the latest body. I want my people to do the autopsy or redo it before the body is processed for burial."

"Do you want access to the ME's facility in Pleasant County?"

"No, we need an order to allow transport and take the body from the ME's possession."

Robert drew a long breath and sighed into the phone. "Why do I get the feeling you aren't telling me everything?"

"Honestly, Robert, I'm chasing rumors and suppositions here. My gut instinct was to say no to this case, but I know and respect the person that has called us and asked for assistance. He's always been a straight shooter, so I'm taking a chance. There will be no egg on your face. If this blows up, you're the hero. If there is nothing, we walk away with minimum ripples in the water."

"Ripples? As in plural. What besides the body the ME is holding?"

He smiled. Fuck, he loved talking to extremely intelligent people. "Caught that did you?"

"I'm a lawyer. I make my living dissecting

people's comments." Robert's rueful chuckle followed.

"We are going through legal channels to exhume the two other bodies. From the information I've been forwarded, the families will agree." Based on compensation Guardian was willing to provide.

"What are you hoping to find?"

"I'm hoping to find absolutely nothing. I want this to be a nonissue." He had too much on his plate as it was, and having Maliki in the middle of Virginia playing junior league detective with little to no training wasn't ideal in any scenario. But if they found anything to tie the murders together, he'd have hard-core investigators down there so damn fast that backwater sheriff's head would spin.

"I don't have a problem with any of your requests, Mr. King. Perhaps someday when I call you, you'll have the same consideration."

Ah, tit for tat. The standard currency of politics. "Understood, Robert. You have my number."

CHAPTER 9

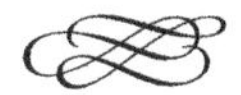

> Safe to come up?

Maliki hit the button to send the text. He'd been sitting outside the apartment building watching the smattering of traffic and a few people walking past. There wasn't anyone in vehicles nor did he see anyone lingering around her building. She'd demanded the caution, but he couldn't help but feel it was overkill. If the sheriff discovered they were seeing each other, he couldn't fire her, not without one hell of a lawsuit filed, and he'd be happy to fund her defense. The pushy bastard had no say in who Poet could or couldn't see. It wasn't like he was a fucking suspect.

He shifted, moving the butt of the forty-five that was now hanging in a shoulder holster under his jacket. The new holster and credentials had been waiting for him at the front desk when he'd gotten back to the hotel. His phone vibrated.

> Coast is clear

He pocketed his phone, grabbed the keys and groceries before he locked the vehicle, and headed across the street. He punched the elevator call button and waited, watching the numbers light as the elevator descended to the ground floor.

The door opened, and he was nearly bowled over by a five-foot nothing whirlwind.

"Oh, damn, I'm really sorry!" The woman glanced up at him and smiled. "I never watch where I'm going. Here, what floor?" She held the door open and paused with her hand over the buttons.

"Thanks, fifth floor."

"Fifth?" She squeaked and then flashed a huge smile and pushed the button. "Fifth it is! Have fun!" She moved as the door closed, keeping her eyes on him until the last moment.

"Well, that was completely awkward." He

shifted the plastic bags in his hands and waited for the world's slowest elevator to inch its way up to the fifth floor. When the door opened, he headed to Poet's door and shifted the bags again so he could knock.

She opened the door with her phone to her ear. She nodded, and he moved past her and into the kitchen.

"Yes, Tillie. Uh huh. I agree. No, that's not going to happen. Uh huh. Right. Okay. No, don't do that. I won't answer it, and I'll call someone to take you to jail. You know I can do it." She threw back her head and laughed as she entered the kitchen. "Law enforcement doesn't use those types of handcuffs that way. You need to do more research."

He chuckled at the conversation.

"Right. Talk to you later." Poet dropped her phone to the countertop. "Sorry about that. Tillie, my neighbor and best friend, saw you at the elevator. She thinks you're hot."

"She knows who I am?"

"Ah, no, that was a leap of logic on her part. We are the only two single women on this floor. There are two other married couples and Mr. Kroeger, who we rarely see. Tillie thinks he's a vampire and uses the apartment as a feeding station."

He stopped moving and then slowly turned his head in her direction. "Say what?"

"Tillie has a very active imagination."

"Obviously."

"Is that new hardware you have there, Doctor?" Poet nodded to the forty-five under his arm.

"It's legal, ma'am. I have a permit to carry it." He shrugged from his jacket. "Where do you keep yours when you're at home?"

"Top of the refrigerator or on the coffee table until I go to bed, then on my bedside table."

"I didn't notice it beside your bed last night."

"Nope, the first night it has stayed on the fridge since I moved in. You made me forget the basics."

"I'll take that as a complement."

"You should." She took the holster as he dropped it from his shoulders and placed it on top of the stainless-steel refrigerator where her nine mil was sitting.

He continued to remove supplies for dinner. "Salmon, saffron rice, and fresh peas."

"Wow. I would have settled for burgers and fries."

"I had a steak the size of my head the other night over at Shorty's. I was in the mood for fish."

"Oh, Shorty's steaks are so good." She leaned

against the wall. "What do you need me to do to help?"

"I'll need a saucepan each for the rice and peas and a frying pan, preferably stainless steel, if you have it."

"Why stainless?"

"Crisps the skin better."

"Ah, of course." Poet rolled her eyes and ducked past him to the cabinet where the pots and pans were stacked.

When she handed them over, he nodded to the wine. "If you could open that and pour us each a glass, we can talk while I start dinner."

She smiled and spun to rummage around in a drawer. Her fit, tight body filled a pair of soft, almost white jeans. Her slender curves wore the denim well. She held up a wine opener. Her hair spilled over her shoulder when she moved.

"Hand me two of those glasses on the top shelf of that cabinet, please?" She pointed to the bank of cupboards behind him.

He opened the one she'd pointed to and reached up to the top shelf, bringing two large wine glasses down. "Okay, here you go."

“Thanks. Now, what did your bosses say?"

"I am your official Guardian liaison. The

marching orders dictate we don't make waves. Guardian will exhume the bodies and search for anything they can find. It is a legal process, and if they can get the families' permission, it will take time. The likelihood of finding anything is very low. Also, Guardian will do a background on all the girls, but they are stuck in queue behind cases with more priority. Since Watson up-channeled the snuff websites to the BCI, Guardian will defer to the state to make the right call. All in all, it could take a while, but I'll stick around."

"Okay, well you might want to contact your bosses again. Shauna Cochran died this afternoon."

His eyes snapped up. "What happened?"

"Don't know. According to the sheriff, he went into the room to sit with her because Daryl and Jennie had gone home to shower. Her alarms started going off. He called for the nurses, but they were already on their way, alarms on the machines alerted them."

"I assume he's contacted the Bureau of Investigations at the state?"

Poet shook her head. "He wants to get an autopsy first."

"What? You mean a clinical autopsy?"

"Nope. Forensic. Shauna's body was taken to

the ME's today, and they are doing the autopsy there."

"That doesn't make sense. This was an attended death. They have the bullet, the wound, and even the surgery and procedures the doctors performed can be detailed ad nauseum at a trial. A clinical autopsy I can see, to determine exactly what killed her, which makes more sense than a forensic autopsy. Unless the sheriff suspects something?" After picking up the wine she'd poured for him, Mal crossed his arms and leaned against the counter.

"Or--"

He lifted his gaze to meet hers. "Or?"

"Or, keep in mind this is the same ME who performed the autopsies of the previous young women who showed up dead."

He lifted his eyebrows. "You think the sheriff and the ME are...?" He let the question hang there.

"I know, I know. It sounds so far-fetched. God, I hate to cast aspersions where there might not be any, but Shauna was on the mend. She'd talked to her parents and to the doctor. Not much, but she was awake and getting better."

He shifted so his ass was leaning against the counter and shook his head. "I would caution you on that line of thinking. Shauna had major surgery. So many things could have gone wrong. We surgeons like to think we are demi-gods, but in reality, things can be missed. Hell, she could have thrown a clot, had a reaction to drugs, any number of things. There's an old saying in the medical world. When you hear hoof beats, look for horses, not zebras."

She chuckled and ran her hand through her hair. "You're right. Damn it."

"I'm not saying we can't look at your suspicions, but temper them with logical steps forward. Have you retrieved Shauna's cell phone data?"

She narrowed her eyes at him. "I'm having a hard time believing you're not a cop, ya know? But to answer your question, I have a request in the system for a warrant to access her information. The judge hasn't signed off on it yet."

"Why do you need a warrant? Why not ask her folks if you can look at her phone?"

She inclined her head and smiled. "You really sure you're not a cop?"

"Pretty damn positive, but why get a warrant? She wasn't a suspect in anything."

"Lining up my ducks. We don't know what happened that night. I assumed she was an innocent victim but hedged my bet in case she was involved in something."

"Well, as she no longer can be prosecuted if she was implicated in a criminal activity, I'd recommend you ask her parents. I'd bet they'll want to know about anything we can find."

A slight smile curled her lips. "We? I like that. It's been a minute since I've been able to openly discuss these cases. I couldn't risk involving one of the deputies. I'm willing to put my job on the line, but I couldn't ask them to do that. Most of them have kids, and the ones that don't are married or have parents who they care for."

"If we look into this and find nothing, what are your plans?"

She crossed her arms and stared at her socks before she shrugged and lifted her eyes to meet his gaze. "I like it here, but there is nothing holding me in this county. I'm not wearing rose colored glasses. I know the sheriff will eventually find out Guardian is involved, and it won't take a huge leap of logic to determine who called them in. So, at a minimum, I'm looking at discipline for going against his direct orders. In all likelihood, I'll be fired."

"Do you have a plan if that happens?"

She chuckled and ran her hand over her t-shirt, smoothing it. "Yeah. My parents won the lottery a couple years back. Not one of the half billion dollar winners, but enough they could retire early and live in a nice condo in Florida. They've set up a trust fund for both me and my brother. Because my brother is in the Navy, his trust stipulates he can't access it until he leaves the service. That was the only way he could still serve. The service seems to think if you have access to riches your loyalty won't necessarily be with them."

He glanced around the small apartment. It was homey, but there were no outward signs of wealth. "So, you don't need this job?"

"Oh, I need it. I'd go insane if I didn't work. I like law enforcement, and this gig has been great."

"Most people I know would chuck the day job and live off the trust." Which was what some of his friends had done. Some, like him, had a passion or calling they followed.

"I use it for plane tickets to go see my folks." She looked to her right and to her left, then leaned in and whispered, "First Class."

"Ah... extravagant," he whispered conspiratorially.

"Right? But damn, it's nice." She winked at him

and took a sip of her wine. "The bottom line is I can afford to risk the job. I know something's going on here. My gut tells me these women aren't getting a fair shake."

He spun and picked up the frying pan and set it on the stove. "Oil? Why didn't you call the state and tell them?"

He watched her grab a jar of olive oil from the cupboard. "Ahhh... nothing to connect them in the evidence or in the ME's reports. Jim would spin it to make me a laughingstock at the state level, but damn it, I know something's off."

"And talking to me?" He opened the fish and retrieved the seasonings he'd purchased from the shopping bag.

"Well, that's easy. If you said I was crazy, the chance you'd go back to my boss and inform him of my concerns was pretty low, you know with the immediate, intense, dislike he had for you."

She had a point. A well thought out, calculated point. "Hand me that vegetable stock. He has a chip on his shoulder where I'm concerned. Damned if I know why."

"Here." She handed him the carton and watched as he started the saffron rice. She peeked into the bags. "Ah, hell. You're a health food freak."

He shrugged. "I'm a doctor, and I'm aware of what I put into my body, but freak? Not so much."

"Uh huh, right. What do you have for breakfast on a normal day? Bet it isn't donuts and coffee. Probably not bagels and coffee either."

He couldn't stop the smile. "Usually, I have a protein, berry, and kale or spinach smoothie after I get done with training."

She laughed and lifted her wine glass. "I believe our definitions of health food freak may be different. But FYI, I'm not going to complain because whatever you make is perfect. Anything I don't have to cook is fine by me."

"You don't like to cook?"

"I don't like to cook at all. Then on top of that, I hate to mess up all those pots and pans just for me."

"Which is exactly why I have a smoothie for breakfast. I can grab lunch and sometimes dinner at the cafeteria, but I enjoy cooking."

"The cafeteria? You mean at the hospital where you work?"

He glanced up from what he was doing and smiled, hopefully covering his surprise at sharing that bit of information. She was easy to be himself with, yet he shouldn't be sharing anything about his day to day with anyone. "Yep."

"I end up eating crap, but I work out so…" She shrugged and lifted herself up onto the counter next to where he was prepping dinner, dangling her legs as she sipped her wine.

"We should go for a run together." He still needed to find a gym to get his weight training back on schedule.

She snorted a laugh and her eyes gleamed. "Hell yes! I saw you the other morning. I'd love to try to keep up with you. You fly."

"It was only six miles." *Only*. He was dog tired when he'd finished that run. He stirred the broth and saffron with the rice and rolled his eyes when his back was to her. What the hell was he doing? Showing off?

"Only six, huh? Well that's double what I normally run. I feel inadequate now. How many days a week do you hit the gym?"

"Here, none so far. At home, I'm in the gym every day."

"Yeah, I'm not that dedicated. What about self-defense? Do you practice any particular discipline?" She drained her glass and set it aside.

"Mixed martial arts. A little of this, some of

that." He'd started working out with different partners as they came through the program before they paired up and worked only with their assigned partner. Each encounter taught him a little more than the last. It was a hodge-podge approach, but he wasn't technically part of the program. "What about you?"

"I studied Krav Maga for a short time. It comes in handy."

He glanced at her. The wine had put a soft blush on her cheeks. "I can imagine. Is there much call to use it here in Pleasant County?"

"There didn't used to be." She made a face. "I can't help thinking that something connects these women."

"From what I've read in the case files, there isn't. So, we need to go back through and re-interview all the witnesses, without causing an uproar or questions that will make their way back to the sheriff. Do you have any vacation time?"

"I do. What's the plan?"

"A day here and a day there. Make up some logical excuses for taking the days, something that won't cause anyone to become suspicious. We contact the witnesses right before we talk to them."

She hopped off the counter and grabbed the wine bottle. "Did you buy two of these?"

He chuckled and pointed to the canvas tote on the table. "I did indeed."

"Perfect." She filled her glass again.

"Not on call tonight?"

"Nope, not my night. Two nights off in a row. It doesn't happen often."

He checked the rice and started the peas before he turned on the burner under the frying pan. "What do you think about starting with the most recent case and working backward? I would assume the recollection would be sharper for the more recent cases."

She stood beside him and watched as he laid the salmon into the pan. "We can do that. Are you considering Shauna the most recent case?"

"I don't know. I need to talk to my--" *Boss? Friend? Handler*? "—with someone at the office. I'll run the specifics past them and hopefully we can determine a way forward."

He glanced at her and did a double take. She stood with her eyes closed, her hand gripping the counter. "Hey, you okay?"

She nodded and spoke, with her eyes still closed. "Thank you." She opened her eyes and turned to meet his gaze. Her blue eyes were filled with emotion, stopping him with their intensity.

“For what? Going forward to my organization with your request?”

“Yeah. Exactly that and for actually listening to a hick deputy with a gut feeling.”

He leaned over and kissed her forehead before flipping the salmon. “You are not a hick deputy. I listened because every class I’ve ever attended started and ended with the instructors reinforcing the mantra of ‘trust your instincts’ or ‘if you feel something is wrong, trust your gut’.”

"Still, it matters."

He smiled at her and gave her a wink. "Let’s finish dinner, and then I'll make a call." He could hear Joseph now. A smile spread across his face. Who knew that hard-boiled son of a bitch would turn into a damn good friend, especially after the fit he'd thrown when he heard another doctor was being assigned to The Rose? Fuck, he was a territorial son of a bitch about the complex for some reason. *Because they told you it would be your facility to run.* Plans change, right?

~

Poet enjoyed the meal, relished the subtle flirting and an easy conversation about the bases where they'd been stationed. As she wiped dry the last pan, Maliki grabbed his phone. He dialed and held the phone to his ear while he leaned back against the counter.

He released a low rumbling laugh. "Fuck you. I did send an email, but I have a concern I need to run past you that won't wait until tomorrow's update." Maliki shot her a glance and winked again.

How could one man be so damn sexy? His blond hair, blue eyes, tanned skin and that damn sexy reddish blond beard. She shivered a bit at the memory of that beard on her neck.

"The young lady I assisted the first night I hit town passed away."

She watched as he nodded, put his free hand on his hip, and explained the events of the day the exact same way she'd told him. No enhancements, no deviation. *Not a cop my ass.* He had to have had training.

"The fucked-up thing is, I can see the need for a clinical autopsy, not a forensic examination." He glanced up at her and listened to whoever was on the other end of the line. He nodded. "Yeah, it is a reach. Four cases. Absolutely no discernable connection between the victims, other than the same ME and the Sheriff's Department." He chuckled, "Yeah, the ass wipe wants this autopsy before he calls in the state."

His head jerked up. "Why? I don't need any backup. We don't even know if we have a link. It could be a series of unfortunate events and a single murder case." He glanced at her and shrugged as if in apology for the comment. She drew a deep breath and sighed because the bottom line was he was right. "Well that makes sense. Why didn't you say that?" He laughed and shifted, standing instead of leaning on the counter.

"Can you do that?" He lifted an eyebrow and listened. "No, we are starting with the most recent case and working backward, hoping memories will be sharper." He nodded. "I can do that. No, no, I agree. Uh huh. Yeah, sure, I've been there." He paused and cleared his throat. "Thanks. What was that? Oh? How are you going to do that?"

He laughed and shook his head. "I have no doubt. Yeah, I'll keep my ass down. What? You and your chickens. Yeah, fuck you, Henrietta." His laughter rumbled around the kitchen as he hung up the phone.

She grabbed her wine and his and handed it to him as she left the kitchen and made her way to the living room where she sat down on the couch. He took a seat next to her.

"So?"

"So, my contact is going to run it up the flagpole. He said not making waves might not be an option. If Guardian assumes responsibility for both of those cases and the forensic autopsies, the players, if any, are going to know we are onto them."

"He thinks you need backup?" She ran her finger around the top of the wine glass, not sure if she was offended or not. *She* was his damn backup.

"I'm not a cop. I've had some training in outlying areas that tend to align with law enforcement efforts, but I'm a doctor. If this case starts to link up, he wants someone in the area who can take charge of the investigation for Guardian. Until we uncover something, though, we are on our own."

"Jim is going to know something is going on as soon as they take the bodies."

Maliki nodded. "You tossed me a snowball. I got it rolling."

"And a potential avalanche of shit is heading down the hill."

"*Or*, we take the bodies, find nothing, and life goes back to normal." Maliki set his wine down on the table.

"What else did he say?"

"That he was going to contact the person in charge of Cyber and push the backgrounds up the queue."

"Does he have that type of power?"

He laughed and rubbed the back of his neck. "He has… connections. If anyone can get it done, it's him."

"I want to say I'm sorry for involving you, but I'm not. If this turns into be me being paranoid and stupid, I'll feel like an ass."

He shrugged. "Gives me something to do."

"I thought you were supposed to be visiting your parents."

"I did that. My father isn't well. My mom is coping. I've promised my mother I'd try to clear the air with my old man." He closed his eyes and leaned back against the couch. "He's had a stroke and has dementia."

Damn, if her dad was sick, all the horses in the world couldn't pull her away from his side. She wasn't sure what problems he and his father had, but she hoped they could work it out. "I'm so sorry." He looked so damn tired resting there with his eyes closed. "Are you sure you need to get involved in this investigation? I could do the interviews if you need to be with your parents."

He opened one eye and then closed it. "According to my mother, my father is most lucid in the mornings. I'll spend mornings with them, and we can do the interviews in the afternoon. I'll need something to keep me out of my head."

"There aren't that many people to talk to in any of the cases. It's almost like they were picked because there wasn't much connection to family." She sighed at the lack of information the interviews were going to provide.

"That leaves Shauna out. She has parents in the area."

"Shauna is the anomaly all the way around. As far as we know, she wasn't missing. She was shot, not found alone in her vehicle in the middle of the county."

"Which are similarities the others share." Mal leaned forward. "What's the likelihood that three women would drive to isolated locations and die?"

She leaned forward, too. "Exactly what I've

been asking for the past year. See, the lack of connection doesn't take away from the way they died. They weren't suicides. No notes, no history of depression, they turned up in the county, in their cars, dead."

"Cars."

"Yep."

"Why their cars? Were they processed for trace and fingerprints?"

"Yep, well fingerprints. They were clean except for the owner's prints and there were very few of those."

"Someone could have sanitized the vehicle?"

"Absolutely."

"And the sheriff didn't think that was unusual?"

"Not when the ME ruled the first to be an overdose and the second to be natural causes."

He tapped his fingertips together. "What is our first move?"

She stared at him for a moment. She had her chance. "I'll get Shauna's phone tomorrow after we do some interviews. We'll start with victim number three, the alcohol poisoning. I can take the afternoon off as long as I'm on call tomorrow night. I can tell them I have an appointment."

He nodded. "It's a start. Now for the hard questions."

She angled her head. "Fire away."

"Am I staying or leaving?"

She chuckled and set her wine glass down. "I don't know about you, Doctor, but I'll admit I'm exhausted. You wore me out last night. How about we grab our service weapons, hit the mattress, grab some shut-eye and maybe experiment with morning sex."

She watched as he stood and stretched. God, he was perfection. He extended his hand for her. "Or we could exhaust ourselves further, sleep well and *then* experiment with morning sex."

She took his hand and teased, "Insatiable."

"Not true. I want to enjoy the woman I'm with, for the time I'm with her." He cradled her against his chest and lowered his lips to hers.

She whispered, "Nothing wrong with that."

CHAPTER 10

The tickle of Maliki's beard on her shoulder and the springy feel of his chest hair at her back woke Poet from a deep, relaxed sleep. She pushed back into him and felt his chest rumble as his lips nipped the top of her shoulder. She gasped as his hand slid down her waist over her stomach and split her sex. She rocked her hips slowly between his hardening shaft and those fingers that knew exactly how to massage her sex to crank her up to maximum bliss in minimum time.

"Lift your leg." His words caressed her skin as he continued his onslaught of feather light kisses and teasing nips.

She moved her top leg, tucking her knee up toward her chest. She felt his heat move away from her back for a moment. The sound of foil crinkling made her smile. He was back moments later and reignited her with those sensuous little kisses. His beard trailed against her sensitive skin. A shiver of desire reverberated through her nerve endings as he centered under her and slid in.

Maliki's hips moved in a steady, slow tempo. She sank into the sensations of the man behind and inside of her. The fast pace of last night's frenzied sex was nowhere to be found. She rocked her hips back and forward, matching his unhurried pace that built a low, hot need deep inside her. She moaned and reached behind her to urge him to go faster.

"Wait, be patient." His whispered command frustrated and enticed her in the same measure. His rhythm didn't deviate even though her need grew. She dug her fingernails into his skin, which only earned her a low rumble of laughter and a patient, "Not yet."

She pushed back into him. "Now." She wasn't afraid to ask for what she needed.

"Not now. Soon." He applied a bit more pressure against her sex with his fingers, but the easy back and forth of his hips as he entered and withdrew never deviated.

"Ahhh... stop teasing." She turned her head, and he lifted long enough to kiss her. In the awkward position the kiss was hot, messy, and indescribably sensual. She lifted her hand from his hip and grabbed the back of his neck, holding him close when he would have moved. She opened her eyes and stared into his. "Now. Now, please."

His hips crashed forward and his fingers were firm against that tight nub. She held him, and their stares collided. The smoldering need in his eyes had to be echoed in hers. He was arresting, riveting and entrancing her, compelling her with a desire she couldn't deny. The need his body had built between them was every bit as real as the air they shared. The swell of sensation tightened deep inside her and formed a ridge, one she crested moments before he did.

She closed her eyes and relaxed back against him, their ragged breathing the only sounds in the small bedroom. Her eyes flicked open, and she glanced at the clock. 5:00 a.m. Damn, time to get up and get ready for work. Soon. Instead, she sighed, "That was a very good way to wake up."

He dropped a kiss on the top of her head. "Very good."

"I should shower and get ready for work." But she didn't move. Not a muscle.

"I should leave before the building starts to wake up." She made some kind of noncommittal noise and closed her eyes.

His chest rumbled under her, "Neither of us is moving."

She stretched and rolled over to face him. She ran her fingers through his beard. "I'm usually not a lazy person. Give me a kiss to hold me until tonight." She couldn't resist tugging on his facial hair until he lowered her lips to his. They shared a sweet kiss, lips pressed together.

"Do we have a date tonight?" His smile was brilliant, and his eyes flashed.

"Standing date for every night you are in the local area." She kissed him again and sat up. He moved his hand under her hair and rubbed her back. "Damn... that feels good."

"Every night? Not going to get my money's worth from that hotel room, am I?"

She swiveled and looked at him. "Meh... plausible deniability. I have a special fund if you need help with the bills."

He barked a surprised laugh. "Ah, that would be a no. I have one of those special funds, too, and

Guardian pays very well." He sat up beside her and yawned. "Where do you want to meet and when?"

She blinked and rubbed her eyes. "Ummm..." She racked her brain for a place she could leave the SUV that wouldn't compromise her story at work. "I need coffee."

"Your wish is my command." He laughed and stood up.

Her eyes followed him as he grabbed his jeans. "Really? Where have you been the last five years of my life?" She watched his muscles flex and move as he stepped into the denim.

He zipped his jeans but didn't button them. He lazily scratched his chest hair and yawned, "That's classified."

She snorted and tossed a pillow at him. He caught it and tossed it back down on the bed. "Damn woman, no violence before six in the morning. It's in the manual." He sauntered down the hall.

She leaned forward to look as far down the hallway as she could. "What manual?"

"The great sex with an almost stranger manual." His words floated back from somewhere down the hall.

She flopped back in the bed and blinked at the

ceiling. *Well, fuck.* That put the last forty-eight hours or so into perspective.

Maliki stepped from his SUV and glared hard at the sheriff's patrol vehicle parked in front of his parents' house. The bastard. The maid met him at the door. "Dr. Blue. Your father is in his quarters. Your mother is in a meeting in the sunroom."

He nodded to the woman and headed to the back of the house and the sunroom.

He heard his mother's voice, sharp and filled with an authority he'd never heard before. "I find your suggestions offensive, Sheriff. My son is--" she caught sight of him as he entered the sunroom, the sheriff's back to him "—here. Maliki, do you know Sheriff Watson?"

Watson spun, his eyes widened and then narrowed.

"Mother. I've made the sheriff's acquaintance. I believe we have a common friend, Virginia's Attorney General." He sauntered in the door, unbuttoned his long sleeved shirt back behind his new badge, and showed the butt end of his .45.

"Do you have a permit to carry a concealed

weapon?" James Watson lowered his hand to his weapon.

"The authority *and* proper permits." He slowly reached into his pocket and extracted the laminated card and extended it to the sheriff.

"I thought Guardian didn't have business in the area. Why are you armed?" Watson reached for the permit.

Mal snorted. "I believe it's obvious."

The sheriff jabbed the permit back at him. "Spell it out for me."

"You, Sheriff Watson. Your hostility and paranoia have put this county on Guardian's radar."

"Paranoia. I'll second that." His mother sat down in a rattan, wing-backed, chair and crossed her legs. "Sheriff Watson had the utter gall to suggest you were forcing your presence on us. I explained you were here at our request."

"I'd still like to talk to your husband."

"As I told you, my husband is ill and not to be disturbed."

"Ma'am, I feel it's necessary to check on him, for his own safety." The sheriff raked his hateful gaze up and down Maliki as he spoke.

"Sheriff, if you have any further questions or concerns, you can contact my lawyers. My husband is not receiving any visitors other than family."

"I could come back with a warrant."

"You could, and I can contact every one of my neighbors and explain how you harassed us. The Boswell name still holds weight in this county." She smiled sweetly. "If you have any future business with us, conduct it through my lawyers. Lucinda will give you their card on your way out." She nodded to the woman who'd let him in moments ago. The woman curtsied and spun on her heel, probably to gather the card before the sheriff hit the front door.

As Watson strode to the door, Maliki caught his arm and whispered, "A word of advice, Sheriff. Stay away from me, stay away from my family, and stay away from anyone I have contact with. If you don't, I will call down the full focus of Guardian on this county. I'll find those secrets you're trying so desperately to hide. Don't ruin my vacation. I don't consider you worth the manpower my organization will expend to tear this county into shreds, but believe me, if you push one more time, I'll call them in."

A tick near Watson's eyes jumped and his jaw locked shut. Oh, the bastard was pissed. He and his mother had backed him into a corner. He had Guardian on his side, and she had a brick wall of impressive legal minds on hers.

Watson jerked his arm from his grip and stomped away.

"Well, that was particularly unpleasant." His mother sighed and dropped back further into her chair.

"How long was he here before I arrived?"

"Not long. I offered coffee, and we made small talk before he started those horrible innuendos."

Maliki took a seat across from her. "About?"

His mother waved her hand. "Utter nonsense. He suggested your father assumed the responsibility of that incident because he was protecting you. I disabused him of that notion immediately."

"What else?"

"He intimated you could have been the one to kill Clarissa."

"Excuse me?" His mouth dropped open. *What the ever-loving fuck?*

She nodded. "That man is insane."

"Mom, when did Clarissa die?"

"Oh, dear, that was in July or August of the year you left."

He shook his head. "I can account for every day

from June 3rd of that year and for two years after. I was in technical training in the Air Force."

She leaned forward; a line of concern formed on her brow. "You *do not* have to justify yourself to me, but if that... dullard is going to make accusations, I wanted you to be aware. I'll also contact my lawyers. That man needs to behave."

"Did he actually say he suspected me of being involved?"

"No, he said it was curious how you disappeared, leaving your fiancée so suddenly, and then she was dead. The unadulterated gall of the man."

"Clarissa left me, as everyone is well aware. Her rather public display when she hurled my ring back at me was witnessed by more than one person. I'm not worried about my reputation, but I'll let my employers know what he's doing now. I'm sure they'll handle anything that comes my way." The sheriff had just boosted his ass from paranoid hick to deranged and suspicious. *What the hell?* He tapped his boot against the beautifully crafted marquetry floors. A wave of dread hit him. "Mother, exactly what type of security do you have on the estate?"

"Oh, well at night, we employ a service. They do periodic checks. The night nurse watches your father. During the day, we have Martin. He maintains the gate, signs for deliveries and checks the fencing."

"Would it be all right with you if I were to upgrade your security, at least until we know what the hell is going on?"

She snapped her head back and brought her hand to her chest. "Do you think your father and I are in danger?"

"No, but it would allow me to rest easier if we manned the front gate and perhaps put cameras on the perimeter of the estate. I happen to know some of the best security contractors in the world. All it would take is one phone call."

His mother stared at him for a while before she nodded. "I believe it would allow me to rest easier, too. Your father isn't mobile anymore, and we have a host of people entering and exiting the grounds. Yes. Yes, indeed. Thank you so much for taking this on for me, for us."

He leaned forward and took her hand. "I don't know what prompted that scene, but I do know I would never let anything happen to you or… him, if I could prevent it. I don't want you to be afraid in your own home, but with the wealth and opulence in this house, having the extra security isn't a bad thing."

"Opulence?" His mother blinked in surprise. "Dear, this house is minimalistic compared to the others in the area."

Maliki chuckled. "It's all about perspective, isn't it? Is he having a good day?"

She smiled. "He is, although it was a bit too windy this morning, so we didn't venture outside. He's in his rooms. Will you see him?"

Maliki stood and took a deep breath. "That's why I'm here. I'm trying."

She smiled and the sheen of tears filled her eyes. "That's all I've asked of you. Thank you, for trying." His mother stood and walked with him to the grand stairway.

He leaned down and kissed her cheek. "I won't be able to stay for lunch today, and I have a friend meeting me here. I gave her the combination to the gate. We're going to park her vehicle near the garages and go together, if that's okay with you."

"Her?"

Maliki chuckled. "Actually, she's one of the sheriff's deputies. As you can tell, he's on a tear about me for some reason, and I don't want to make it harder for her. So, having her vehicle here, parked behind the house near the garages, will keep our secret from the sheriff and her away from trouble."

"Of course, that won't be a problem. My staff is trustworthy and very discrete. Is this a new... relationship?"

"Very new and nothing serious. But we need to keep it tightly under wraps. If anything were to get back to the sheriff, she'd be in trouble." He wasn't going to let his mother know about the investigation. Better she thought he and Poet were sneaking behind the paranoid and obnoxious sheriff's back to see each other rather than conducting an investigation.

"I am the fount of discretion." She beamed up at him. "I shall not tell a soul."

"Thank you." He winked at her and headed up the stairs to his father's suites. He found his father in his den, sitting in one of two massive recliners that hadn't been there when he was growing up. Neither had the large flat screen television he watched. Mal glanced at the screen. A documentary on Winston Churchill. "I didn't know you were a history buff?"

His father turned at his comment and a lopsided smile tugged at one side of his face. "I'm not. I hate soap operas." The words, as usual, were slow and slightly slurred.

"Well, that we have in common. I also despise reality television." He sat down in the recliner next to his father.

"Bah… attention seekers. They want the celebrity and... money." His father lifted the remote with his good arm and turned the volume down.

"I would agree with you. How are you feeling today?"

"Today is good." His father turned to look at him. "I was a horrible father."

Maliki closed his eyes and took a long breath. He agreed wholeheartedly, but he was here to find a way beyond that part of his life. "That is in the past."

His father shook his head. "No. That is reality."

He held his father's gaze. "We'll get there."

"Tell me about you. I missed so much." The words his father strung together were tinged with hopefulness. Maliki's immediate instinct was to remind his father *why* he missed so much, but he stifled it. Neither of them needed the past dredged up. His old man had apologized. Getting past the hurt of the event was his baggage to lug around. His father's condition limited the time he had to make amends, and fuck it, he was trying to let it go.

"Well after I left, I joined the Air Force..."

Poet drove up to the estate gates and rolled down her window. She gave one final look down the long, deserted roadway she'd traveled on before she keyed the number and waited for the wrought iron gate to open. The drive to the house took her breath away. She'd never been to the Boswell estate, but the beauty and splendor rivaled anything she'd seen. Topping the ridge, she slowed to a stop. The home was absolutely stunning, but what drew her eyes were the manicured gardens that extended like a lace fan beyond the home. The hedges formed a one-hundred-and-eighty-degree arc behind the house and a multitude of colors filled the artistic creation with a breathtaking splendor.

"Oh wow." She sighed the words and let her foot off the brake. She parked the SUV where Maliki had told her to park and got out of the vehicle. She straightened her summer weight blazer that covered the gun she carried in a holster at her back and the handcuffs that were tucked into a pouch secured to her belt. Her badge was clipped to the other side of her belt, also out of sight. She carried a weapon, even off duty, but today was different. Today she was taking purposeful steps to actively disobey her superior.

The clothes were perfect for a follow up investigation, but not for... this. She stared up at massive columns and the front of the imposing architecture. She swallowed hard and wiped her sweaty palms on her jeans. *Damn.* Her nerves were on edge and the towering mansion she walked around was out of her league. She took a deep breath and spoke to herself, "It's a house." She snorted and shook her head. *Maybe compared to the Taj Mahal... maybe.*

She walked up the limestone steps to the inlaid beveled glass doors and rang the bell. *Holy shit.* The muted sounds of Westminster chimes echoed from within. She could see someone approaching the door and stepped back a bit. The door opened, and a little woman wearing a maid's uniform smiled up at her. "Yes, miss?"

"Ah... I'm supposed to meet Maliki here."

"Oh, yes, please come in."

Oh, wow. The wooden floors were exquisite.

Darker inlaid boards outlined beautiful geometric designs along the outer edges and intricate patterns repeated from the front door to the... oh, the gardens! The house was split in half by the three-story high hallway. Two grand staircases led to different sides of the house. Three crystal chandeliers that rivaled the size of her patrol SUV were suspended from a fresco painted ceiling. "Wow." Her whisper echoed in the cavernous hall.

"It's rather big, isn't it?"

She whipped around at Maliki's voice. He trotted down the right staircase.

"Big? Big is probably the understatement of the millennium." She pointed up to the light fixtures. "That's big. This--" she spun around with her arms extended from her side and her head tipped back "--this is ridiculous!"

He laughed at her and grabbed her hand, pulling her back toward the door. "I'll give you a tour another time." He rushed her from the house.

"What was that? What's the hurry?" she asked as he encouraged her down the stairs and toward the big black SUV he drove.

"Unless you feel like going through an inquisition, I strongly recommend we get going." He let go of her hand and darted to the driver's side door, flicking the fob on his keychain, unlocking it.

She jumped into the vehicle and put on her seatbelt. "I'm a big girl, I can handle a few questions."

"Ah, well, after I brief you, you can handle a few questions."

"Why? What did you do?"

"I... Okay, let me back up a minute so you'll understand why I did what I did." He put the vehicle into gear and headed back to the front gate.

"So, spill." She crossed her arms and lifted an eyebrow at him in a silent challenge.

"When I arrived this morning, Sheriff Watson was here."

"No, God, he went through with that asinine plan?" She dropped her head back on the high seat-back and groaned. "Fuck, what is wrong with him lately?"

"I have no idea. I told him if he came after me, my family, or anyone I spent time with, that I would bring Guardian down here, and I guaranteed they'd run a probe so far up his ass they'd examine his fucking tonsils. I think that got his attention."

She closed her eyes and shook her head. Things

were getting crazier and crazier. Admittedly, she'd been responsible for upping the stress level by asking Guardian for help. Hopefully, Jim was just a territorial asshole. She shook her head and stared through the passenger window without seeing the manicured landscape. Something told her Jim was treading water and getting ready to go under. Something had him rattled. He was scared, and he was posturing and threatening to stop her from asking questions. The trip to Maliki's parents', that was to try to get something to hold over him. Why? What the fuck was he so damn afraid of? She waited until they left the estate and turned onto the county road before she remembered the dash from the house. "So, the inquisition?"

"I may have led my mother to believe we were dating and sneaking around behind the sheriff's back, so you didn't get in trouble."

She blinked at him. "We aren't dating. We're hooking up."

"No baggage, I remember." He glanced over and winked at her and then lit her up with that brilliant smile.

"Then why..."

"I had to have a plausible reason to leave your vehicle at the garages, out of sight, especially after your dickhead of a boss insulted my mother and tried to intimidate her." He shrugged. "You could do worse than me."

She lifted a finger. "One, I get the rationale, I do. It was just a shock to be told I was in a relationship." She lifted another finger. "Two, you didn't tell me that Jim insulted your mother, nor did you indicate he tried to intimidate her. You only mentioned he insinuated things, and you threatened to rain down all types of shit on him if he didn't behave. And three, I have no doubt I could do worse, but I doubt I could do much better. For a hookup, you're top-shelf."

"Top-shelf?" He laughed at her.

"Hell, yeah! You're a doctor, and my next door neighbor has deemed you as a sexy as fuck catch. You're prior Air Force, that gets you mega points. It's so nice to talk to someone who knows what AFSC, AFI, PCS, TDY, Elements, Flights, Squadrons, Groups and Wings are!"

"Speaking the same language does help, doesn't it?" He smiled that perfect toothpaste commercial worthy smile at her. "Speaking of which, I need to call in and bring my organization up to speed on the sheriff's latest."

"There is a gas station about fifteen miles up the road if you need privacy. I'll step out."

He shook his head. "I don't have any secrets." He grabbed his phone and hit a speed dial number before he put the phone on speaker.

A voice growled, "I am so over this bromance."

She swung her gaze to Maliki.

"Senior Deputy Campbell is in the vehicle with me."

"And?"

"Can you conference Jared in?"

"Standby."

She glanced at the phone and dipped her head toward it. "Hell of a way to answer a phone."

Maliki chuckled and scratched his beard. "Yeah, well, we've been talking a lot lately. I'm his favorite."

"Bullshit." The disembodied voice spoke, and she allowed herself a laugh at Maliki's expense.

"I'm on." Another, deeper voice came across the speaker.

"Jared, Deputy Campbell is in the truck with me. I needed Joseph to bring you in because I believe the sheriff has become an issue rather than an annoyance. He was at my parents' residence this morning. He insinuated a host of things; my primary concerns are simple. I'm worried about their safety, not only because of the weirdness of the situation, but because they don't have good security. Would you make some phone calls and get them hooked up? I'd prefer a manned front gate, a camera system, and they need the house rewired. They have an alarm system, but it's ancient, probably easily manipulated."

The deeper voiced man responded, "Consider it done. What is your secondary concern?"

"He insinuated I was responsible for the hit and run accident that killed my former fiancée. It happened in July or August of the year I enlisted. I went straight from basic to tech school. My attendance is documented."

There was silence before the first man responded. "I'm getting very tired of this guy. Can we get the background on him included with the original request?"

The second man said, "I'm going to do better than that. Maliki, I want you to stand down on the interviews. This guy is tracking off course, and my gut is telling me he's volatile. We are going to push this up in priority and bring in a trained investigator."

The frown on Maliki's face rivaled her own, but

she held in her displeasure. Mal didn't. "I'm not going to fuck this up. Deputy Campbell is here to make sure I don't."

"I'm afraid I'm going to insist. Until we have a better understanding of exactly what is going on down there, Deputy Campbell and you both need to watch your six, better if you are working together. Your sheriff is hiding something. He's terrified of you and trying to shake you or your parents into making you leave. When he gets notification that Guardian has taken not one, but two bodies from his medical examiner, he's going to do one of two things, lie low and pray shit blows over, or he's going to strike."

"He has a third option." The first voice said. "He could run."

"He could, but he can't hide." Maliki pulled over to the side of the road. "And what are we supposed to do in the meantime?"

"Do what you were there to do in the first place, and keep Deputy Campbell close, real close. With the information you've given us, I make this guy as a snake in the grass, and while we don't know what's driving him, he is hissing and ready to strike."

"I have a feeling being seen close to Deputy Campbell may be an irritant to the situation."

"I'd rather you had backup, and a deputy sheriff that works for the man is a formidable obstacle for him to plow through to get to you. He wants things kept in the county, and quiet, remember?

She spoke to the phone. "Will the investigator keep it below the radar?"

"They will until we have the background information we need. Then we'll take what we find to the AG. You two watch your six. Dom Ops out."

"Keep your asses down, ears open, and don't fucking get killed."

Mal chuffed a humorless laugh. "I hadn't planned on dying."

"Good. Too damn much paperwork. Whatever it takes, Mal."

"As long as it takes."

The connection dropped, and her eyes shifted from the phone to Maliki. They were parked on the side of the road with nowhere to go. "Well, what now? I've requested time off like we talked about."

"You should probably take the time off, so you don't raise any suspicions. Do you have enough vacation time?

"Well, despite what I tell my mother, I have plenty of vacation time accrued." She waved him off when he angled his head in question. "She always wants me to visit. I love them, but it's like they think I'm still a teenager when I go home. It's magic, I swear. I lose fifteen years of confidence, paying my own bills, military service and working as a deputy, not to mention all that time of living by myself. I'm twelve again, at least in their eyes."

Maliki smiled sadly. "I'd covet that. My parents and I have never had a close relationship. We're working on that."

The mood shifted. She reached over and clasped his hand, threading her fingers through his. "Care to talk about it? I've been told I'm a good listener."

He shook his head. "We promised no baggage."

"Meh, that's not baggage, that's history. Baggage, for the purposes of this hookup, should be defined as... anything that will make us parting company messy." She'd miss him, sure, he was a fantastic lover, but she was also a realist. He wasn't staying, and she'd probably be looking for a job by the time Guardian finished the investigation. Hell, she was tempted to put feelers out now. Jim's personality changes recently were troublesome.

She'd started to notice the other deputies ducking away whenever he was around. It wasn't just her who wanted to avoid him.

He lifted his hand and stroked his beard before he winked at her. "You better watch out, I'm easy to fall in love with."

She threw back her head and laughed, "I'll take the risk." She knew, if she let herself, she could develop feelings for the sexy doctor.

"You've been warned." He gave her a dazzling smile and put the truck into gear. "It's a long story. Have you eaten?"

CHAPTER 11

"Do you want dessert?"

Maliki leaned back in his chair as their waitress took their plates. He glanced at Poet and lifted an eyebrow in question.

She smiled a carefree, wide smile and nodded. "Let's share a piece of apple pie."

He was full, but he'd indulge a bit. "Sure, and more green tea for me, please?"

"Ice cream on that?" The waitress juggled the dishes as she asked.

Poet nodded. "Yes please, two scoops."

"You got it. Be back with it in a second." The waitress turned on her heel and headed toward the kitchen.

"So, nobody told the truth?" She leaned forward, her thick red hair fell over her shoulder and she tossed it back with an aggravated flip of her hand.

"Eventually, someone came forward. I don't know who. I guess it really doesn't matter. I'm assuming an investigation was completed and my father handled the repercussions through legal channels. I was unavailable for two years and had legally changed my name after I hired lawyers to protect my trust fund and give me access to it via my new identity."

"So, have you spoken to your father?"

He nodded. "Twice. He's not well. He's had a stroke that left him disabled with partial paralysis. He also has dementia. We were visiting this morning. Nothing too deep or emotional. I don't think either of us is ready to go there, although we brushed up against it the first time we spoke. Today, he was quiet for a moment and then looked at me, and I could tell he was lost or maybe confused as to who I was. He became agitated then. It has to be terrifying suddenly not knowing where you are or who you're with."

"What did you do?" She reached over and covered his hand with hers. The gesture felt normal and sincere. He turned his hand and their fingers slotted together.

"Directed the conversation to what was on television. He seemed to settle down, so I sat with him for a while, thinking about my life since I left." He leveled a stare at her. "I've been through events and situations that rocked me to the core. Experiences I would never wish on anyone, but those crises made me who I am today, and I'm okay with this guy. He's a better man."

She smiled at him and whispered, "I like this guy too." The waitress sped by and delivered their dessert and his tea. Poet squeezed his hand and leaned back, disengaging their contact.

Contact that he missed almost immediately. Probably because he'd never had anyone to talk with about his family or about the things he'd been through. Of course, his employers knew the basics, but he didn't discuss the details, his feelings, or his hopes with them. Hell, he hadn't talked with anyone like that since... Clarissa. Those conversations were a pale, superficial substitute for what he longed for now.

She handed him a fork before she took a bite of the pie. He placed his fork on the table and sipped his tea instead. "Aren't you going to have any?"

"Maybe in a minute. You eat what you want."

"Might not be any left."

She cut a healthy portion of the pie with her fork and waved it in front of him before she ate it. "I'll risk it."

He lifted his tea and toasted her.

"What experiences?" She scooped some ice cream and paused to look at him.

He blinked at her. *What?* "I'm sorry, I'm not following?"

She ate the frozen cream and then used the napkin to wipe her lips. "You said you've gone through experiences you wouldn't wish on anyone. Were you in the Air Force or with Guardian when they happened?"

His internal armor rose. He watched her for a moment. What happened with Foxtrot Team wasn't something he'd ever broached when others were around. That night had devastated him. He was the only one to escape. The man he'd carried out of hell with him never really returned. His body came home, but mentally, Trucker stayed in that pit where their teammates lost their lives. The men's names and the events of that night were almost sacred to him. "You're quite the investigator, aren't you?"

"Actually, no. I haven't been to any classes for investigation. I'm just a deputy. I have my basic law enforcement certification, and I'm damn good at paperwork. The Air Force taught me to do it right the first time. The sheriff would never sign off on the cost for an advanced course like that. He can send three through other classes for the cost of one person going through the investigator's course. I get it. But I am diligent, I pay attention, and I know when someone redirects the conversation. Not something you care to talk about?"

He put his tea down and leaned on his arms. "Dark times. I don't want to disrespect the memory of those who didn't come home by discussing it in a chain restaurant where there is no privacy. It seems..."

"Wrong. I get it. Sorry I pushed you."

He shook his head. "You didn't push; you asked."

"So, Doctor Blue, what are we going to do for the rest of the day?"

"Do you have anything important to get back to?"

She tipped her wrist to look at the face of her watch. "No. I cleared the afternoon. Although I'm back on call at six. Let me tell you, being sidelined by your boss sucks."

"I agree, but I acknowledge my limitations. It's better if Guardian takes this. I wouldn't want to be responsible for messing up the investigation. My training is evolving, but I know nothing about interviewing witnesses."

"Yeah, what do you know about?" She dropped her chin into her hand and stared at him.

Wow. Okay, you opened that door, shithead. "Oh, you know, run of the mill stuff." *Like how to disable a bomb, fly a drone, build and use a remote triggering device.*

"Hmmm… evasion again. Okay, let me redirect the question. Why would a doctor, a surgeon in fact, be training to do anything *but* medicine?" She blinked at him and then lifted her eyebrows, taunting him to answer.

He drew a breath and asked, "Have you ever been so incredibly bored with your life that you needed to do something, anything, to validate you were in fact… alive?"

She leaned back. "Well, I've jumped out of an airplane, and I rock climb. It makes my blood pump, and I get a charge from it. We've already established *you're* an adrenaline junkie. Run of the mill classes wouldn't keep your interest." She narrowed her eyes and leaned forward; her voice lowered to a whisper. "You said you were assigned to a team when you first worked for Guardian. I think maybe your dark times happened with that team; *they* are the people you won't disrespect. Maybe the reason you take these 'less than basic classes' is because you're afraid of letting what happened then happen again. Although knowing what little I do about you, I believe you did everything in your power to stop whatever was happening. You don't seem to give by half measures."

The sounds of the restaurant dwindled to nothing as he stared at the woman across from him. A woman who'd known him for less than a week had split him open and cut out his heart. A movement in the corner of his eye caught his attention, and he lifted his hand signaling the waitress for the check. He dropped his eyes to his empty cup.

She reached across the table and touched his arm. "Should I apologize again? Did I insult you?"

He shook his head. "It's hard to be insulted by the truth."

Maliki let the GPS navigate them through Charlottesville but turned it off once they were on the county road heading back to Pleasant County. Poet hadn't said a word since they'd left the restaurant. He glanced at her before he spoke, "It was hard to hear."

Her attention rested on him. "I'm sorry."

He attempted a smile. "Don't be. I don't know how to explain the suspension of reality in which I've existed recently. You ripped the blinders off, and the reality of what I was doing and possibly why I've been doing it is rather jarring. That revelation requires a moment to digest." He was an intelligent man. He'd been called gifted. He'd made his life decisions based on fact, hadn't he? Where had the deliberate shift of his focus from medicine to the thrill of the danger involved with Guardian's newest teams come from? When had he lost his edge? Where did he deviate from his goal to be the best surgeon he could be?

Ah... well, yes, then. He'd lost the zeal for his profession when his father accused him of negligence. Nothing else he'd accomplished had come close to the sense of achievement of a successful surgery. Perhaps that was why he was still searching?

He set the cruise control and let his mind wander. Poet was right. He never wanted to let a team down again.

He cleared his throat. "Guardian supported me, and the decisions I made that night."

Her hand landed on his thigh. "I'll listen if you want to talk about it. If you don't, I understand."

He ground his teeth for a moment before the words came. Words he couldn't stop, and he wasn't sure he wanted the memories to ebb. "I was on the team's six, taking my turn on trail making sure we weren't being followed. When I made it to where the others were, my team leader and the second in command were squared off in one hell of an argument. Loud. Too fucking loud. We didn't have a chance of avoiding detection. The situation around us devolved into an epic clusterfuck. They could have fucking avoided detection, but the argument between Skipper and Drago put us on the scope. Our second in command was taken out with a first-round volley of hand grenades. The skipper led us through the streets and into a small compound. He knew exactly where he was going, but as far as I knew we didn't have intel on the area. Sandy, the youngest and most inexperienced on the team, was wounded. I picked him up and

Trucker hauled his ass with us as overwatch. Skipper didn't stop, didn't slow down, he was hell bent on getting to wherever the fuck he was going. Of course, we followed.

He led us down a street to a compound that was fortified. We were pinned down. Fuck, we fought like animals for over thirty minutes. We were running out of ammo. The skipper ordered us to cover him and he made it into the next building. I split my time between caring for Sandy and keeping the insurgents from overrunning us. Trucker, damn we'd all be dead if it wasn't for that man. We heard the skipper yell for us to get down. We hit the dirt. The skipper tossed a hand grenade, and I watched as he hauled a chest from the building and sprinted toward us in our defensive position we'd been using. Sandy lost his fight for his life about the same time Skipper bought it. Skipper was shot through the neck at the edge of the small shelter we were defending."

Maliki drew a shuddering breath at the memories. *He'd fought to keep his skipper alive, but it was useless. He pushed the chest over, using it as cover for his teammate as he worked on him and then as a base to steady his M4. A volley of bullets broke the case open and the contents spilled out.*

"Motherfucker!" Trucker swore and glanced at Mal.

Mal shook his head. "Forget about it. We need a way out."

"I'm on it. Keep them off me, Doc, then we play dead."

Trucker rigged two claymores and they baited the bastards in by not firing. When the fuckers were close enough, Trucker popped the explosives. Mal shivered at the recollection of the mist of blood and the fall of body parts. He and Trucker hauled ass. They fought their way out. He was hit in the shoulder; Trucker took a bullet to the head. His helmet slowed the projectile and angled the wound, skimming the man's skull before it embedded. He triaged his teammate and carried him until he met up with friendly forces. His skipper, the son of a bitch... he'd put all their lives on the line for fucking money. A fucking chest of gold.

Poet shifted beside him, extracting him from the past. He cleared his throat and continued, "Trucker was shot, but I was able to get us help." Not enough and not soon enough for Trucker. The man lived in a convalescent home and didn't recognize his family.

"What was in the chest?"

Maliki gripped the steering wheel with a death grip and shook his head. He'd briefed Guardian and only Guardian knew what was in the chest. "We never found out. Survival became paramount."

"That I get. Do you think that was why your skipper and the second in command were arguing?"

"Again, I don't know. I wasn't there long enough to figure it out before we were running down the back alleys and streets of that little town."

"What about Trucker? Did he hear?"

"We'll never know. He suffered a brain injury. He has little to no cognitive ability. He can feed himself, he doesn't speak, doesn't act like he recognizes anyone."

"You got him out?"

"I'd die before I left him there."

They were quiet for a long time. "Maliki?"

"Yeah?"

"I'm really glad you made it out, too."

He covered her hand that was still on his thigh and squeezed it. He may have made it out, but he'd never been able to leave that experience. Never. That day had shaken his faith in his organization, in his own judgement, and in humanity in general. He'd trusted his team with his life, and his skipper had violated his trust. Three dead, one critically injured and him... alive but grieving.

"Would you like to come over tonight? Same time? You're cooking. You're better at it than I am, and you can afford it. I saw your house, today, remember?"

Her question dragged him away from his thoughts, and he gave thanks for the distraction from the somber memories. "What? This coming from another trust fund baby?"

"Oh, hell, my trust fund is like a three-year old's piggy bank compared to yours."

He threw back his head and laughed. "How would you know?"

She gawked at him. "I. Saw. Your. Mansion!"

"Not mine, my parents."

"Ah huh. Money. Old money. Lots of old money. So, you buy dinner or bring the ingredients and we'll cook together."

"I'll do that, but only because I don't want my arteries to harden in the time I'm here."

"Whoa! That earned you a whole week's worth of cooking."

"Thank God."

She blinked owlishly at him. "Oh, my God, I think I was insulted."

"Not at all. Besides I want to be there when you call in and tell them you're back and take over your call. I'm curious how the sheriff handled Guardian assuming control of the autopsies on the latest victims."

Poet groaned, "Oh, damn, that is a good question."

CHAPTER 12

Poet drove into her apartment complex and parked. She had another two hours before she had to check in, and she was going to use every last second of her 'non-call' status. For the first time since she'd been promoted to Senior Deputy, she didn't want the events of the night to interrupt her plans.

She locked the SUV and headed to her apartment. Instead of taking the elevator, she used the stairs. Not many did, but she enjoyed the quiet of the rarely used stairs. She'd been replaying Maliki's words since he'd dropped her off to retrieve her vehicle. He was going to pick up something for dinner and come over, which made her smile. She hated to cook and the mac and cheese dish she made the first time she invited him over was about the only thing she could make that wouldn't kill someone. She'd never tell anyone it came from a box, but it did. She added some cheese on the top and shoved it in the oven. The ham she'd picked up was from a small charcuterie place at the edge of town that also sold heat-and-serve meals. She was a bane to her poor mother who thought a woman should be able to feed her eventual mate. Hell, she could feed that imaginary man... take out, frozen pizza, burritos, sandwiches.

She let herself into her apartment, locked the door, and dropped her keys into the dish on the small table inside the door. Her gun went on top of the fridge, her handcuffs and badge traveled back to the bedroom with her. She lost the professional clothes and tugged on some soft jeans and a t-shirt, no shoes, no socks, before she padded back into the kitchen and retrieved her cell. She'd put it on silent and turned off the vibration alert before she drove to Maliki's parents'.

She waited for the facial rec to unlock the phone and groaned at the first missed call she saw. Jim Watson. She put the phone on the counter, fished her pitcher of sweet tea out and poured herself a tall glass of instant energy. She was going to need it. The corner of the sectional welcomed her like a lover, forming around her and holding her in a comfortable embrace. She opened the phone again. Avoiding the sheriff's call probably wasn't the smartest idea, but that is exactly what she did. She answered several texts and read her emails. She read her brother's email, twice. He wrote about once a month. He was career Navy, and he loved submarine duty. They were as opposite as people could be, but she envied his commitment to the service, even if, in her opinion, he picked the wrong one.

She finally looked at her recent calls. Tillie'd called and left a voicemail. She chuckled at her friend's rant on her students' lack of responsibility. The profanity laced diatribe was so typical of Tillie. Her mother called. Just checking in. Without any other reason to delay the inevitable, she hit the play arrow on the sheriff's message.

"*Deputy Campbell, if I find you are responsible for the AG pulling strings and taking over the medical investigation on those two cases, I will take swift and immediate action. You will call me as soon as you hear this message. That is not a request.*"

"Well, not as bad as it could have been." She tossed the phone onto the couch beside her.

Career aside. Well, she'd been aware of the consequences when she invited Maliki into her insanity. In the long run, it didn't matter, as long as those women received the justice they deserved. Now, talented investigators were taking over. If they found nothing, and she was fired… well, she'd find something to do. She had money to live comfortably for many years—as long as she was careful.

She took a sip of her tea and glanced at the time. Maliki should be arriving shortly. She smiled, happy for the companionship. She enjoyed spending time with him. He was so damn intelligent and even cagey at times. His past... damn. She'd read accounts of missions going bad, and suspected some of them had been far worse than what she'd read online since the details had been glazed over. As he recounted that day, watching his emotional reactions was heartbreaking and painful. She'd caused him pain by asking him to retell the events. Her damn quip about him not wanting to let down people in the same way had been uncalled for and so damn presumptuous on her part. He'd lost three of his teammates and one was gravely injured. He was a doctor. He'd been trained to save lives, and if he couldn't do that for the people he trusted most, he probably felt like he failed his team. Damn, she wished like hell she'd never said anything.

Tonight wasn't for bad memories. She needed to pull the curtains back and let fun and laughter into his life. Sexy times, too, for sure, but they needed to do something fun, something to lighten the mood. Oh! Yes!

She bolted from the corner of the sectional and landed on her knees in front of the wall unit she'd bought in Japan. She opened the bottom cabinet and smiled as she carefully unboxed her ancient Nintendo gaming station and the games she'd kept from childhood. *Super Mario, Donkey Kong* and *Tetris*.

She unboxed the unit, found all the cords and hooked up the machine before she powered it up. The NES logo bounced on her television screen. *Score*. A knock at the door sent that direction in a sprint. After taking a peek she unbolted the door and once again yanked Mal into her apartment.

"Whoa, woman. Did the sheriff show up here again?" He leaned into the kitchen and set the bags he was holding on the small kitchen table.

She bounced on her toes as he set the bags down. "No, but I need to call him. He left a message. Come look."

He threw her a suspicious look but followed her from the kitchen. She stopped in front of the television and waved at the gaming system, doing her best Vanna impression. "Ta da!"

He looked from the television, to her, to the game. "I take it by your expression I'm supposed to be surprised."

"Well, yeah! It works!"

"What works?"

"It's an original Nintendo!"

He crossed his arms and glanced at the setup again before he turned to her. "Yeah, I don't know what that is."

Her jaw dropped. "No way. You're lying."

"I assure you I don't know what that is."

"*Super Mario*? *Donkey Kong*? Old-school video games. The best games on the planet?"

He shook his head. "Sorry..."

"Oh, man you have had a neglected childhood! What did the rich kids do after school when you were growing up?"

"My life was pretty regimented. I went to private boarding school in the states until high school and then I went to a prestigious private school in Switzerland. Video games weren't allowed. We had organized sports and study time."

She ass planted onto the arm of the couch. "So… no video games?"

"No, although I played a few of the stand-up machines in the arcades during summer break."

"Huh." She glanced at the game and then at him. "So, I'll be able to beat you senseless, huh?" She rubbed her hands together.

"Really, you're going to take advantage of my lack of knowledge?"

"Oh, damn straight, Doc. Let's make dinner and then your education really begins." She headed into the kitchen but stopped and spun on her heel. She walked up to him, put her arms around his neck and urged him down for a kiss. He folded his arms around her and pressed her against him. Their lips slid together until his tongue encouraged her to open for him. She attacked and countered as he took control of the kiss. When they finally parted, he placed his forehead against hers. "What was that for?"

She stepped back so she could see his face. "I'm happy you're here." She spun and practically skipped into the kitchen.

"I told you woman. You better watch yourself, or you're going to end up falling in love with me."

She laughed and tried to slide a serious

expression on her face, almost certain she didn't master it. "I don't know, Mal. No Nintendo experiences? What other serious character flaws do you have? I mean, this type of void in your personality development is very concerning. I'm not sure I could love a man who can't play Super Mario."

"Well then, I guess you'll have to teach me. I'm obviously lacking in your opinion." He popped her on the ass on the way into the kitchen.

She rubbed her hind cheek and watched him disappear into the kitchen. *You don't lack a thing, Dr. Blue. Not a damn thing.*

"Get in here, woman. You said we were cooking together." Mal stuck his head out from the doorway of the kitchen. "You are my sous chef. Veggies need to be cleaned and chopped."

She dropped her head back between her shoulders. "Veggies? What are you trying to do to me? Please tell me you have something unhealthy in those bags." She followed him into the kitchen. An array of different color veggies and dark green lettuce like leaves, a carton of nuts, a... pomegranate and strawberries lined the counter.

"What does that make?"

He turned and looked at the counter and then

at her. "Ah... that would be a salad. How rudimentary do we need to go on this cooking tutorial?"

She closed one eye and pursed her lips as she stared at the veggies and fruit. "Why would you put fruit in a lettuce salad?"

"That's baby kale and you put fruit in because it's good."

"Kale?" Her skin crawled. She'd heard horror stories from other deputies whose wives had made them eat kale.

He nodded and pointed to the counter. "Wash all of it. Chop everything but the kale and the pomegranate."

She reached for a knife, drawing it from the butcher block holder on the counter. "You're a slave driver."

"Right... Stop bitching and start chopping."

"Please tell me we are having meat." Her voice may have been a titch petulant.

"Depends on your definition of meat."

She stopped gathering the veggies and rolled her head toward him. "Explain that. Are we having a meat-based protein, or am I going to be forced to become a rabbit tonight?"

"We're having blackened shrimp and cheese grits with our very healthy salad which will be dressed in a balsamic vinaigrette." He leaned over and dropped a kiss on her lips before he hip checked her and sent her in the direction of the sink. "Rinse and chop."

With one eye on the clock she worked on the salad and was fussed at for eating more of the strawberries than were making it to the bowl. She side-eyed Maliki before popping another quarter slice into her mouth. Another glance at the clock and she sighed. "Okay, I can't avoid it any longer. I need to check in and call the sheriff back."

"Did he leave a message?" Mal stopped peeling the shrimp and glanced at her.

"Oh yeah, hold on, let me play it for you." She made quick work of retrieving her phone and playing the message.

"Well that's easy. You didn't request anything. I did." He sliced the back of the shrimp open and removed a long black strand.

"What is that?"

"What?"

She pointed to the sink where he'd tossed the strand. He chuckled and asked, "Don't you need to check in?"

"Yeah." She slid out the chair, sat down and called dispatch, putting the phone on speaker.

"Hiya, Faye. I'm back in the county and taking back my call. What do you have going on?"

"Hey, Poet. Nothing right now. Quiet at the moment. I do have a message for you from day shift. The sheriff wants you to call him immediately. He said to check your messages."

"Damn, I had the phone on silent. I'll do that now. Thanks, Faye."

"No problems, sweets. Hope I don't have to talk to you again tonight."

"Yeah, me too. I have a video game challenge I plan on winning." She winked at Maliki when he turned to look at her.

Faye snorted. "That sounds completely boring."

"Hey, I don't bust your ass about your quilting."

"True, you don't. Enjoy your mind-altering digital fix."

"Thank you, and don't sew your fingers together."

"I haven't done that in *at least* a year. Hey, don't forget to call Jim. According to day shift, he was in rare form. Everyone was on patrol. No one wanted to be in the office with him."

"Sounds like I picked the perfect day to have a doctor's appointment."

Faye's voice lowered, "Everything okay?"

"Yeah, annual stuff."

"Eww... gotcha. Hate it, but yah gotta do it."

"Ain't that the truth. Let me go, I'll call Jim next."

"Have a good night, I'll log you in as on call."

"You too, and thanks."

She hung up and hit the speed dial for Jim before placing that call on speaker too. The phone rang and rang and rang. *"This is Sheriff Watson. If you have an emergency hang up and call 911. If you have business with me, please leave a message and I'll return your call."*

When the beep sounded, she said, "Jim, this is Poet. I got your message, and I don't have a clue what you're talking about. I absolutely did not request anything from the AG. You told me not to call the state. I would never violate a direct order, and I've not spoken to anyone at the state about any case. Give me a call if you have any questions."

She hung up and drummed her fingers on the kitchen table. "Well that was really anticlimactic."

"Probably for the best, though." Maliki stood at the stove.

"Yeah. Anyway, I'm on call, but I have some sweet tea or sodas if you'd like a drink."

"Oh, so you're on call and that means I can't

drink?" He used the whisk on a white creamy mixture. The grits, maybe? She'd never tried them, even in basic training where they were a staple for every chow hall breakfast line.

"Do you want a drink?" She pointed to the living room and her little bar.

He shook his head. "I'll be fine with water. I need to stay sharp so I can beat you at Super Donkey Brothers."

She rolled her eyes and had no idea if he was joking or not, but something told her he wasn't.

"Jump!" She laughed as Mal's Mario fell off the floating bricks.

"I jumped! Aww, man that was my last life, too." He held the controller, jabbing the button.

"You didn't jump soon enough, but you did really well this time. You haven't gotten to this level before." She was sitting cross-legged on the floor next to him. "Try it again." They'd been playing for about an hour, and watching Maliki master the controller and then learn the game had been far more entertaining than winning on every level, so they went to one player and she tried to help him advance.

Her phone, which she'd put on ring after she'd checked in, shrilled as he started a new game. He hit the pause button silencing the annoyingly repetitive music. "The sheriff?"

She glanced at her phone. "No. Dispatch." She swiped the face and answered, "Campbell."

"Poet, we have two units on the way to Doc Giles' residence. His son called in. He found his father hanging from the rafters in the garage."

"En route. Has the sheriff been informed?"

"I haven't been able to contact him."

"All right, I'm en route. ETA, ten minutes." She hung up and sprinted to the bedroom as she yelled over her shoulder. "The medical examiner is dead."

Mal's voice came from directly behind her. "Want me to come along?"

"Do you have a current license to practice medicine in Virginia?"

"I do. Why?"

"Because our medical examiner usually declares the victim deceased at a death scene. We're going to need a stand in."

"Done." He spun and headed down the short hall.

She threw on a long-sleeved t-shirt and shoved on a pair of boots. Mal entered the bedroom wearing his automatic under his light jacket and presented her with her service weapon.

She clipped it to her belt along with her badge and handcuffs. She snagged her cell phone from the front room and grabbed her keys on the way from the apartment. It took twenty seconds to secure her apartment before they launched down the hallway and into the stairwell.

Maliki buckled into the passenger's seat and she lit up the parking lot, running her emergency lights, but waited to hit the siren until they cleared the residential area.

"I'm calling this in. The investigator assigned will need to know."

"It could be a total coincidence." She rolled through a four way stop and hit the gas again.

"You don't believe that any more than I do." He grabbed the 'oh shit' handle as Poet took a corner on damn near two wheels. He jabbed the button to contact Joseph. His friend answered, "I'm sweaty, sandy and hungry. This better be damn good."

"The medical examiner is dead. We are on the way to the death scene."

"Why are you going?"

"I have a license to practice in Virginia. The ME is the person who usually declares the decedent dead. Deputy Campbell asked me to fill in."

"Well, fuck. Keep your phone with you." The connection dropped and Mal pocketed the device. "How much further?"

"About two miles from town." She hit the county road and flipped on the switch for the siren.

Minutes later she decelerated quickly and turned into a driveway. The whirling lights of two other sheriff's vehicles directed them to where they needed to be. They parked near the garage. Poet stopped, and they both hit the ground and headed toward the open garage door.

"Granger? What do you have?"

"Hey, Poet. The man stood up from beside the now prone body of Doctor Giles. "His son, Martin, came home and couldn't find his old man. His car is parked out front. The kid called his phone. Heard it ringing. He opened the garage door and found his old man swinging." He pointed to a red nylon rope that had been tied to the crossbeam of the garage. It had been sawed in half, frayed and jagged.

"Who cut him down?"

"Dobson and I did. The kid had grabbed his father's legs and was trying to keep pressure from his neck."

"Have you moved anything else?" Mal leaned down next to the man. The break in his neck was obvious. Mal glanced around.

"No. We cut him down. There was no pulse. He was grey and cold. We didn't do CPR."

"Thank you." He turned so his back was to the other officer and glanced at Poet and then motioned to Granger with a tilt of his head. Her eyes widened in understanding. "Do we have a suicide note?"

"Dobson is inside with the kid. He's pretty shook up; I don't know if they looked yet."

"Do me a favor, head in and get the kid's permission to take a look."

"Roger that." Granger headed into the house.

Mal adjusted his weight on one knee and waited for the door to close. "What's missing here?"

"Missing?" Poet looked around. "Cars?"

"No. This man's neck is broken. To do that requires a substantial torque, such as a significant drop. It doesn't appear as if he choked to death—no petechial hemorrhages of note—and the break is inconsistent to the area where the rope tightened." He pointed to the break and then the area of the neck where the rope had obviously been wrapped. "Notice the lack of bruising around the ligature marks. That indicates blood wasn't flowing while he was hanging. There is nothing in the garage he could have stepped on to get up to that noose. Nothing that he kicked away or slipped off of. This is not a suicide by hanging. No, there are too many things missing."

"Murder. To what end? Is someone covering up something with the two bodies that were taken today?" She whispered her question.

He stood and shook his head. "I don't know. We need validation of my opinion. Let's call it a suspicious death. Until an experienced ME can get x-rays and do an autopsy, I wouldn't hurry to classify it as a suicide."

"Hey, Poet, we got a note." Granger held a single sheet of paper in his gloved hand. She held up her hands. "Hold that for us, we don't have gloves on yet." Granger complied.

. . .

Martin,

I'm sorry to leave you this way. I love you. Forgive me.

Dad

"It isn't signed." Poet glanced at him and then back to Granger.

"It was in the printer in the Doc's office along with his wallet. I've bagged that, and I'll get this in an evidence bag, but I figured you'd want to see it."

"Thanks. Good work. Do we have an ETA on the ambulance?"

"The one that covers this area is transporting a patient into Charlottesville. The other rig is coming over from the west. Five more minutes maybe. You going to have them transport to the county morgue?"

He shook his head. "No, he should go to the hospital's morgue."

"Why's that?" Granger angled his head and narrowed his eyes. "You keep showing up. Who are you?"

"I'm a doctor with Guardian Security. I was with Deputy Campbell tonight when this call came in." He crossed his arms over his chest and sighed.

"Look, this guy was the Chief Medical Examiner. Are you really going to make his own people see him like this?"

Granger blinked and then glanced down at Giles. "Damn, didn't think about that."

Poet propped her hands on her hips. "Yeah, damn good call, Dr. Blue. Granger, have Faye call the hospital and make the arrangements after you get that note into an evidence bag."

He waited until the officer retraced his steps before he spoke. "The computer needs to be taken as evidence. The keyboard needs to be dusted for prints."

"I'm on it. Are you good waiting here with him?"

Mal palmed his vibrating phone from his jacket. "Yeah, I'm good." He swiped the phone and watched her jog into the house as he answered. "Blue."

"Jared here. Joseph's on the line, too. What do you have?"

He swung his eyes to the door and moved away. He lowered his voice. "I'll need someone to validate my suspicions, but I believe we have a murder someone staged as a suicide. The deceased was discovered hanging by his neck in his garage.

There is a note, all printed, no signature and generic. The break of the neck vertebra isn't consistent with the positioning of the rope. There was no bruising or typical strangulation indications other than the damage to the exterior dermis, and there isn't a box or chair that this guy could have stepped off. My opinion is someone killed him, and then strung him up."

"What the hell did you get yourself involved in?" Joseph's question rolled through the connection. Yeah, that question was foremost in his mind, too.

He walked to the driveway to make sure no one could overhear him. "I don't know, J. Gut instinct says Deputy Campbell found a frayed edge, and now, whatever is happening around here is coming unraveled. Why would someone kill the ME?"

"Why does anyone kill? Greed, lust or power. Our investigator will be there tomorrow. Asher Hudson will hit the ground running. He has the case files you sent but will want to sit down with you and the senior deputy. The switchboard will patch him through to you. I'll give him this update but be prepared to sit down with him tomorrow. Do you have a place the three of you can meet where there won't be any interruptions?"

"Yeah, either the deputy's apartment, or I can use my folks' place, but I don't want to bring them into this if I don't have to do it."

"I understand that. If nothing else, use your hotel room to talk to him. You can put the deputy on the phone and do it virtually. Oh, I arranged for a contractor to look at your folks' place tomorrow. They are taking some temp guards with them to leave in place until they get the systems online and make permanent hires."

He sighed and rubbed the back of his neck. "Thanks, I'll rest easier."

"Based on your professional opinion that this was a murder, are you and the deputy safe?" Jared's concern was obvious.

"I've been watching my six since the sheriff's original confrontation. The deputy has worked with this guy a long time. She's tuned in to the man's actions." He'd double check with Poet on that before he left her tonight, or tomorrow morning.

"All right. Hunker down until Asher gets there. He'll bring the full authority of this investigation with him; it is now officially an open case with Guardian as the lead agency. The AG is acutely aware of our interest and wants constant updates, but hopefully Jason can keep him from sending someone down to muddy the investigation."

Red flashing lights bounced against the front of the house as the ambulance drove down the driveway. "Roger that. We're sending his body to the hospital morgue, not the ME's office. I didn't want it to turn up missing."

Jared acknowledged his actions, "Good thinking. I'll up channel the request for authority over the postmortem. Let me get that sorted. Do you need anything else?"

"I'll let you know if something comes up."

"All right. I'm clear." Jared exited the conversation.

"I don't think I'll let you go on vacation again." Joseph added.

"Hold on." He directed the ambulance crew to the dead body and told them to transport to the hospital, not the county morgue. "All right, I'm back."

"See if you can keep yourself and that deputy alive long enough for the investigator to arrive."

"I'll work on that." He chuckled a bit and rubbed the back of his neck as he watched the ambulance crew spread a body bag. "This isn't what I expected when I was working with the teams at the facility."

"What exactly did you expect?"

"I thought... Hell, I guess I thought with two people, the shit that happened with Foxtrot Team would be impossible. That communication would be clearer, the work would be... different."

"The work will always be the same. Answer a question for me. Can you read minds?"

He drew a deep breath. "No."

"Well then, stop beating yourself up about what happened in the past. You couldn't have prevented it. Survivor's guilt will eat you alive. Cut yourself some slack." Joseph didn't seem in a rush to close the conversation tonight.

Mal leaned against the deputy's vehicle and watched Poet as she entered the garage. She was all business but glanced around until she found him. He raised a hand, and she returned the gesture before she went back to work.

"You make peace with your old man?"

He glanced up at the dark night sky. A few stars twinkled—the rest hidden by the light of the house and the strobe lights. "Trying."

"Worth the effort. Keep your ass down."

"You keep telling me that. Awful worried about

my ass, aren't you?" Mal waited for a moment and then looked at the face of his phone. The fucker had hung up on him. He chuckled and shoved the phone into his pocket. He glanced at his watch. *Where was the sheriff?*

CHAPTER 13

Poet dropped Maliki off at his hotel as the sun was coming up. The crime scene had been processed and taped off. Doc Giles' kid was staying with friends and the doctor's body was safely transported to the hospital.

She headed to the office and trudged up the steps into the waiting area. "Hey, Faye. The sheriff make it in yet?"

Faye shook her head. "No, but Carter Hopson came in this morning—said the sheriff was taking some days off due to an emergency. Carter said the County Commissioner called him and told him he was in charge until Jim got back."

"Well that makes sense. Even though he works the other side of the county, Carter is the most senior deputy we have." Poet leaned against the counter. "I'll go brief him."

Poet waited for Faye to hit the release button on the hall door and then ambled down the hallway. She stopped at the break room and grabbed a cup of coffee, doctoring it liberally with French Vanilla creamer. The sugar and the caffeine might help her stay awake. With the adrenaline of last night waning, she prayed they would give her a boost.

She made her way to the sheriff's office and found Carter under a pile of paperwork. "Hey."

"Hey, Poet come in, have a seat. Faye briefed me on the suicide last night. I swear this county is going crazy."

"Seems like it." She sat and took a sip of her coffee.

"I'm trying to make heads or tails out of Jim's schedule and the cases we have open."

"I looked at the rosters, they're good to go. They just need a signature." She pointed to a folder that had almost tipped off his desk.

"Good. Damn, payroll needs to be submitted. It was due three days ago and the commissioner asked me to send him the budget requests for next quarter Jim owed him last week." Carter sighed heavily.

"What the hell has he been doing?" She looked at the mess Carter was dealing with and cringed.

"I don't know, but he's going to be gone for an indefinite period of time. He couldn't give the commissioner a return date, so I'm digging in for a while." Carter held up a file. "Who is Doctor Maliki Blue? Jim has a file on him and the only thing I can understand is that the man works for Guardian."

Poet drew a deep breath and leaned forward. "Jim has been acting strangely for a long time, but lately it's gotten worse. May I shut the door and talk with you?"

Carter narrowed his eyes at her and angled his head. "I'm not going to like what I'm going to hear, am I?" Poet shook her head. "Well, shit. Shut the door and let's talk."

Poet presented the events of the last year and then detailed Maliki's involvement with Shauna's shooting and told him Maliki was the Boswells' son.

He rubbed his face and dropped his elbows on the desktop. "Why does Jim have a file on this guy?"

"Why would Jim order me not to make contact

with Doctor Blue? Why would Jim go to the Boswell estate and threaten his mother? Maliki is having Guardian upgrade the security system on the estate with armed guards."

"That's not unusual for the estates around here."

"True, but the reason they are upgrading isn't usual. Doctor Blue accompanied me to Doc Giles' house last night. He pronounced death and according to him, the physical indications contradict suicide."

Carter blinked and sat back in his chair. "This Doctor Blue believes someone killed Doc and then what, strung him up?"

"Yeah." She drank the rest of her tepid coffee.

"We need to call in the BCI, for both this case and Shauna's. I've been looking for the referral to BCI, and I can't find it. Do you know when Jim sent it in?"

"Jim refused to call BCI, but we don't need to call. Guardian is sending an investigator down today. They've been called in by the AG. They've taken over the investigation of the murders and now Doc Giles' case."

Carter lifted forward and searched the stacks of paper on Jim's desk. "I don't see any indication of that."

She put her hand on Carter's. "I did it behind Jim's back. I requested Doctor Blue's help. He briefed his superiors, and as things started to get more and more weird, they agreed to take over the investigation."

"Weird?"

"Yeah, it started back at the first murder when Jim turned in the snuff films to the BCI."

"The what?"

"He turned over a phone with links to four separate snuff films to BCI. It was found near the crime scene, but not close enough to say it belonged to the scene, you know?"

"No. I didn't know." Carter dropped back in his chair and closed his eyes. "What a fucking mess. Why didn't Jim let BCI do the investigation on the murders?"

"I wish I knew."

"When will this investigator be here?"

"Today. We were going to meet with him at the inn or at my apartment."

"Nonsense. We have the conference room here. He can set up and run his inquiries from here. If Jim comes back while the guy is here, you and I will take the ass whipping, but we're doing this the right way." Carter groaned and pointed at her. "I've got three weeks' worth of paperwork to plow through, and you're already armpits deep in this investigation. I'm putting this on your shoulders, but I want to know what's happening. You keep me briefed, and I'll check with the investigator daily. I'm going to make a call to the AG to assure him we will fully cooperate with the Guardian investigation and let him know you're our liaison."

"That would be a good start." She yawned and shuddered. "Damn, I need more coffee, maybe an energy drink."

"Get your statement done and then get some sleep."

"Granger is bringing in the evidence. I'll help him with it, do my statement, and be around for him if he needs assistance. It's his and Dobson's case. I was there in a supervisory position. Dobson took Doc's boy to a friend's house. His ex-wife has been contacted. She's making arrangements to come pick up her son. He was here for the summer." She stood up and stretched.

"Did he leave a note?" Carter stood up, too. The man was as big as Maliki, but his sandy brown hair, slightly crooked nose, and permanent five o'clock shadow put him in the 'bad boy' category compared to Maliki's 'too sexy not to notice' classification.

"Generic. 'Sorry and I love you.' Not signed and found in the printer tray."

"Damn, that right there is fishy as hell."

She stopped and looked at Carter. "You know what? You'd make one hell of a sheriff."

He gave a humorless laugh. "I'm not sure the headaches would be worth the promotion. Now get out of here and take care of the night crew then all of you get some sleep. I want to meet that Guardian investigator and that doctor. Let's plan for later this afternoon after you get some shut eye."

She yawned again and grabbed her coffee cup. "You got it. I'll call and set up the meeting."

She headed down the hall, but Carter's voice halted her. "Hey, in case you haven't been told lately, damn good work, Deputy."

"Thanks, Carter. I needed that."

"Figured. Let's find out what's going down around here and clean house while we have the keys and can get the job done." Carter tapped the side of the door frame twice. A boyish grin flashed before he stepped back into Jim's office. "And while we're still gainfully employed."

She grabbed her phone from her pocket and called Maliki.

"lo..."

"Did I wake you?"

"Ummm… I was shutting down. Still awake, but barely. What's up?"

"Jim took vacation. Some emergency. Carter Hopson is standing in for him. I told him everything, and he wants to meet you and the guy Guardian is sending down. He wanted to call in the Bureau of Criminal Investigations about Doc Giles' case and was pretty upset that the BCI hadn't been contacted about Shauna or the other cases. He said he'd rather the Guardian guy work from our office, and he wanted to be kept apprised of the situation. He made me the department's liaison to Guardian." She chuckled. "I'm the liaison to the liaison."

Mal hummed a laugh. It was low and sleepy. "Come over and liaison with me."

God, what she wouldn't give to be in bed with him now. Not just for the sexy stuff, but sleeping next to that warm, strong body was so damn comforting, and the feeling of peace that overcame her when she was with him... perfect. "Oh, don't tempt me. I've got to do my statement and help with evidence."

"I sent you my statement already. Emailed it to you."

"Doctor Blue, you are far too efficient."

"Learned it in medical school. If you don't do your notes and charts, that shit will bury you. I do the paperwork, so I don't get smothered with it." He yawned over the last words.

She lowered her voice, "Get some sleep."

"Going to catch three or four hours then head to my parents'. I want to check on the security team and catch my dad before he starts to degrade. He's best in the morning."

She sighed and closed her eyes. "I'm keeping you away from spending time with your parents."

"Not at all. I've been gone a long time. There is some rough water between us, but we're building a bridge a little at a time. I'm being deliberate about repairing our relationship. It may never be perfect, hell for that matter, it may never be good, but we will find a way to create a peace we can all live with. Spending time with you is a respite from that turbulence."

"I get that. You're pretty cool to hang out with, too." She smiled so wide it hurt.

He yawned and softly said, "I told you, better watch it, you could fall in love with me."

Boy howdy, she could see how easily it could happen. "I can see that. Call when the investigator gets a hold of you. We'll meet here."

"Will do. You get some sleep, too."

"That's the plan. Talk to you later." She waited until he hung up and spun around smiling.

Granger stood not more than five feet behind her. "Man, I knew it. You're banging the doctor." Her coworker's shit eating grin challenged her to deny it.

"I'll be denting your head if you make a comment like that again." She nodded to the box with Doctor Giles' computer, printer, day planner, cell phone and wallet. "Ready to start logging that into evidence?"

Granger slid the box onto the large table in the corner of the office space they shared. "Coffee first, yeah?" He rolled his shoulders. "Dobson is stopping at the diner. I don't know about you, but I'm starving."

"Please tell me he's getting donuts." Poet reached for a pair of latex gloves.

"A dozen, plus sausage biscuits, and jelly. I told

him I'd make a fresh pot of coffee." He nodded toward the break room.

"Go, make coffee. I'll start logging this into the system. What about prints?"

"I wore gloves, so did Dobson. We got the kid's prints to exclude and the Doc Giles' should be on file." Granger's voice rose as he went into the break room. "Can we get the BCI's mobile crime scene techs down here to lift prints?"

"The AG has given the case to Guardian." She flipped through the day planner looking for anything obvious to snag her attention.

"Say what?" Granger was beside her, a coffee pot full of water in his hand.

"I asked Doctor Blue to look into a few things when he first showed up. Guardian has coordinated with the AG to take over a couple of the homicides and now Doc Giles' case."

Granger narrowed his eyes at her. "Why?"

"Because Doctor Blue noticed a few things that didn't add up at the crime scene." She placed the day planner back in the box with the rest of the evidence.

Granger put down the pot. "Thank God." He scrubbed his face with one hand. "Dobson and I have been talking. There was something off with those deaths. We couldn't pinpoint what the hell it was."

She snapped her mouth shut. "You didn't say anything."

"What were we going to say? Wait, did you find a tie-in? Is that why you called in Guardian?"

She shook her head and pointed to the pot of water. "Suspicions and questions only. Go make coffee. When Dobson shows up, we'll talk."

"Damn, Poet, we were sure you and the sheriff were in agreement. You didn't let on." He picked up the water and headed back into the break room.

She slid out a chair and dropped into it. No, she hadn't let on, that would have been subversive. She only had suspicions, gut feelings, no evidence. But she had questions. So many questions and with Jim acting strange, those questions had come to a head about the same time he seemed to go over the edge. She wasn't going to tell Granger or Dobson that. She'd told Maliki, but casting Jim in a bad light to his employees without solid evidence? No, she wasn't going there. Not yet. She glanced at her watch. The Guardian investigator couldn't get here soon enough.

~

Maliki smiled. His mother stood beside him watching the technicians Jared had sent. Old monitors were removed, new ones installed. A wireless camera system was installed at key points around the perimeter of the house. The alarm system for the house was being rewired. A portable gate shack was being unloaded at the gate and the codes for the gate had been cleared. New codes were established and given to only those in the family. The employees were listed on an entry authority listing and would be allowed entrance when they were scheduled to work. The men manning the gate would remain for a month so the security agency could recruit and train from the local area or move volunteers from other locations to Virginia.

His mother leaned toward him and whispered, "They're very industrious. Is your company always so efficient?"

"Always."

"Were you able to talk with your father? He wasn't sharp this morning when we had breakfast." She glanced at him and gave a small smile.

"He wasn't comfortable today when we spoke. Agitated and confused, but I turned on the television, and we talked about the old programs. It seemed to settle him down." Maliki watched as a technician removed an old control panel.

"Have you been able to talk with him about... that time?" She looked up at him, worry evident in her creased brow.

"We've touched on it." He didn't know how much longer his father would have even momentary clarity. The disease was relentless and even with meds pushing it back, the end was inevitable. His father was a trained physician. He knew his prognosis. Perhaps that was why his old man was trying to repair the past. Knowledge of impending death had a way of leveling pride, tearing down differences, and balancing regrets against actions. The more he sat with his father, the more he realized that the great man, the surgeon, a titan in his profession, was just a scared human.

"He's trying." She slipped her hand through his arm.

"I know. He wants to make amends, but in reality, there are none to make. Changing anything in my life would change where I am today. And yes, I'd give anything to repair my relationship with him--"*or save the men of Foxtrot company* "-- but changing my past would change who I am today.

The man I have become is who I want to be even though I'm not quite sure about a path forward."

"Path forward?" His mom smiled at him. "Are you considering staying, going into the practice?"

He covered her hand with his. "No, I can't see myself working in the practice, but Guardian has presented me with a few opportunities over the last year or so. I may take a chance and try something new." He'd been offered The Rose as a place to hide and heal. The massive training facility didn't really need him, and now that he'd healed and licked his wounds, what was next? He sighed. The Rose wasn't for him anymore. He could go back and complete the training to become a part of a team of operatives, but during the time he'd been here, he'd rediscovered his true purpose and first love was in fact medicine, not the teams.

His phone vibrated. He retrieved it and glanced at the screen. "Excuse me, I should take this."

"Of course, dear. I'll stay and watch the activity. It's rather exciting." Her gaze bounced from person to person.

He chuckled and headed into the library, shutting the door behind him. "Blue."

"Doctor Blue? Asher Hudson. I'm about an hour outside of town. I need to check into my hotel and call in to Guardian before we get together. There are several loose ends to tie up on the case I left yesterday. Can we meet, perhaps, for dinner?"

"I'd suggest we meet at five at the sheriff's office."

There was a pause. "I thought we were persona non grata at the sheriff's office."

"Did Jared brief you on the ME's apparent suicide?"

"The one you don't believe is a suicide, yes."

"Well, the sheriff never showed up at the crime scene. This morning, the deputy who reported all these anomalies was told the sheriff went on vacation. Some kind of emergency. The deputy acting as interim sheriff wants us there and wants to be involved."

"That will help. The body should have been picked up this morning from the hospital. Guardian's ME is doing the autopsy. We should have preliminary information by tonight. I've got Cyber doing background checks, and we're pulling electronic footprints for all the decedents. I have an associate coming down in a couple days' time, and we'll re-interview everyone on each case, get the new medical data and run the backgrounds the way they should have been run. Is the crime scene from last night protected?"

"Yes. It's locked up." He'd watched Poet and Granger secure the home and seal all the doors with crime scene tape.

"I'll want to go there before the meeting with the sheriff. Not doubting your intuition, but I want to immerse myself in the middle of the case, see what you saw. I'll need to talk to the deputies and the person who found him. That was the son, right?"

"Yes. The kid was broken up. He's staying with friends."

"Evidence collected?"

"The deputies on scene did the best they could. None of them are investigators. Normally, the BCI is contacted and responds."

"But the sheriff has muzzled his deputies, and now we have jurisdiction."

"Correct. I'm not usually a jump to conclusions type guy, but something tells me the sheriff knows more than he's letting on. Is there justification for investigating him as well?"

Asher drew a deep breath. It took several seconds before he responded. "Legally? Probably not, unless we have evidence tying him to the crimes, but I have some resources that can check off the books. If we find anything, *then* we find a way to tie him to the investigation and that gets us PC to find the information or evidence legally. We'd be spinning our wheels going after him now. I don't want to waste any more time chasing false leads. Would you arrange for me to visit the crime scene and swing by my hotel so I can follow you to that location?"

"I can do that. Where are you staying?" Mal glanced through the window and watched as one of the technicians walked by with his mother. He could tell by the man's hand gestures that he was explaining the system to her.

"I'm staying at... ahh, here it is, The Paintville Inn."

He chuckled, "That's where I'm staying. Room 307. Knock on my door when you're ready to go."

"I can do that. Meet you soon."

Maliki swiped his phone to clear the call and then called Poet.

"What?" The word was muffled. She sounded half asleep and pissed.

"Did I wake you?"

She groaned, "Who says I'm awake?"

He chuckled. "Guardian's investigator is an

hour away. He wants to visit the Doc's house before he meets with the new deputy in charge. Can you meet us there?"

"What time is it now?"

Maliki looked at his watch. "It's a little after one."

"Okay. What're you doing?"

"I'm still at my parents'."

"You should come over."

He chuckled and lowered his voice, "Why's that?"

The laugh she gave he'd heard before when they were alone and intimate, and it was fucking sexy. "I wanna beat you at Mario. Why do you think?" Sarcasm dripped from her tone like slow, sugary syrup.

He glanced at the library door to make sure he was still alone. "And here I thought you wanted my body."

"Oh, that? Well, okay, if you insist." A sexy, purr-like, sound crossed the connection.

Damn. "I insist. I'll see you in half an hour." He smiled when she said goodbye and tossed his phone into the air. Even with all the shit swirling around him, he'd found a small piece of Utopia, and fuck if he wasn't going to hold onto that sublime, blissful relationship as long as he possibly could.

He liked Poet. Hell, it was more than that. He was attracted to her in ways he hadn't been attracted to any woman before her. He stopped and thought for a minute. He ticked off the women he'd had any relationships with in the past, and damn, he was right. She *was* different, and he could list the reasons she was distinct and authentic. She had a wild sense of humor, a childlike wonder that hadn't been tainted by the harshness of the world, yet she was tough as nails and smart, shrewd, intelligent. She was irreverent and gave him shit *all the time*. Most women he dated were a variety of the same mold. Polite, socially acceptable, professional. Poet could play all those roles, and yet she spoke the same language he did, and had a shared military background that made them unusually compatible. Their differences were such that every minute with her provided a new revelation. Yeah, he'd embrace this contentment even as the world swirled around them. Hell, they both deserved a break.

CHAPTER 14

Poet dragged herself from the bed and into the bathroom. She splashed cold water on her face and brushed her teeth. A quick glance at the clock on the wall told her she'd clocked a solid three hours of sleep, about six hours too little, but she'd worked on less. She looked in the mirror and grimaced. The dark circles under her eyes were about as attractive as morning breath, but until she got some solid sleep, those charcoal colored slashes would be her new fashion statement.

She chortled at that thought. She had zero fashion sense. She wore jeans when she wasn't on duty and a uniform when she was. That left two dresses, three pairs of slacks and one blazer in her closet. Four long sleeve button downs completed her professional and going-on-a-date attire. Maybe she needed to go shopping? That thought went into the mental trashcan. She didn't need new clothes. It wasn't like she was going to need them, although she wondered if she'd change her mind if Maliki... but no, he was here for a short time, and they had a good arrangement. Those burgeoning thoughts of hearts and flowers were ill-advised.

She tugged on an oversized t-shirt and padded to the kitchen. She needed a caffeine infusion. Stat. It would be bad form to fall asleep during the middle of sex, although with the way that man moved, sleep would be the last thing she thought about. She placed her cup under the drip spout and started the machine. Leaning against the counter she sighed at the thought of his hard, muscled body. She was screwed because she really liked the guy. More than really liked him. Granted, it had started as purely sexual. She wasn't going to apologize for making moves on him that first night. She was an independent and sexually liberated woman. She could, and did, let men know when she was interested. *But how do you let him know that the attraction has morphed into a desire for something more*? Particularly when she'd been so emphatic about it being just sex.

Her coffee gurgled its last few drips into her cup. She cradled the warm mug in her hands for a moment before she took her first sip. Maybe more wasn't in the cards, but damn it, that man made her want it. Content in her life, she'd never really given much thought to sharing it with anyone. Marriage? A chuckle bubbled up. Not once had she dreamed of a white dress and a fancy wedding. Being a tomboy her entire life, outrunning the boys, out throwing them, being competitive and proving herself better, not equal to them, had been her focus. But now? Now she'd admit having someone to run with, not against, intrigued her. She'd never considered the possibility of finding that special someone who... She snorted a laugh into the empty kitchen. "He completes me."

Did you really just think that? Yes, yes, she did. As a matter of fact, those thoughts had coalesced since meeting Maliki Blue. He seemed to be the key to the new ideas. Of course, he was here temporarily. She took a sip of her coffee. Well, hell, as far as that went, she could be here temporarily, too. Depending on how the investigation shook out.

A soft knock on the door startled her. A glance

at the microwave clock produced a smiled. She set the cup down and padded to the door. After lifting on her toes to see through the peep hole, she unlocked the door and swung it wide.

His eyes traveled down and then back up her body. The heat in his gaze brought forth a shiver of excitement. She lifted her foot and scratched her shin with her big toe. The t-shirt hiked up, exposing her thigh almost to her hip. His eyes followed the material's movement and she smiled. "Ready to play games?"

He shook his head. "No. No games." He stepped in front of her, grabbed her waist and kicked the door shut behind them. He bent down, wrapped his arm around her thighs and hoisted her up. Scrambling to grab his shoulders and lock her ankles behind him, she dropped her head back and laughed. His mouth found her neck, and the humor of the situation turned to lust.

He walked toward the bedroom, holding her and kissing her neck and shoulder. His knee hit the mattress, and he leaned over the bed. She loosened her hold and dropped onto the cool sheets.

He lowered until he was on top of her, keeping most of his weight from crushing the breath from her. "You should be sleeping."

"I can sleep when I'm dead. You're worth losing a couple hours of rest." She ran her fingers through his beard.

He smiled. "You like my beard, don't you?"

She nodded; her eyes focused on what her fingers were doing. "I've never like beards, but there is something about you and this." A small tug on his beard brought him down to her lips again.

He reached over and found that half empty box of condoms and tossed a couple on the bed. His clothes and her t-shirt fell away in the midst of soft, slow touches, softer kisses, and eventually, deep penetrating thrusts. He allowed himself to feel the way her body molded to his. The way her sighs and kisses not only surrendered to him, but also fueled him with more than desire. When he made her feel good, the small sounds she made drove him insane. The way her legs curled around him to keep him deep inside her, how her hips lifted to meet his thrusts—countless small things propelled this act of sex to something more.

He hadn't been looking for this--the emotion behind the act of sex. He'd given up thinking there might be someone for him. Poet could be that woman. She was magnificent in bed, her body in tune with his in ways no one else had ever been.

He stared down at her, at the flush that painted her chest and neck, magnified her plump red lips, and those beautiful, expressive eyes. He held her gaze in a silent commune. He could see a lifetime with this woman. She would be worth the effort.

Her nails dug into his back, and her body clamped against him tightly. Eyes closed, he followed her over the edge. With his forehead resting on her shoulder and the weight of his upper body sagging on tired arms, he sucked panting breaths into his lungs.

Her fingers trailed over the muscles in his back. "It keeps getting better, doesn't it?"

He nodded. Not lifting his head from her shoulder, he replied, "It's because you're falling for me. I warned you."

"That's true, you did—and I have. What was I thinking?"

He chuckled. "We weren't thinking, which is probably why it seems so easy. I agree. It's rather unexpected."

Her fingers stopped trailing. "But... okay?"

The hesitant tremor in her voice brought him up so he could see her eyes. "Yes, I think so. Worth exploring at the very least."

She frowned at him and pouted, "Damn right

I'm worth exploring. I'm fabulous, sexy and irresistible."

He laughed and nodded. "Obviously. You've snared me. Whatever will we do?"

"What? I would never *trap* you. You had your eyes wide open. Don't even think that I would use my seductive feminine attributes to entrap you." She sniffed in hauty mock derision.

"I apologize. You are fabulous, sexy and irresistible. So much more than I anticipated." He gazed down at her.

She traced his lips with her fingers, and he kissed the tips. "You're not staying."

"You might not be either." He dropped a kiss on her lips. "Look, we can worry, or we can move forward and see if what's between us is going to last. When we know, we dictate what we want and make it happen."

"That easy, huh?" She tugged on his beard and brought him down for another kiss.

He lost himself in her taste for long minutes before they separated. "It could be that easy, if we want it to be." God, he really wanted it to be, but she needed to be on board.

"I want it to be easy. I want it to be good, and I

want to see what is around the next corner—with you."

"So do I." He glanced over and groaned. "But we need to grab a shower and get over to the hotel."

She turned and lifted her head. "Damn."

"Yeah. Should we conserve water?" He waggled his eyebrows at her making her laugh.

"Do we have enough time?"

He dropped his forehead to her shoulder. "I have no idea. We agreed he'd drop by my room when he was ready."

She patted his back. "That will teach you. No ambiguity, Doctor Blue."

He grabbed her and rolled so she was on top of him. Her long auburn hair fell over them. "Lesson learned Deputy Campbell. You want the shower first?"

"No, but I'll take it." She dropped a loud smack of a kiss on his nose and slipped from his arms. He watched her stand, perfectly nude and gloriously beautiful. Her skin damn near glowed against her dark red hair. Her hips swung gently as she walked away from him. Yeah, he wanted to see what was around the next curve, too.

Maliki stood in the front room and waited for Poet. Evidently blow-drying hair was a process that took time. Finally, she walked from the bedroom. He glanced at her and smiled. The wait was worth it. She was beautiful. Obviously tired, but beautiful, nonetheless.

She stepped into his arms and put her head on his shoulder. He wrapped one arm around her and kissed the top of her head. "I'm impressed by your awards. You were successful in the Air Force."

She turned and glanced at the one he'd been looking at. "Well, in hopes of not sounding vain, I guess I'm proud of who I am and of my accomplishments. I don't have a medical school diploma like you do, but I can look back at each of those achievements and say, I gave it everything I had. Sometimes knowing I did the best I could makes me feel... validated. What time do we have to meet the guy?" She covered a yawn.

He chuckled. "His name is Asher Hudson, and he'll be at my room by four at the latest. We should go." He brought her back into his chest and hugged her.

"Hard to go when you're holding me still."

"I think you could get away if you wanted."

"Who says I wanna get away? I kinda like it

here." She snuggled closer, and he tightened his grip.

"This isn't getting us to the inn." He dropped his arms and grabbed her hand. "Come on, Deputy. Work calls."

His fingers intertwined with Poet's, and he led her down the interior hallway of the Paintville Inn. It had been a hell of a long time since he felt this way. Smooth, with no rough, irritated edges. The snags, grit, knots, and coarseness of the world had been sanded away.

"I need about ten energy drinks." Her soft comment came as she leaned her forehead against his back when he stopped at his room and withdrew his magnetic card key.

He took a peek at her over his shoulder and caught her mid yawn. "You were the one who wanted to play the Mario Donkey thingy." He smiled, inserted his key.

"There was a donkey sized thingy involved, but it had nothing to do with Mario." Her laughter and a weak ass attempt at a swat at his shoulder had them both laughing. She followed him into the room and dropped onto the bed. She rolled over, taking the comforter with her, and cocooned herself. "Wake me when he gets here."

He glanced at the clock. If the guy was prompt, she could maybe grab a half hour power nap. He dropped into the one and only chair in the room and put his feet up on the bed. While he was tired, his mind wouldn't shut off. He glanced around his hotel room. There was nothing of himself here. Just like the small apartment back at The Rose. Nothing. Sure, he could paper the wall of that small apartment with military plaques, awards, diplomas, certificates from residency and internships, boxes full of laudatory commendations, and yet he hadn't bothered to display any of them. Perhaps it was because he didn't want to look back, exhume the bones of his past and examine them—resurrect memories he'd buried, or thought he had. He closed his eyes as memories flooded his mind. The regrets, the wrongs, the missed opportunities and the events he couldn't change but desperately wished he could. He remembered Poet's words and measured each event against those words. He *had* done the best he could. He opened his eyes, dropped his feet from the bed to the floor and leaned forward. *He'd done the best he could.* He stared at the door and thought of his father. Perhaps his old man had done the best he could, too.

Fuck. He needed to talk to his dad tomorrow morning, if his father was cognizant. He needed to let his father know he'd forgiven him. At the time, they'd both done the best they could do. The revelation and forgiveness, of himself and his father, cascaded over him in a wave.

CHAPTER 15

Poet's eyes popped open at a bracing knock on the door. It took a couple of seconds to remember she was in Maliki's hotel room. She rolled off the bed and brushed her hair into some semblance of order as Maliki walked to the door, flipped on the light and looked back at her. He cocked his head in question. She ran a hand down her shirt and smoothed her hair again before she nodded.

He opened the door and extended his hand. "Asher?"

"Maliki. Good to meet you. Jared is a common friend, I believe." A deep voice resonated through the room. The door blocked her view of the new Guardian.

"Yes. Please come in. I'd like you to meet Deputy Campbell. She's the one who brought us into this situation." He moved back and another massive man entered the room. He had to be at least six three, with black hair and hazel eyes. She moved forward and extended her hand. "Poet Campbell."

"Asher Hudson." He shook her hand. "Would it be possible to see the ME's house before it gets dark?"

Poet waved his concern off. "Absolutely. Do you two want to follow me? We have a meeting with Carter Hopson, the deputy who has assumed the sheriff's responsibilities while he's gone."

"Perfect. If you don't mind, Doctor Blue, we'll take my vehicle. It has all my equipment in it."

"That works for me."

Asher put his hands on his hips. "Deputy, was there any indication why the sheriff would suddenly need to take vacation? Sick parents, siblings..."

"Honestly, I've been wondering that myself. His parents have passed. They died in a horrible accident years ago. From what I've been told, their heater stopped working during the middle of the night. His father used a portable gas heater and didn't vent it correctly. They died of carbon monoxide poisoning. I've never heard him mention any family. Even though we work together, we aren't close. Talking about our families isn't something we do." She sucked her bottom lip into her mouth and thought about it. "Carter Hopson has been at the department the longest. He might know something." She glanced at her watch. "We've got an hour to look at the crime scene before we meet with him."

Asher nodded and gestured toward the door. "I'm ready when you are."

Poet drove into the office lot, parked and exited her vehicle. Rain threatened, and she didn't want to get caught in a downpour. Maliki and Asher had been caught by one of the town's three stoplights and would arrive shortly. They'd spent a little less than an hour at Doc Giles' home. Asher walked through the house, asked a few questions and inspected the garage carefully. He'd agreed with Maliki. Based on the lack of chair, box or anything to use as a step to get to the rope, the death was not only suspicious, but one he'd consider a homicide. The doctor's autopsy was scheduled for tomorrow morning, and they should know then if Maliki's belief about the injuries not being consistent with hanging was correct.

She hustled through the parking lot as the rumble of an afternoon thunderstorm growled in the distance. She'd been kicking herself in the ass for not considering the lack of box or chair last night. She'd totally missed it. It was little consolation that Granger and Dobson had missed it, too. What it reflected was a lack of training. The department needed an investigator. The funding to send one to school shouldn't be prohibitive. She glanced back at the parking lot. All of their patrol vehicles were new, the equipment inside the vehicles was top notch. Perhaps priority could go to training at least one of the deputies to handle these big cases. The BCI covered the entire state and helped when called in, but their lack of training handicapped the responding deputies.

She opened the door and entered the building as the first drops of rain started.

"Hey, Poet." Faye leaned toward the counter.

She smiled and lifted a hand. "Hey, what are you doing here? Your shift doesn't start for another hour."

"Sharon's kid had a school play. She'll pay me back when I have an appointment or need to leave early."

"Ah. Did the sheriff ever call in?"

"Not that I know of. He could have called Carter directly, but nobody mentioned it to me. Strange, huh? I didn't know he had family left." Faye pointed to the door.

"Not yet. I'm waiting on Doctor Blue and--"

Maliki ran up to the door and opened it as both men sprinted into the lobby. A flash of lightning preceded an almost immediate clap of thunder.

"Damn, that is one heck of a storm." Asher wiped his face with his hand.

"We get them occasionally." Poet laughed and nodded to the door. Faye hit the button and they entered the office area. "The bathroom is over there if you want to mop up."

"Nah, I'll drip dry. Doc?" Asher looked at him.

"I'm good. I've been told I'm not made of sugar, so I doubt I'll melt."

"All right then, Maliki, you know the way to the back. I believe we'll be meeting in the conference room. I'll go grab Carter." She watched the men walk away before she headed the opposite direction.

The door to the office was open so she knocked on the door frame. Carter lifted his eyes to her and then shifted his gaze to the clock. "Damn, time flies. Are you ready?"

"They're here and waiting in the conference room. You okay?"

Carter threw his pen on the desk and dropped back against his chair. "Shut the door." She stepped in and did as he requested. "I swear, Poet, I have no idea what the hell Jim's been doing. The more I look, the more I find, and it's not good. This desk is a powder keg of incomplete work, pending issues and demands from the county commissioners. I've been on the phone with three of the five commissioners today. They didn't say it, but I firmly believe Jim was heading for a disciplinary session."

She sat down on the edge of the chair in front of the desk. "I knew he was under pressure. Like I said, he hadn't been acting like himself for--" she shook her head "--hell, a long time now. Has he called anyone? Do we know what emergency he's dealing with?"

"Nope. I've known him since high school. Unless he has extended family, I thought he was all alone."

She stared at Carter for a moment. He furrowed his brow. "What?"

She debated her question for a moment before she leaned forward. "Have you found anything illegal or potentially problematic in the paperwork you're going through?"

Carter shook his head slowly as his eyes scanned the piles of paperwork. "Other than being criminally behind? No. Why?"

She shrugged. "Just grasping at straws. I thought maybe some of this might be what he is trying to get away from." That and Guardian taking over the cases, although the last message he left her indicated he believed the AG was taking over.

"I couldn't see that. Why would he want anyone to see the mess he has going on here?" Carter stood and stretched. His back popped, and he groaned. "Death by paperwork. Are you ready to do this?"

"Absolutely."

"Wait, there was something. Hold on." Carter sat back down and started opening drawers. "I couldn't find any logbook entries about this, and yet, it's bagged and tagged. Do you know what it is?" He held out the evidence bag that contained the phone they'd found at the first death scene.

She walked forward and looked again, to make sure she was right. "Yeah, it's a phone we found at the first scene. The one with the websites on it that led to snuff films. Jim said he was going to get BCI to look into it."

"Does the phone work?"

"No."

"Maybe he just sent in the websites?" Carter turned the phone over in his hands.

Poet's gut clenched. "Yeah, maybe."

Maliki sat and watched as Poet presented the cases to Asher and Carter. He filled in tidbits of information as he knew them, but basically stayed out of the woman's way. It took over an hour to cover the information they had on all the cases, including Shauna's and Doctor Giles'. "You need to know that Carter found the phone Jim told me he had sent on to BCI. Carter suggested that perhaps Jim just forwarded the website addresses."

"Websites?" Asher looked from Poet, to him and then to Carter.

"Snuff films. Poet though that one of them could have been filmed in the local area."

"Do you still have those URLs?" Asher looked at Poet.

"Yeah, I deleted them off my phone, but I have them stored on my computer." She motioned toward the office space outside the conference room doors.

"All right." Asher glanced at the files spread in front of him. "Please send me those sites and I'll have Guardian confirm that the BCI has taken steps with the information. The crime scene photos of the older cases are helpful. I'll spend the night going over the new information. Deputy Carter, I appreciate the use of the conference room for this briefing, but I won't need the space on a day-to-day basis. For the most part, my SUV is my office. Guardian has hooked it up with everything I need. My partner is heading down tomorrow. We will go through each case, re-interview witnesses, family, friends. The medical examiner's reports are being checked and the initial autopsies of the two bodies Guardian has already seized have been completed. I don't have the results. It takes a couple days for them to make their way through the system and then a month of Sundays to get toxicology and pathology. We have a priority on this, but those tests take time, even Guardian can't change science. Yet." He winked at Mal and they both chuckled.

"Do you need anything else from us?" Carter stood and asked.

"If I do, I'll call Deputy Campbell or drop by the office and speak with whomever is working. I believe I have all I need. If I've made any headway I can release without hindering further investigations, I'll call and brief you after I've informed my chain of command."

"I guess that's all we can hope for. I'll release Poet to her work then. Doctor Blue, I just read my people's report on Doctor Giles' apparent suicide. Our thanks to you for responding to the scene. Gentlemen, if you need anything, the sheriff's department is at your disposal."

Maliki leaned forward after the acting-sheriff left and asked Asher, "Do you need me for anything?"

"Honestly, Doc, I don't think so. I appreciate the offer, but I think I have it. Keep that piece on you. We may need you to step up if shit gets hairy, but for now, Jared said you were down here on vacation, right?"

"I'm splitting time between visiting my parents and a new relationship." He winked at

Poet and watched her eyes widen and her cheeks flame.

Asher laughed and started gathering the paperwork. "I'm damn good. I pegged that when you opened the hotel room door."

Mal stood up and blinked in surprise. "How's that?"

"The light was off. You turned it on before you opened the door. Someone was sleeping." He pointed at Poet as he spoke. "I didn't want to assume… ah hell, that's bullshit. I totally assumed, but before you leave, can you point me to a good restaurant?"

"Shorty's had good steaks, but it's been closed since the shooting. Shauna's folks own it. The diner is closed by now, so you are stuck with fast food." He turned and lifted an eyebrow at Poet, asking without asking.

Poet yawned and stood up. She pointed to him, "He's a great cook, come have dinner with us."

Asher looked at him and winced. "Normally, I'd defer, but I'm starving and didn't have time to grab anything to throw in my hotel fridge. I promise not to stay late."

Asher watched Poet as she walked from the conference room. Mal hummed, agreeing, "I'll kick your ass down the stairs if you outstay your welcome."

Asher laughed again.

Strange, he hadn't meant it as a joke.

Dinner was simple, pasta carbonara and a salad. He had it on the table within twenty-five minutes of them walking in the door, and Asher was good to his word. He left as soon as dinner was done, stating the review of the new documentation was his priority.

He and Poet cleaned the kitchen. He grabbed her hand and led her into the bedroom where he undressed her, tugged her into bed with him, and turned off the light. She curled into him, and they found a comfortable position. She was asleep within minutes. He closed his eyes and drew in a contented breath.

Poet's alarm blared, jarring them both awake. He slapped at the damn thing and finally determined he needed to slide the toggle to shut it up. He dropped back onto the pillows. "That is the most obnoxious alarm clock ever."

"Right? I got it after basic training."

She yawned and stretched against him. Her soft, sleep-warmed, skin slid against him. "What time do you have to be at work?"

"Thirty minutes." She sat up and stretched.

He glanced at the clock and then at the windows. "It's still raining."

She turned her head and narrowed her eyes at the window. "Accidents."

He blinked trying to follow her train of thought. "Say what?"

"Rain equals accidents. People driving too fast, hydroplaning, driving too slow and causing a hazard." She groaned. "I'm not looking forward to what today is going to bring."

He sat up and slid behind her. "Then focus on what tonight will bring." She turned toward him and smiled questioningly. He leaned in and kissed her shoulder. "A hot shower, together, dinner, and then fantastic sex."

"I like that." She leaned forward and kissed him. "What are you doing today?"

"I'll go to see my parents. Spend the morning with Dad and the afternoon with Mom." He needed to speak to both of them. His new found forgiveness–enough for not only himself, but for them—gave him hope he could find a balance.

He lazed around until she finished her shower. He dressed in yesterday's clothes and walked from the apartment with her. She had to drop him back off at the inn as he'd ridden with Asher yesterday. They parted with a long, warm kiss under the overhang of the front door of the inn. It took him no time to get ready and head to his parents'.

The men at the gate wore rain gear, and they were damn thorough, making sure to check his ID against the authorized entry listing. He parked in front of the house and sprinted up the stairs, making sure to wipe his feet, while he waited for Lucinda to answer the door. She smiled and stepped back allowing him access.

"Good morning. Where's my father?"

"It's a good day today, sir. He's in the sunroom watching the rain."

"Thank you." He strode down the hallway and into the sunroom.

His father turned toward him and gave a lopsided smile, speaking with care, "Came in the rain?"

"Of course. I wanted to spend time with you." He sat down beside his father. "Is that coffee fresh?" He pointed to the coffee service on the table. When his father nodded, he reached forward to pour himself a cup. Mal pointed to his father's insulated cup with a straw stuck through the top. "Do you want me to freshen yours?"

"No, I'm good." His father's words were careful and slow. He watched as his father leaned down and took a sip from the straw.

He settled back into his chair, and they stared at the rain trailing down the glass enclosure of the sunroom. "So, I've been doing a lot of thinking."

His father nodded. "Me too."

Mal took a drink of his coffee. It was tepid at best. Perhaps his father had forgotten or lost time again. "What have you been thinking about?"

"Regrets. You. Your mother." A tear fell from his father's eye. "Missed you."

He leaned forward, put his coffee cup on the table, and took the opportunity to turn his chair so he faced his father. "It's okay—"

"No!" His father's good hand clenched into a fist. "No. So wrong."

Mal put his hand on his father's arm. "I forgive you, Dad. Life isn't about perfection. It is about doing the best you can do, each day. You're doing that today and so am I. I think we both deserve the chance to move past something that happened years ago. Let's do that."

Old, tired, eyes swung toward him. His father's head shook. "How?"

He wasn't quite sure what his dad was referring to, but he took a stab at it. "How did I forgive you?" He got a nod in confirmation. He drew a hand down his beard, stroking it as he carefully considered his words. "I'm seeing a woman who said something that struck a chord. Here's the thing, Dad... neither of us can change the past. No amount of wishing or beating ourselves up will change a single moment of time, or a word, or an action. It simply is what it is. But today, in this time we have, we need to strive to be the absolute best version of ourselves that we can be. In order to be that person, for her, and for myself, and for you and Mom, I need to let the guilt, hurt, and regrets of the past go. So, I accept your apology and I'll face today without the past keeping me from doing what I need to do." He reached up and wiped another tear from his father's cheek. "You were my hero. What happened hurt both of us. It's over, Dad. We need to move past that pain."

"I love you." Tears spilled down his father's cheeks.

"I know. I love you too, Dad." It was a fragile feeling--tenuous and new, but it was there. He blinked back the emotion and smiled at his father before he enfolded the man in a hug. His father's good arm wrapped around him, and he felt his father shoulders shake as he cried in his arms. He held him tighter and breathed, "We're okay, Dad. I promise. We're okay."

CHAPTER 16

Maliki parked his SUV behind Poet's apartment building. The last two weeks had been a blur of activity punctuated by many, many moments of sublime pleasure. He'd introduced his mother and father to Poet. His father had days when he didn't remember their conversation about forgiveness. It didn't matter. He'd repeat the words to his father as many times as it took. He and Poet had endured an uncomfortable dinner with his mom and her lover, Richard Prentiss. The man was attentive and polite, but the fact he and his mom were 'keeping company' while she was still married to his father made for an awkward evening. One he hoped to never repeat.

Asher checked in every other day or so, and

while he didn't get updates on the case, per say, Asher assured him they were getting closer. Guardian's inquiry about the websites had earned a resounding no. They hadn't been forwarded, so Guardian shipped them to the FBI. That bruised the state's ego and ruffled feathers. They'd had to subpoena telephone records for several of the victims, which took time, Asher was hopeful he'd have all the records by the end of the week. He confirmed there was a link between the cases. He wasn't divulging what that link was, but he validated Poet's initial concerns, and for that, Mal was grateful.

He now had a key to Poet's apartment, but still maintained a room at the inn. When she was called out at night, he left and spent the night in the hotel. They weren't living together... yet. He smiled and hoisted several grocery bags from the passenger seat of his SUV. He was early, but his mom had a date, and his father's mental acuity deteriorated in the afternoons, so he went to the store, purchased ingredients for dinner, and headed over to her house. He'd texted her he was going to start cooking, but she hadn't responded–normal for her. If she was busy, she'd text back when she could.

He took the stairs two at a time and used his butt to push the crash bar on the fire door to open it.

Tillie walked from her apartment at the same time as he entered the hallway. "There you are. Dude, I need to talk to you and Poet. You need to settle your jets; you know what I mean?"

He stopped and shook his head. "I have no idea what you mean."

"Look, I know you're all like macho man and everything, but that noise this morning was not appreciated. Some of us need our beauty sleep."

He narrowed his eyes. "What noise? I wasn't here this morning. Poet was called out last night."

Tillie's eyes rounded to the size of saucers. "But–"

He dropped the groceries and flashed to the door, shoving the key in the lock, only it wasn't locked. The door swung open.

"Holy fuck!" Tillie gasped behind him.

"Call 911." He withdrew his automatic from its holster and glanced back at Tillie, who stood staring into the apartment. "Call 911, now, damn it! Get into your apartment." She nodded and spun, shoving her hand into her purse.

There were drops of blood on the beige carpet.

Pictures hung lopsided on the wall, several of Poet's plaques had fallen from their mounts. Her mementos from the countries she'd been stationed in had fallen from their perches and several were broken. A bloody smudge on the oak colored shelf chilled him to the bone. He moved forward. The footstool had been tossed on its side, and the television hung off its shelf, dangling from the cable connection at the rear of the screen. He moved past the couch when he saw the spray of blood. Not much, nothing life threatening, but blood, nonetheless. He worked his way past the living room. Her bedroom wasn't disturbed. Her sheets had been thrown back, as if she'd just gotten up. He squatted at the far side of the living room and looked at the mayhem. He palmed his phone and called her. The phone went to voicemail immediately. He tried again. And again. He heard a siren in the distance. He placed a call to Carter Hopson.

"Hopson."

"Carter, its Doctor Blue. Have you seen Poet?"

"No, not today. I got a text from her about seven this morning. She said she was going to Ohio. Her mom was sick. She didn't tell you?"

"No. Ohio? Her mom and dad moved to Florida

some years ago. No. Carter, her apartment has been trashed. There's blood in the living room."

"Holy shit. I'm on the way."

The line went dead. He called Asher and relayed the information.

"Fuck, okay, we're en route. We're on the other side of the county. Don't let the locals process the crime scene. Don't disturb anything."

"Understood."

He carefully made his way from the apartment. Tillie stood in the hall. "She's going to be okay, right? Poet's going to be okay?"

He dropped his arm around her and folded her into a hug, not answering her, because he didn't know. Questions spun through his mind, but one stuck. Who the hell would know that her parents lived in Ohio, but wouldn't know they'd moved to Florida? An acquaintance, a coworker... her boss.

Two deputies he'd seen before but couldn't remember names of emerged from the stairwell. "I've cleared the apartment. Guardian is en route as is Deputy Hopson."

"Is Poet..." The man's question trailed off.

"She's not in there. There's a small amount of blood. There was a fight. By the looks of the room, one hell of a fight. Tillie, what time did you hear the noise this morning?"

"Oh... it was five… a little after five."

Carter Hopson threw the stairwell door open and entered the hallway at a jog. "Hannaford, Mellette, our job is to secure the scene. Her vehicle isn't here. Hannaford, you stay on that apartment door. Only Guardian goes in or out. Mellette, we need to find her vehicle. Miss, are you a witness?"

"I heard a disturbance this morning. I thought it... I didn't think she was being attacked."

"No problem. I'll take your statement." He looked up at Maliki. "You need me?"

Maliki shook his head. "No, I know what to do." He turned and headed toward the stairwell.

"Doctor Blue?" He looked over his shoulder. Carter stared at him. "Find her."

"I guaren-fucking-tee it." His phone was in his hand before he hit the first step.

"And here I thought we'd stopped these hen parties."

"Someone has taken Poet."

"Whoa. Hold on. Poet? The deputy?"

"Yes."

He heard Joseph's muffled voice and then the sound of a door closing. "Details. Now."

Maliki gave him a run down. "I need a location on Sheriff Watson."

"Why do you think it was the sheriff?"

"Because whoever it was knew her parents lived in Ohio but wasn't close enough to her to get the intel that they'd moved."

"That's thin." Joseph growled in response.

"I know. Have you been briefed on the cases here, the ones Asher took over?"

"No and that was because I was told you were out of it. I'll pass on your concerns to Jared, but you need to stand down."

"The fuck I will." Before he left Poet to the bastard who had her, Maliki would slit the throat of Hades himself, remove the Prince of Hell's beating heart, and eat it.

"What's your damage, man? The investigators assigned can handle this."

"Would you sit on your ass if Ember was the one taken?"

"Ember? Oh, fuck. Son of a bitch. Motherfucker. You fucking fell for the damn local yokel."

He ground his teeth together and seethed, "Watch yourself."

"Yeah, yeah. Got it." Joseph drew a big breath

and released it. "Damn it, Blue, you're a pain in my ass."

"I need a location on that sheriff."

"Why have you zeroed on that dick? It could be any of her coworkers or anyone else she knows."

"My gut says if that bastard isn't involved, he knows who is."

"Fuck. Stay by your phone."

Mal headed to his SUV and opened the back hatch. He retrieved an M4, loaded it, and placed it in the rack built into the passenger side seating area. Velcro straps tightened a bulletproof vest around his chest. He filled his pockets with zip ties, extra ammo for both weapons, and snatched a taser and pepper spray, clipping both to his belt. He found a medical kit. The tabs attached to the vest and secured in a second. The lid of the armory was once again locked down, and he jumped into the driver's seat of the SUV. He had no idea which way to drive so he sat and waited... and prayed.

He focused on the clock and watched the minutes change. Minute after minute, the blue digital display grew, and his feeling of inadequacy mounted in exact proportion to the passing of time. He should be doing *something*.

His phone vibrated. "Blue."

"Mal, this is Jewell. James Watson has a residence in Paintsville. I'll text the address."

"I can't see him taking Poet there, Jewell. This is a small town. People notice shit. She wouldn't go willingly, and if she wasn't willing, she could be unconscious or..."

"We aren't going to go there yet. Tell me more. Her apartment was broken into. There was a struggle. What else?"

He took a breath. "Her vehicle is missing, too."

"Vehicle? What kind?"

"SUV, patrol vehicle. Newer model."

"Hold on. I'm accessing the Pleasant County data base. I need to bypass the firewall and disable the... yeah, here it is. A list of county assets, buildings, vehicles, no... bulldozers, graters... here… normal vehicles. I'm scrolling... there, SUVs. Okay, snagging these and accessing the sheriff's office computer system. Standby, this won't take long. I've been in their system before. Come on, come on... good, let me in and… perfect. I'm in. Now, files... personnel, payroll, disciplinary actions, assets. Good, okay, yep here we go. Vehicle maintenance... and assignments. Got it. Hang on. There. Okay. I have the VIN number. I'm going to request the manufacturer enable the vehicle's tracking software. It will take a couple minutes." He could hear her fingers flying across the keyboard as she spoke.

"While that's working, let's see what is in Mr. Watson's background."

"I thought you couldn't run him unless we could tie him to a crime with solid evidence?"

Jewell snorted. "You can't. I can. I have an operative telling me he believes this man is involved in a felony and the life of a law enforcement officer is in jeopardy. That, my friend, is probable cause." He could hear her fingers tapping. "Okay, I got notification that the manufacturer is flipping the switches. It will take a moment to acquire."

"Do you know Watson's mother and father's names?"

Maliki blinked. "Ah, no."

"That's okay, I'll get it. There it is. Okay, I'm sending a pin to your phone. The vehicle is stationary about fifteen miles to your west on County Road 1837."

Maliki put the vehicle in gear and tore from the parking lot. "Tell me if it moves."

"I will. While you're driving, I'm pulling this guy's past apart. Damn, sucks about his folks." She tsked a bit and then got quiet. The only thing he heard was periodic staccato sprints of typing. "All right. I've reached Jared. He's sending his people to the sheriff's primary residence. They are inclined to believe the sheriff may be involved, based on telephone records my people have requested."

"I'm coming up on the vehicle."

Jewell made a sound, acknowledging him before she added, "I have state police responding. They were closest."

"I don't see anyone in the vehicle. Standby while I clear it." He slammed his foot on the brake and slid to a stop on the blacktop. With his automatic in his hand, he jogged to the SUV. A quick look through the windows proved it was vacant. The driver's side door wasn't shut all the way and the passenger side door was likewise open. A small amount of blood was smeared on the passenger headrest and center console of the vehicle.

He jogged back to the Guardian SUV and spoke to Jewell. "There's nothing except small amounts of blood in the interior. He must have transferred her from that vehicle to another."

"He has two personal vehicles registered to him. A car and a truck. I'll get a bulletin released on both of them."

"What now?"

"Now you head east."

He put the truck in gear and after ensuring the road was clear, made a U-turn. "Where am I going?"

"To a property that is still in his mother's name. Hold on. Tax records show it has been improved and has a residence."

"Does it have power?"

"Damn good question. Let me check."

"How far on this road?"

"Ah... keep going past the town. I'm looking for utilities." Strangely her familiar tempo of start-and-stop typing comforted him.

He drove past the town and continued on.

"There. Yes. Electricity and water. Where are you?" Her phone rang in the background. "Standby Mal."

He kept driving, staring at every turn off as if he could see back to the properties. Fuck, he was going insane.

"Sorry about that. Jared decided to yell at me for helping you. Evidently his people found nothing at the primary residence and want in on the chase."

"Give me the address and you can bow out."

"Fuck that. I gave him the address and patched

Jared through to Jason. Let them duke it out. Okay, I've got your SUV on my screen. Three miles up on the left, there is a two-lane road. Take that."

Mal followed her direction and turned on the road. "Ten miles up. The property is on the left. I don't have current satellite coverage so I can't watch real time or tell you if there are any vehicles at the property."

"I'll stop short and work my way in. I don't want to alert him that I'm coming."

"Do you have comms?"

"What?"

"An earpiece paired to your phone?"

"No."

"Dude, damn it. Okay, well, put your phone in your pocket, but mute me. If there is anything emergent, I'll text you and it will vibrate. Understand?"

He pulled over and carefully maneuvered the SUV off the road. "How many of these operations have you run?"

"Me? None. I'm the geek behind the keyboard. Do as I say. Remember to use your training, Mal, and I don't mean the one where you apply bandages to boo-boos. You are going in alone. You have backup en route. Waiting for them might be the right choice."

"I'll make that call when I get into position."

"Good luck."

Mal muted the phone and pocketed it. The damn thing was already on vibrate. He unclipped the M4 from the rack and slung it on his back for rapid travel. With silent deliberation he closed the vehicle door and locked it with a key, not risking the remote chirping. Not far from the edge of the road, the earth sunk under his feet and he buried to his knees in mud. "Damn it." He pulled himself from the boggy area and adjusted his gear. He got his bearings and started to jog, his eyes and ears alert for movement in the trees.

CHAPTER 17

Poet's stomach lurched, and she dry heaved. Again. Her head throbbed and her vision blurred. She curled in on herself. The cold tile under her was hard and unforgiving. She blinked and tried to sit up only to collapse on the floor again.

Pain gouged white trenches across the darkness of her closed eyes as the sole of a boot smashed against her back, catching her under her shoulder blade. She curled tighter, trying to move away from the pain.

A knee dropped on her and her arm was wrenched backward. Cold steel circled her wrist and she was dragged across the floor by her arm. He lifted her by her arm, nearly dislocating her shoulder. She scrambled to her knees and heard the other cuff snap lock against something. The sound of heavy footsteps diminished. She panted, trying to force air into her lungs. She opened one eye a fraction of an inch and blinked several times. She closed her eyes and swallowed back another wave of nausea before she opened both eyes. A camera. Video camera.

She opened her eyes again. She couldn't see behind the camera. That side of the room was dark.

"What did you tell Guardian?"

She startled at the words. They were the first he'd spoken since she opened the door this morning. His voice was higher, more nasal than usual. "I didn't."

"Liar." The emotionless word hung for a moment and then she heard him walking back toward her. He crouched down in front of her and gripped her chin in a crushing hold. The black mask couldn't conceal his identity from her. She recognized Jim's eyes. "I'm going to beat you until you die. It is going to take days and days and days." He stroked her hair gently while holding her chin so tight he could fracture her jaw.

Between her clenched teeth, she ground her reply, "Why did you kill them?"

He started to chuckle, released her, and then stood. An eerily high-pitched laugh echoed in the small room. "This isn't a TV drama. I'm not confessing my sins so your knight in shining armor can ride in and rescue you."

"Do you record all the deaths?"

He turned his head to the camera and waved at the lens. "I'm not recording. I'm broadcasting. No audio. They don't pay for audio."

"Pay?"

That eerie laugh again. "To watch women die. There's a lucrative market."

"Please, you don't have to do this!"

He walked back toward the darker side of the room, his back to her. "Oh, but I do."

"Why?" She tugged on the handcuff and the bar it was clamped to. It moved a little.

"Simple. I want to." He moved further away.

Oh God. She shoved her shoulder under the bar and pressed up with her legs. The pipe shifted about a half inch. She arched and screamed as her body jolted and convulsed under a current of electricity until the world went blank.

Gentle slaps on her cheeks roused her from unconsciousness.

"Wakey, wakey, Deputy. No escape for you. My ratings would take a hit if you escaped. Did you enjoy the taser? I would rather drive my fist into your face, but I suspect you have a concussion, and I need you conscious. They like the fear, the suffering. I'll avoid your head until I'm ready to kill you."

She moaned and tried to move. It was useless. She lifted her head and tried to clear her vision. Her arms and legs were tied to boards bolted against the wall.

She panted back the nausea lifting her head caused. "They'll know it's you."

He shook his head. "How? There's no evidence to tie me to any of those women."

She winced as he approached her with a metal police baton. "What appendage should we break first?" He tapped her right arm, then her left before he turned away. She swallowed hard to try to combat the nausea and was unprepared for his spinning slash of the metal rod. The rod crashed into her right forearm. She screamed; the pain shot up her arm to her shoulder and down to her hand. The door on the far side of the room burst open.

Darkness tunneled her vision as she watched Jim lunging forward. She welcomed the oblivion.

"Poet, God, please, wake up." She moaned and curled in on herself. *Free*. She wasn't bound, and boards wrapped her arm. A splint. She opened her eyes. Jim hovered over her and she jerked back.

"No, no, it's okay. I have to get you out of here."

She pushed further away from him. A terror filled scream stuck in her throat and she croaked, "No!"

"I have to get you out of here before he wakes up!"

"He?" She pushed back, hit the wall, and lifted slightly. She looked around wildly. The man with the hood lay on the ground, not moving. "Who is he?"

"I'll tell you, but I have to get you out of here before he wakes up. Come on!" He lifted her good arm around his neck and helped her stand. "You have to walk; I need to be able to get to my gun if I need it."

She leaned heavily into him and stared at the man on the floor as they passed.

"Up the stairs. Come on, one foot in front of the other. That's right."

She gagged as they passed through a small kitchen and then an empty room before they emerged outside. The sunlight blinded her. "I can't open my eyes."

"Keep them closed then. Keep putting one foot in front of the other. I parked on the main road."

The distinct sound of a round being chambered in a gun stopped both of them. "Stop where you are."

At the sound of Maliki's voice, she crumbled to the ground, sobbing.

Mal watched Poet collapse. Her face was devoid of color and she'd been beaten. Some sort of ad hoc splint supported her right forearm. She wore one of his t-shirts and a pair of shorts.

"Whoa, Doctor Blue, this *is not* what you think it is." Jim Watson raised both hands straight into the air. "I rescued her. Got her away from that mad man."

Maliki moved forward, his .45 aimed directly at the bastard's chest. "Back off! Hands behind your head! Move away from her, now! Jewell, get the rest of them out here, now. I have the sheriff. If he moves, he's dead. I need an ambulance."

"Who are you talking to? Never mind, he's going to come to any minute. We need to get her to safety." The sheriff's question turned into a shouted demand.

"Shut up! Back off. Further." He watched the bastard back up, his fingers linked behind his head.

Watson kept glancing to the small house and shaking his head. "Man, I don't know if he has any guns. You really need to get her the hell out of here."

"Get on your knees." He barked the command and watched the bastard drop. He followed the man and slowly sank to his knees beside Poet. "You're going to be okay, sweetheart. Did he rescue you?"

She folded against him and whispered through her tears. "I don't know. I... I don't know. There's another man, downstairs."

His phone vibrated in his pocket. "Kind of busy here, Jewell. Can it wait?" His gun remained pointed at the sheriff. "One buzz for yes, more for no." He stood and moved to put himself between Watson and Poet. His shirt pocket lit up with multiple vibrations. He reached in his pocket, his eyes boring a hole through Watson, and unmuted the call. "Go ahead."

"There is a live stream coming from an IP address at that location. There is no movement, it looks like a basement. I heard him try to divide your concentration."

Mal narrowed his eyes and sneered at Watson. "Believe me, he has my full attention. He so much as flinches and he has a .45 hole through his heart."

"Keep an eye on the feed, how far is backup?"

"Three minutes."

"Roger." He dropped the unmuted phone into his shirt pocket. The faint shrill of sirens heralded closer.

"Doctor Blue, I can explain everything, but that guy in there is deadly. Please send whoever gets here first down there to secure him."

"Why didn't you secure him when you were down there?" Mal stole a glance at Poet. Her curled form behind him terrified him, but he wasn't dropping his guard and allowing the bastard in front of him to kill them both.

"I knocked his ass out! If you hadn't stopped us, I could have gotten Poet away from here and then brought back reinforcements." Watson shook his head.

"Yeah, and where the hell would you have taken her?" He snarled the question at the bastard.

"I wasn't looking for her, I was looking for him!"

"Who is he?"

"My half brother. He's sick, he was saying crazy shit. That's why I took vacation. I had to find him."

"Your brother?"

"Yes, damn it! Why was she here?"

"I don't know, you tell me." Maliki could see the man's wildly frantic eyes; he didn't trust the bastard.

"I was taking her to my radio in the car, for help. I couldn't carry her and reach my weapon if he woke up and came after us." He nodded his head to the holstered weapon on the belt of his jeans. "She had to be awake. She had to walk up from there. Come on man, you know me! We grew up together!"

He stared at the crazed expression on the sheriff's face. He shook his head slowly from side to side. "I have no idea what you're talking about."

"My old man worked on your parents' estate

while I was in high school. You talked to me! You know me!"

"I don't know you." Mal's gut lurched. He really couldn't remember the man, but it didn't matter; the bastard wasn't going anywhere.

Maliki heard the vehicle racing up the drive. He held his gun on center mass of Watson's chest. Asher was out of the vehicle first. Mal held his weapon and shouted. "Downstairs! Another suspect."

"On it!" Asher and another man sprinted to the house.

"Handcuff this bastard!" Maliki bellowed.

"I've got it, Doc. I'm approaching now." Carter Hopson came into his view and walked behind the sheriff. "Jim, I'm handcuffing you now."

"I didn't do shit except get her the fuck out of there."

Hopson grabbed his right hand and angled it behind his back. "If that's the case, we'll get it sorted, and you can fire my ass. Until that happens, I'm following Guardian's directions like the AG directed me to do."

Mal holstered his weapon the second he heard the handcuffs click around Watson's wrists. He was beside Poet a heartbeat later.

"Okay, babe. We got them." He pushed her hair away from her face. The huge hematoma above her temple worried him. The break to her arm was obvious. Thankfully, the bones hadn't penetrated the skin. "Talk to me, Poet."

"Concussion. Nausea. Blurry vision. He broke my arm."

"Yeah, I can see that." The ambulance drove up, and he waved them over. "I want a backboard and collar, and we'll need an IV stat. Where is the nearest trauma center?"

"Charlottesville."

"Take us there."

"Sir, that is out of our catchment area."

Mal lifted his eyes from his examination. "I don't give a flying fuck. We are going to Charlottesville."

"They'll fire our asses," the man mumbled as he removed the backboard and cervical collar from the gurney.

"I promise you they won't." Jewell's voice rang from his pocket. The man's eyebrows lifted, and he shook his head, but got to work.

They prepped Poet and rolled her onto the backboard after stabilizing her neck. The female EMT tugged the t-shirt she was wearing down and patted Poet's leg. "We'll get you onto the gurney and covered up, honey."

Mal stood up as they secured her to the gurney for transport.

Asher headed his way. "Doc, there's a guy downstairs. He's dead."

"Dead? No! I didn't hit him that hard! He can't be dead!" Jim Watson howled, snapping their heads toward him. "He's my brother! God, no... please, no!"

"And that was unexpected. I'm on it." Jewell's voice snapped both Asher and Maliki back from Watson's spectacle.

"So who do you have in your pocket, Doc?"

He took the phone from his shirt. "Jewell King, Asher Hudson."

"Hi, Asher. Jared talks highly of you. I'm taking over this case as a favor to another brother, and man is he going to owe me for this one, because I'm busier than a supercomputer cracking an unsolvable problem. Forward me anything you need that hasn't been provided by my team. I'll get it to you ASAP along with the sheriff's genealogy as far back as the Niña, Pinta and Santa Maria. Mal, it was good to talk to you. I'll handle the EMTs' issues and take care of getting the billing sent to Guardian. Anyone need anything else? No? Good. Toodles."

Mal stared at the phone and then glanced at Asher. "Was that all in one breath?"

"Damn, I think so. That woman lives up to her reputation. Take care of your lady, give me a call when you can, and we'll get this settled."

"Roger that." He jogged over to the ambulance and helped the team load the gurney into the back of the bus. He grabbed the handle and stepped up into the back of the ambulance and the driver closed him in the back with the female EMT. He took Poet's hand in his. It was cold, but her pulse was strong. "It's over, babe."

She squeezed his hand a bit. "He said he killed them. Snuff films."

"Who said that?"

"The man in the mask."

"Jim?"

"I thought so. But... everything's blurry."

"Yeah, you probably got a wicked concussion. When did that happen? This morning?"

She squeezed his hand again. “Fought. Bit him hard, on the chest. Blood. Tasted blood.

"Was it Jim?"

"Mask."

"Okay. We'll talk about it later."

"You found me." She squeezed his hand again.

"I did. I'd never stop looking for you."

She smiled a bit, her eyes still shut. "You better watch it; you're going to fall for me."

"Yeah, too late, I already have."

She made a humming sound and the female EMT sniffed. He glanced up and the medic shifted her gaze to her clipboard, smiling.

CHAPTER 18

Maliki leaned against the hospital corridor wall and closed his eyes. Poet had undergone a CT scan to rule out any acute, life threatening, issues to her brain. Thankfully, there were no hematomas or edema that required emergency surgery. If her symptoms didn't abate soon, they would perform an MRI to make sure there weren't micro-hemorrhages, or contusions. Her injured arm needed surgery, but it was stabilized, and they were waiting for a second orthopedic specialist to consult. The ER doc had directed a rape kit be completed and forensic technicians had scraped under her fingernails, gathering evidence. He'd witnessed the procedures many times, this time... he drew a deep breath and opened his eyes.

Thankfully, Guardian had forwarded his certifications and license to the hospital. He'd been allowed to see her records, and the doctors and nurses briefed him on what was happening. The kit had come back negative, thank God.

She was being transferred to a private room, and he'd taken the nurses' advice and let them handle the transition. Still, he couldn't get the image of her on that stretcher, her body broken and bruised, out of his thoughts. The pain she'd endured... Her head injury had bled, but that wouldn't account for the condition of her fingernails. Her fingernails were broken and bloody. She'd fought with everything she had. The contusions and bruising, plus the shattered radius and ulna evidenced a horrific series of events. He'd called Asher, but he was interviewing Watson, and then Poet was wheeled to radiology. He followed her, his protective instinct overriding the probability that she'd be safe. What if he hadn't stopped by early? If he'd shown up at six instead of the middle of the afternoon? Would she still be alive?

"Hey."

Mal's eyes popped open, and he stood away from the wall. He was enfolded in a massive bear hug seconds later.

"What are you doing here?"

"Meh, it's a small up and down jaunt in a jet. We wanted to make sure you're okay." Jacob finally released him.

"We?" He glanced around Jacob. "Holy Shit." Jade and Jared walked down the hall toward him. "What in the hell? Who's running the operation in D.C.?"

"That's what I asked." Jade pushed Jacob out of the way and wrapped her arms around him, giving him a warm hug.

While still being hugged by Jade, he reached and shook Jared's hand. "Seriously, why are you here?"

Jade stepped back a bit and slugged him in the shoulder. "Because you're family, stupid."

"Ow. Damn." He rubbed his shoulder. "I don't think I want to be in your family. It's rather abusive."

"Ha ha. Stop being a wimp." She flipped her long black hair over her shoulder. "Joseph sent a mayday. You aren't answering your phone."

"What?" He reached into his pocket and extracted his cell. "Fuck, its dead. I had Jewell on the line forever today. It must have drained the battery. Still… three of you?"

"If we were in trouble, you'd come running? True?" Jade glanced up at him.

"Absolutely, but I'm not in trouble, Poet was." He threw a confused glance from one to the other.

"Uh huh. Well, I never took you for a slow one, Mal. We show up in force when our family or friends are in trouble. Your woman is in trouble. She qualifies as family." Jade shook her head as a slow smile spread across her face. "I wanna meet the woman who bagged you."

"Bagged?" Mal blinked at her, and then at Jared and Jacob, both of whom wore identical shit eating grins.

"Caught, tied up, enamored, fell in love with? Or is it still lust? Damn, where are the Double Ds when you need them?" She reached in her purse. "I'll call them and get more words."

"Ah, no. I get it." He smiled at her and shook his head. "It's still new. It might not be what you're insinuating."

"New? Right. How long did it take you to fall in love with Tori?" She pointed at Jacob.

"One airplane ride and one date." He shrugged. "She was it for me. I knew it the second she kissed me. Wasn't going to fight destiny."

"And you, before all the bullshit with you and

Christian, when did you fall for that man?" She pointed at Jared.

"One night. I woke up with him in my arms, and I was a goner." Jared smiled and winked at him. "And all we did that night was sleep."

"Nic wormed his way into my heart so fast it had to be a record, so don't drop that 'it's new' shit on us." She smiled up at him like a cat who'd not only found the cream but lapped all that shit up, too.

"So, how is she doing?" Jared asked.

"She's pretty banged up. A concussion, but the CT doesn't show any emergent issues. She'll have surgery to repair the arm the bastard broke. Do we know who he was?"

"I'm having that information sent to me as soon as we get it confirmed. Do you think she'll be up to answering a few questions?" Jared nodded down the hall where Poet was being settled into her private room.

"She's been given a very mild pain killer to take the edge off, but nothing that will interfere with the concussion protocols. They're bringing in a specialist for her break. The bastard shattered both her ulna and radius. She should be able to answer questions, but if we could limit them, I'd appreciate it."

"Have you given your statement yet?"

"No. I haven't even thought about the administrative end of the issue."

"Jewell has typed up hers and attached an audio of the telephone call. I reviewed it on the way down. When did you realize Poet was in trouble?"

"This afternoon. When I got to her apartment, her next-door neighbor was giving me a rash of shit for the early morning disturbance in Poet's apartment, only I hadn't been there. She'd had a call out, and I don't stay in her apartment when she's not there. I opened the door to her apartment, and her place had been trashed. I had the neighbor call 911. The deputies responded and secured the scene for Asher and took a statement from Tillie."

"Tillie?" Jared interrupted.

"The neighbor. Poet's friend. I called Joseph, and he called Jewell. The rest is on the recording."

"That is congruent with the rest of the information I'm getting. Shall we see if she can answer a few questions?" Jared nodded down the hall and fell into step with him as he moved to the room where Poet had been taken.

He checked in with the nursing staff before he and the Kings entered the room. Poet opened her eyes and blinked several times before she saw the way Jade was holding onto his arm. She crooked her finger, and he started toward her.

Poet lifted her hand stopping him. "No, her." Jade walked forward and stood by her bed. Poet nailed her with a stare. "He's mine. Hands off."

Jade threw back her head and laughed. "Oh, damn, Mal, I like this one." She patted Poet's arm. "Honey, I got my man. I don't want yours. My name's Jade DeMarco. That is my brother, Jacob King, and my other brother, Jared King. We work at Guardian. Jared is a cop like you. He'd like to ask you some questions. You okay with that?"

Poet nodded. "Memory is fuzzy."

Maliki moved up and took her hand. "That's to be expected." He swiped his thumb over her fingers, avoiding the IV catheter in the back of her hand.

"Poet, may I record this?"

"Sure."

Jared held his phone and hit some buttons. "This is Jared King with Poet Campbell. Also in attendance are Jacob King, Jade DeMarco and Doctor Maliki Blue. Poet, I'd like to discuss the events of today. Can you tell me in your own words what happened?"

She swallowed hard. "I was asleep."

"In your apartment?" Jared asked.

"Yes. Alone. Mal doesn't stay over when I get called out. He goes back to the inn. I got in late. I fell into bed. There was a light knock at the door. Early. It was still dark. I thought it was Mal. I stumbled to the door, and I didn't look through the peep hole. I unlocked it and opened the door. Someone pushed it into me and then came after me. We fought. He was fast and big. I got in some good punches. I kicked him in the balls. Hard. He shoved me off. I tried... I couldn't get to my room, for my gun. I fought him. He punched me in the jaw. I think I hit the wall." She closed her eyes, swallowed hard, and drew a deep breath.

"What happened then?"

"I woke up in my patrol vehicle. I tried to get away, but I went black again. The next time I woke up, I was in the basement of that house."

"Do you know who it was who took you?"

"I thought it was Jim."

"Jim?" Jared prodded.

"Jim Watson, the sheriff. When he leaned down in front of me, his blue eyes. I've been looking at those eyes for years. I could have sworn it was him."

"What happened then?"

"He beat me. Kicked me. My head again. I passed out. He lifted me up, hit me repeatedly. I don't know how long. He tased me. I lost consciousness again."

"How was your arm broken?"

"He tied me up on boards attached to the wall in the basement. I noticed the camera. I thought he was recording it. He said he was streaming it. That he got paid well for snuff films. I think that was why the other women were killed. Umm... he asked what I said to Guardian."

Jared nodded. "So you never saw his face?"

Poet closed her eyes for a moment. "No, he wore a black mask. Ski mask. Knit. I saw his eyes. Blue eyes. Voice sounded like Jim... sometimes. Sometimes it was high pitched and different."

"How did you get away?"

"Jim, he woke me up and was desperate to get me moving. Told me the man would come to and we needed to leave."

"Did you believe him?"

"There was a man on the floor, wearing a black mask."

"The clothes, were they the same?"

"Yeah. Jeans, denim shirt. Boots?" Her brow drilled down and furrowed. "There's something about the boots." She closed her eyes. "Something about the boots."

Jade interjected, "He kicked you with them?"

"Yeah." She opened her eyes, the furrow still tightly drawn.

Jared cleared his throat before he asked, "If you were asked to identify your assailant as James Watson with certainty, could you?"

She opened her eyes and stared at Maliki before a tear pushed clear of one eye and trailed down her cheek. She slowly turned toward Jared and spoke one simple word. "No."

"All right. We'll let you rest now. Don't worry, we're still on this case." Jared clicked his phone off and nodded to the door. Jacob and Jade walked from the room, but Maliki remained. Jared lifted an eyebrow in question.

"I'll be right there. Give me a couple minutes?"

"Take your time." Jared smiled at Poet and headed from the room.

Another tear slipped down her cheek. He reached up and wiped the trail away.

"I can't be sure."

He leaned down and kissed her nose softly and then swiped a soft kiss across her lips, avoiding the massive bruising on her face. He spoke quietly, "It doesn't matter. We'll get to the bottom of it. I promise."

"Who was the other man?"

"I don't know. I've been with you. I haven't been briefed."

She squeezed his hand. "You need to find out. You need to work this. I don't know them. I know you. I *know* you. Please, I can't... I'm..." Her eyes held his. The desperation in her plea gutted him.

Mal pushed her dark auburn hair from her eyes. "You're safe. I promise."

"Am I? With him out there?"

"One of them is dead, the other is in custody. They're contained."

"For how long? If I can't identify Watson, how long until he's cleared? I swear they were his eyes, but that voice wasn't..." She squeezed his hand. "I'm sorry. I'm not making sense."

"You're making perfect sense. Do you want me to contact your mom and dad?"

"No. No, they don't need to get involved in this. I'll call her later, after."

A nurse stepped into the room.

"I'm going to let her do her job. I'm not going far." She squeezed his hand again, and he lifted it carefully to his lips. "Rest."

He walked from the room, finding Jacob waiting for him. "Jared and Jade have headed down to the administrative wing to borrow a conference room."

"You didn't need to come. I appreciate it, however--" Mal stopped talking when a Charlottesville police officer slid into place by Poet's door.

"We don't know how long we'll be away. Jared contacted the Charlottesville Chief of Police and asked for the courtesy and promised him a favor should he ever need it. She'll have round the clock security."

Mal reached out and shook the man's hand. "Thank you, we appreciate the courtesy."

"No worries. We take care of our own." The officer hooked his thumbs in his black leather gear and leaned back against the wall. "No one without a Guardian or a hospital badge goes in. We're square."

Jacob slapped him on the shoulder, and they headed down the corridor.

He drew a breath and glanced at the man he'd

known for years as Alpha. "Back to what I was saying--"

"Look, you're not getting the big picture here. You and a few others were in on our ground level and build up. When we were elevated in the business, the people we could trust, grow with, and shape the company through, were handpicked. I picked every member of Foxtrot Team. Every fucking member. Your team leader failed you and your team, but the ultimate failure was mine. I didn't use the psych evals to my benefit. Sure, I looked at them. I asked the questions I thought were appropriate, but I failed to take into consideration the evaluator's notes, their intuition. Two of the three evaluators for your skipper warned he could be a risk due to his greed. Three years later, they were proved right."

"There was no way you could have known what he was doing." Mal shook his head. "Hell, I had no idea what was going on, and I was with them. At some point, we have to put those old ghosts to rest."

Jacob stopped and Maliki followed suit. "Have you?"

He shoved his hands into the front pockets of his jeans and nodded. "Yeah, you know what? I have. I'll always remember it, and I will probably always wonder if there was something I could have done differently, but at the end of the day, I did the best I could at the time."

Jacob's eyebrows lifted to almost his hairline. "Damn, this little trip has been beneficial, huh?"

He shrugged. "I've gained new perspective, listened to a woman who is a hell of a lot smarter than I am, and decided that I need to focus on today, not yesterday."

Jacob nodded. "My experience is women know what the fuck they're talking about. Not that I'll let Tori know. She thinks I'm perfect."

He lasted five seconds before he bent over laughing. Jacob gave him a shove. "Dick. Come on, Asher was going to call in."

Chuckling, Mal followed Jacob down the long hallway. They found the conference room with some help from a nice lady in the hospital administrator's office.

Jared held up a finger, stopping all conversation when they entered the conference room. "Okay Asher, I know you gave me a run down, but let's go through it one more time. Jewell, can you run these claims of Watson's in real time?"

"I can send requests for information as Asher

talks. I'll route them to your tablets as they come in. How is the deputy doing?"

"She's being taken care of." Maliki spoke for the first time. "Thanks to you, we were able to get to her in time."

"Yeah? I think it was a team effort, so give yourself a solid high-five, too, my friend. By the way, I have a couple people who volunteered for a little over time. We are going to find who was watching that shit, and we are going to get them. Even though that bastard wasn't recording the films, the people who paid to watch it more than likely have it recorded. According to the whispers on the Darknet, it costs about a hundred thousand for a full access seat at one of these... executions."

"Asher, what do you have?" Jared scribbled something in his notebook as he asked.

"The dead man is Darren Watson. He's half brother to James Watson. According to James, Darren was the result of an affair. Darren was born shortly after James. His mother and father reconciled, and the bastard son, Darren wasn't a part of the family. James said he didn't meet his half brother until his parents passed. He claims Darren was destitute and has lived in their house since his parents died. It was left to James, but he didn't need it, so he allowed Darren to live there."

"I see a birth certificate. The man is six months younger than James Watson. His mother is dead, father, John Watson, passed with his wife in a freak accident."

"Anything else on him?" Jacob leaned forward after he asked and grabbed a pen from the cup in the center of the table. He took a piece of paper from the back of Jade's notebook and was rewarded with a glare and a flip of the woman's hair.

He could hear Jewell type as she spoke. "Digging. Give me ten minutes and I'll be able to tell you his shoe size and what flavor ice cream he eats."

"Asher, how did Watson explain the fact that he 'found' Deputy Campbell?"

"He said he took personal time because his half brother was acting weird and that he was worried about him. He suggested the guy was suicidal. He said he couldn't deal with the job and his brother, so he took vacation. He was doing his daily check on him."

"Hold up." Jewell's voice cracked across the conference line. "Darren Watson was employed in

Charlottesville, a pharmaceutical representative. He has an apartment downtown. He's not destitute. Bank records show bi-weekly deposits in his bank account by Webster-Franklin-Cole Pharma. He pays his bills. Likes Thai and Italian food and has a membership at a crossfit gym and according to his online purchases, drinks a lot of protein drinks."

"So, Watson is lying." Mal leaned forward.

"Or was being lied to," Asher countered. "Don't get excited. We're still sorting the stories."

Mal sighed heavily and leaned back in his chair. Fuck, he wanted to pin this on the sheriff. His gut told him the man was complicit.

"I'm having someone contact Darren's office." Jewell interjected as the ever present tapping continued.

"Asher, what else did the sheriff give you?"

"He said he tackled his brother. He said his brother went limp, and he thought he'd knocked him out. He untied Poet and woke her to get her away from the basement."

Jared concurred, "That is flushing up with the other statements."

Asher asked, "Did we get the body to D.C. for an autopsy?"

"Our jet was loading the body as we left the Charlottesville Airport. He's probably already at the lab," Jacob answered.

"Affirmative. Body received and checked in. We have a certified private lab on standby for the tests. I'm keeping the AG away, for now." Jason's voice interrupted the conversation. "We can hold Watson for twenty-four hours based on the incident and our suspicions. Can we get a positive ID from the deputy?"

Jared sighed and scrubbed his face. "No. She couldn't be sure. He wore a mask and the voice is similar, but higher pitched than James Watson, according to her. But she has suffered a concussion. We'll debrief her further as she heals."

Mal leaned forward, "Within twenty-four hours that man will be back on the street."

Jared nodded and Jade made an exasperated sound and threw her pen onto the table. "You know, sometimes the law really gets in the way of fucking justice."

"We follow the law, Jade. Shortcuts will screw us in the long-run," Jared reminded his sister.

"I know that. I just don't *like* it."

"Jewell, compile everything and zip it to Asher. Asher, you will bring Doc Blue into this investigation. He has a vested interest," Jason dictated.

Asher acknowledged Archangel's orders. "Copy that. Is Deputy Campbell safe?"

"Charlottesville PD is supplying a guard. We'll get our own down here if she is kept more than a week."

Maliki shook his head. "Once her arm is repaired and her concussion issues start to resolve, she should be released. I'll take her home."

All three heads in the room looked at him. "As in…?"

He blinked at the question, before he realized what they were asking. He shook his head quickly. "No, my parents' estate. They have recently updated security and have a manned gate. Asher, you can run your investigation from there, too. If the sheriff is released, I don't like the chances of us being unmolested at the Paintville Inn."

"I can send a new team down. We have six of them that are in training. They can patrol the local area around the estate until we get a resolution on this," Jacob offered.

"I thought we were moving to a different composition of teams?" he whispered to Jacob.

The man winked at him and whispered back,

"Different missions, different compositions. What does one have to do with the other?"

Maliki leaned back and stared at the speaker in the middle of the table. Jared confirmed the team would be useful. Asher, however, declined. "I'll take you up on that if we see any indication of the sheriff doing anything other than being very helpful."

"Then we've got our assignments. Asher, call Mal at least twice a day and give him updates until Deputy Campbell is released. After that, if he is comfortable leaving her at his parents' residence, he can join you for the investigation."

"Roger that. Do me a favor and charge your phone?" Asher chuckled. "There was one pissed off dude looking for you. I swear that was the only time I heard Operator Two-Four-Seven speak with anything but dead calm. Whoever that guy was, he was scary."

Everyone in the room chuckled. Jason's voice broke up the meeting. "Mal, charge your phone. I think Joseph is going to have words with you about that. Jacob, Jared, and Jade, the plane should be on the ground by the time you get to the airport. Get back here. The rest of the world needs us, too. Maliki, if you need anything, you call. Archangel out."

"I'll get that info to you and Asher. The stuff I have coming in can fill a vat six feet deep. You'll have a lot of digging to do."

"It's what I'm good at. I'm going to go after the sheriff again with the new info about Darren's employment, residence and income. Maybe we can chip away at that airtight story of his. Hudson out."

"CCS out." Jewell hung up, too, and then dial tone was all that remained.

Jade stood up and reached over to swat the off button on the conference call device. "Well that sucked."

"We have to do this step by step. You know that." Jared picked up his tablet. "Mal, keep us posted on her condition. Poet has CPD at her door for the next week. If she needs to stay longer, we've got you covered." Jared extended his hand and shook his.

"Thank you, I appreciate everything you've done."

"We'll be expecting you in D.C. for dinner before you go back to the heat and Joseph's bossy ass." Jade lifted up and kissed him on the cheek.

"He's really not that bossy." His friend was

abrupt, brash and a dick at times, but bossy? Not so much.

"Yeah, and a rattle snake is not that poisonous." Jared slapped him on his back and winked as he followed his sister out the door. "Tori and I want to be at that dinner, Jade."

"Cool. We can do a private room at one of Justin's restaurants." She swung and blew a kiss at Mal as he closed the conference room door behind them.

He waved as they headed out of the building. Damn, it was good to have friends. Or rather family, chosen not given.

CHAPTER 19

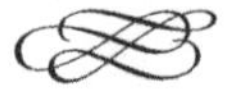

Maliki stepped out and nodded at the new officer on the exterior of Poet's door. She was resting after her surgery yesterday. Rods, pins and screws now replaced her shattered ulna and radius. Her blurry vision had cleared, and the other signs of concussion were lessening. If everything kept progressing, she'd be released the day after tomorrow. He rubbed the back of his neck and made his way down to the end of the hall. There was a window by the stairwell a floor down and on the other side of the building where his reception was best. He called Asher, instead of Asher calling him. It worked better for both of them if he initiated the calls.

"How is she?" Asher answered.

"She's a champ. She's resting now. She should be discharged the day after tomorrow."

"Thank God, something is going right." Asher sounded wrecked.

Maliki's shoulders slumped. "You no longer have him in custody."

"Yeah. We couldn't hold him any longer. We already surpassed the twenty-four hour limit. We exhausted all our probable cause." He swore bitterly. "Until we get something from the lab or the autopsy that ties him to Poet's abduction or any of those women's deaths, he's back wearing his uniform and pretending he's the hero in this event."

"Anything from Jewell and those traces on the video feeds?" Mal sat on the windowsill and leaned back against the glass. The cool feel of the smooth pane against his back felt good.

"Not that I've received. The autopsy concluded the preliminary cause of death for Darren was blunt force trauma."

"He died when James tackled him."

"Allegedly."

"You're not buying it?"

"Too tidy. The sheriff showing up and rescuing the damsel in distress. Poof, all the suspicion is off him and dumped on a guy who we believe was leading a pretty damn normal life. He doesn't have any extra income from the videos. I don't get it."

"What about the sheriff?"

"We need a warrant. Can you believe that shit? He's requested a lawyer, and he's charging our continued inquiry 'without cause' is purposefully maligning his reputation."

"There are no charges for killing his half brother?"

"Since we have jurisdiction, Jared ran it past the US Attorney General. At the bottom of this is the man who was allegedly acting to save another. He didn't use unnecessary force and fled with our victim without engaging again. It reads accident, but they are willing to wait to see if we can find any evidence that links the sheriff to the crime."

"Damn it. You know doctors are sworn to protect lives. I've bent that rule to the protection of my team members when I was assigned to a team, but I really wish Poet had bit the sheriff instead of his brother."

"What?" Asher's voice lowered.

"What, what?" Mal stood and looked through the window. "I can be vindictive. Bites hurt like a motherfucker and human bites tend to get infected. I wish that fucker all the pain in the world, you know what I mean?"

"There weren't any bite marks on the corpse. Fuck, where is that report." His attention snapped to what Asher was saying. "Here. No... no. No bite marks. Are you positive she said she bit him?"

"Absolutely. She said she bit him when she fought with him at the apartment."

"Fuck. How did I miss that? Did I know?" He could hear Asher going through the files in front of him.

Mal tensed. "I don't know if it was ever put in a statement."

"Look, I'm calling this in. We may have proof to nail his ass."

"If he hasn't fled already."

"He hasn't. We're monitoring him."

"And if it isn't enough?"

"Reports are coming hourly. Guardian is trying to track the URLs she gave me, but Jewell mentioned it might not be necessary. They have Doctor Giles' computer in D.C. and she's digging in. I'm buried in paper. There will be something. There has to be. I'm not giving up, and neither should you. Get back to her. As soon as she wakes up, we need to verify this bite information."

"Done." He dropped his phone into his pocket and made his way back to her room.

"Hey, Mom." Poet yawned and pushed the pillow behind her. She maneuvered the bed into a sitting position and put the phone on speaker. It was easier that way until they removed the IV from her good hand.

"How are you feeling today?"

"Ah… just waking up from a nap." She blinked and carefully rubbed her eyes with her good hand.

"Are you sure I can't come up?"

"I'm feeling a lot better and no, not yet, please. My department is working to close the case. Until that is done, I need to focus on work. You can mother me later. I promise to come down and let you fuss, soon." She stared at the gauze wrap on her arm. The doctors told her they would put it in a cast before they discharged her, but right now they wanted the swelling to go down a bit more before they encased the arm in plaster.

"So, are you going to tell me how you broke your arm?"

"I already told you. I was working. I can't say

much more because it is an ongoing investigation. Rules, you know." Poet rolled her eyes. Like she was going to tell her mom that she'd been abducted, beaten and her forearm shattered by a potential serial killer. That would go over *sooo* well.

Her mom made a noise in her throat and snipped, "I don't like your rules."

"I know, Mom, but they are in place for a reason."

"If you say so. So, tell me about this young man you're seeing."

"Maliki?"

"Yes, that is an interesting name."

"He's an interesting man. I told you he's a doctor, and he works for Guardian Security."

"But you said you didn't think it would ever be a relationship."

"Things change. I know I've changed in my attitude. We mesh, Mom. I've never been so relaxed and myself around a guy before. He's an amazing man. He makes me eat healthy."

"Well, that's a point in his favor."

She laughed and continued, "He's kind and generous, and he's been working through an old problem with his parents. That was why he came here to begin with. His dad is failing. He has dementia and has had a stroke. Maliki is mending those bridges. He's spent every day and night here with me, but he calls his dad and talks to him as much as possible in the morning. That's when his father is most likely to remember. Sometimes they talk for hours, sometimes only for minutes. He checks in with his mom, who is taking care of his father. Well, there is a staff full of healthcare workers, but his mother is running that show."

"Sounds like he is a good son."

"I think he is. They were estranged for a long time, but they're working through it."

"And how is he with you?"

She sucked in a breath and whispered, "Oh, Mom, he's amazing."

Her mother's voice lowered too, "You're in love with him, aren't you?"

She blinked back tears and nodded her head. "I think so. I can't imagine not being with him, you know?"

"Wait, you'd leave your job for him? The job you love?"

"Mom, I'd leave the country for him. He hasn't asked me to do that, though."

"Do you think he cares for you?"

"I do, but we haven't spoken those words, and I'm not going to put a decision in front of him." She picked at the woven white cotton blanket that covered her legs.

"One sided love doesn't work, sweetheart. He has to be as committed as you are for a relationship to last."

"I know. But when we started to see each other I told him it was temporary. He's only here for a few weeks longer. He has to go back to work."

"Well, that was stupid. Where does he work?"

"I don't know, Nevada, I think." She laughed again and wiped away another tear. "You call it like you see it, don't you?"

"Yes, and I taught you to do the same. Tell the man how you feel."

"It isn't that easy. What if he..."

"Imagining obstacles and stewing in doubt will get you exactly nowhere. Take it from an old woman. Don't let him leave without telling him how you feel. You're stronger than this. Are you sure you're okay?"

"I'm fine, Mom. Just a little emotional. It must be the meds?"

"Meds? Poet Marie Campbell what kind of meds are you on?"

Shit. "Ahh... something for infection and over the counter pain relievers." She glanced at the IV in her hand and shrugged. Okay, so not so over the counter. "Either that or it's the lack of sleep." She squinted one eye closed and stared at her phone, hoping her mom would buy it.

"Yeah, don't you think for a second that I believed either one of those excuses."

"How's Dad?"

"Changing the subject?"

"I'm attempting to do that, yes." She nodded her head at the phone as she talked.

"Fine, but only because you sound so much better than the last time we spoke. Well, your father is as stubborn as you and your brother. He is doing better on the greens, however he is horrible driving down those fairways..."

She leaned back on the pillow and listened to her mom regale her about her father's swing. According to her mother, he had none.

"Thanks for watching our girl. I'm going to sit with her for a while. You can grab a drink or a bathroom break if you need it."

The officer smiled. "Perfect. I'll be about twenty minutes or so. I need to stretch my legs. The Doc let me grab some food earlier. He'll be gone for a half hour or so. He usually stretches his legs about this time."

"I'll see him when he gets back. Go ahead, take your time."

"Thanks again, and listen, I'm sorry about your deputy. She's been knocked around pretty hard."

"We'll find the son of a bitch responsible. He'll pay for his actions."

"Thanks, Sheriff. I'll pop my head in when I get back."

"That works."

He watched the officer stroll down the hall and moved into the darkened room. She was pale against the white sheets. Her hair around her shoulders was dark in the dim light of the room. The arm he'd broken was wrapped in gauze, but not yet cast. He smiled and recalled her scream. It was... *magnificent*. He'd give anything to finish his performance with her. It was a far better demonstration than the drugs and alcohol poisoning had been, but then he didn't pick the means of death, he only did as his audience requested.

He slid his hand into his leather gloves and

then withdrew the small black case from his pocket. He extracted the syringe of high-test heroine. "Too bad I won't hear you beg for mercy." He placed the needle in the IV port and depressed the plunger, opening the drip until the heroine fed into the tubing and then closed it to the same position it had been in.

Maliki watched on the closed circuit monitor two rooms down the hall. The motherfucking bastard. "This is recording, right?"

"Yes." The technician Guardian had sent down from D.C. confirmed it again. "Redundancy is running, too. Damn, look at that." The tech pointed to the screen as the sheriff pushed the syringe into the IV.

"Wait for it." A sneer lifted Maliki's lip. A man dressed in black walked up behind the fucker. A glint of steel flashed. Mal bolted from the room, and the cop that had left the door moments ago followed him.

He flicked on the lights and rushed to Poet's side. Joseph held a wicked looking knife at Jim Watson's throat. The man's eyes bulged; his face was so red it was tinged with purple. The sheriff dropped the syringe. "He was trying to kill her! I stopped him!"

Poet sat up carefully, moving as far away from Watson as she could get. Mal gently gathered her toward him, wrapping her in his arms.

A low hiss of words rolled from Joseph. "Too bad I won't hear *you* beg for mercy."

Watson roared, "He's the one! He tried to kill her!"

Mal shook his head and sneered before he informed Watson of the sting. "We have everything recorded, Sheriff."

"No! I didn't do it! He did it! I stopped him at the house! I stopped him here!" Spittle hung from the corner of his mouth and his chest heaved, but he didn't move a muscle. "Poet, tell them! Tell them I saved you!"

Mal tore his eyes from Watson. "Joseph, his left pec."

Joseph's knife dug and lifted. The sheriff rose to his toes as Joseph ripped open the front of the man's shirt and exposed a weeping, infected bite mark.

"It was you. You took me, you beat me, and you killed the man who tried to save me." Poet's voice was low and quiet. "You killed those women because you wanted to."

"No! It was him! Can't you see? He did it! *He* did it!" The man wailed and his voice morphed into a high-pitched, hysterical, laugh.

"Cuff him." Joseph held his knife precariously on the sheriff's throat while the deputy slapped the handcuffs on him in record time. When he removed his knife there was a thin red line that oozed several drops of blood. Damn, that fucker had to be sharper than a razor.

"I saved them! I made it right! He killed them." The sheriff's shouts brought a crowd of medical workers from various rooms. Four Guardian operatives split the crowd like Moses splitting the Red Sea and sauntered down the hall toward the room. Two men he recognized from The Rose grabbed Watson, and one of them helped the officer escort the shrieking man from the hospital to the waiting Guardian vehicle. He was in federal custody now and wasn't going anywhere

"Are you okay?" He dropped a kiss to Poet's forehead. She was pale, but steady.

"Yeah. Here, you'll need this." She produced a bag from under the cover. It was attached to the IV, not her, and held whatever Watson had pushed through the port. The second man placed the bag and the syringe that had fallen to the floor into separate bags. "Tech is set up where?" The man asked quietly. Mal directed him, and he exited the room.

She looked over at Joseph who was wiping his knife on the back of his leg, any blood on the steel would be hidden by his black fatigues. "Thank you. I didn't hear you come into the room."

"Poet, this is Joseph."

"Ah, the one on the phone. How did you open the door without alerting him? It's so noisy in the hall." She leaned against Mal, and he felt her relax

"I've been in your room since your nap this afternoon." He nodded to the closet door that stood ajar. "We had a tracker on Watson, and saw he left town this morning. When my men informed me of his movement, I assumed my position." Joseph shrugged as if staying motionless in a confined space for over six hours was nothing.

Her brow furrowed, and she angled her head when she asked, "You've been in there? Since... when?"

"About one. You were sleeping when I arrived. I didn't want to disturb you."

"How did you get in? The officer outside the door, did he know?"

Mal said, "No, I relieved him so he could take a break, then there was shift change at about three and the new officer was in place. We suspected Watson was going to try to get to you because of the heroin Guardian's ME found in Shauna's blood. Watson's lawyers had stopped us from questioning him, but Watson knew Asher left the area."

"How?" Poet bounced her gaze between Joseph and him.

"Because Asher went to the station and told Watson he'd be back. He told the sheriff you were starting to remember what happened. He put you on the hook as our bait. Watson's world was back to the status quo, except for one thing. You." He ran his fingers up Poet's back and gently massaged her neck.

"Right, you explained most of that when we organized the little operation this afternoon, but..." She blinked at him. "You knew he was in here, and you *didn't* tell me?"

"I did know, and no, I didn't tell you. You're one of the bravest women I've ever met. You agreed to be the worm on our hook for this operation, but I wasn't going to let that maniac in your room without someone here. Joseph would have stopped him if he'd tried anything else."

She lifted the sheet and gripped the ass end of her nine mil. "He'd be dead twice, then." She turned and stared at Joseph. "So, you heard my conversation on the phone today?"

Joseph crossed his arms over his chest. "Nope. Couldn't hear shit in there."

Joseph and Poet both glanced at the closet—the closet that had wide mesh ventilation inserts at the bottom and the top.

Mal narrowed his eyes. "Why? What conversation?"

"Nothing." Poet and Joseph spoke at the same time. He stared at both of them and opened his mouth to speak but was interrupted.

"Damn, Doc, someone told me you were on vacation. Remind me never to share a condo on the beach with you." Dan Collins filled the awkward silence.

Mal sent Joseph one more side-eyed glance, which was met with a sneer, before he smiled at Dan. "See you got paired up."

"Meh, who knew that asshole would pair me up with this guy." Dan threw his head toward a man Doc recognized. The one who communicated with sign language. "Sage Browning, this is Doc Blue."

"We've met in passing." Mal extended his hand. "Good to see you again."

The man nodded and smiled.

"This is Deputy Poet Campbell. She's the one who cracked this case."

"I didn't." Poet chuckled and smiled at Dan and Sage. "Nice to meet you."

"Don't sell yourself short." Joseph headed to the door. He stopped at the door and turned around. "And for the record. I agree with your mother." He slipped out, and Dan and Sage left in his wake.

Poet pointed at the place where Dan had stood. "Doesn't he look like that guy from the movies--"

"He gets that all the time, but he's not. Now, why would Joseph agree with your mother?"

"Long story." Poet sighed and lifted the sheet and white blanket up over her legs.

He helped her lie back down on the bed and removed the fake IV cannula from the top of her hand. Her weapon went on the bedside stand, and he picked up a small clear plastic cup with two pills in it. "Take these now. You've got to be hurting."

"I am." She tossed back the pills and took a drink of the water he provided.

He tugged her covers up and tucked her in before he sat beside her on the bed. He grabbed her hand and ran his thumb over it. "Care to let me in on the secret now?"

She smiled and shook her head. "It was some motherly advice. Joseph heard it. Obviously."

"And what did your mom advise you to do?" He pushed her hair away from her face, and she leaned her cheek into his palm, closing her eyes for a moment.

When she opened them, she said quietly, "She told me to make sure you knew how I felt about you."

His heart beat so hard she had to have heard the pounding from where she lay. "How do you feel about me?"

"I don't want this to end."

"This? Us?" He released a shaky breath. "I can't stay here. I've been honest."

"I'm not asking you to do that." She grabbed his hand. "I know it's only been a couple weeks. I'm not asking a lifetime commitment, but I want to see where this goes. If you don't, please tell me now. We've been through a lot. I'll understand if you don't think we'll work."

He took her hand in his and stared at her, gathering in her strength and beauty. The bruising had diminished, but was still there, a yellowish blue hue spotting her face. "Yeah we have been through some shit, haven't we? I want to see where this goes. I need to see where this attraction will lead us, but..."

"But?" Her eyes, huge pools of blue, stared up at him.

"My career path is in transition right now. It could be a while before I know what I'm going to do, or where I'm going to be when I do it." He licked his lips and drew a deep breath. His hands were trembling, but he forced himself to be honest. "It could mean you moving closer to where I am. Giving up your job." He held up a hand to stop her from speaking. God, he had to get this out, for her to have all the information. "I know that is a shit thing to ask. You've built seniority here. You've got a life here, but I can't come back to Paintville. I'll visit because my parents are here, but I couldn't live here. The closest work to this county Guardian could offer me would be in D.C. And that would only happen if they could find a position for me there. If we're trying to see how we fit, being apart, even that limited distance, isn't going to work for me."

She blinked several times and then shrugged. "Do you think Guardian has any employment opportunities?"

"What?"

"I've never looked at their website. Would I be someone they'd look at? I mean, I've got my basic law enforcement certificate. Years of on the job experience. I'm prior military. I have an excellent work record, and I'm a team player... well, minus calling Guardian on my serial-killer boss. But, I'm sure a recommendation from you probably wouldn't hurt. If I worked for Guardian, maybe I could be co-located with you. Unless they have a policy against that?"

A fucking shiver went down his spine. She was committed enough to move to be close to him. He smiled. "No, no policy that I'm aware of."

"So?" She reached up and urged him down to her lips. "Are we doing this?"

He sipped at those lips and took a long deep drink before he slowed and then stopped the kiss. He rested his forehead against hers. They had undeniable chemistry. He liked her, hell, he cared for her, deeply. If she hadn't asked him, he'd have initiated the conversation. Everything felt right. Everything.

He stood, turned and rubbed the back of his neck. He drew a deep breath. "I'm in. Under one condition." He kept his back to her, the smile that split his face hurt it was so fucking wide.

"What?"

The trepidation in her voice spun him around. "You have to teach me how to play Super Donkey Mario Kong."

She closed her eyes and laughed. "Deal, but when you figure it out, I'm going to show you no mercy."

He leaned over her hospital bed and kissed her. "I look forward to that challenge."

CHAPTER 20

Poet's hand rubbed up and down his back. He didn't hear the minister's words or recognize most of the people in attendance. His father's casket lowered into the ground, and he and his mother stood and threw in the first handfuls of dirt. Neither cried. There were no more tears. He escorted his mother and Poet from the family graveyard to the waiting limo. They were going to the house, for a reception.

"It was the way he wanted to go," his mother said while looking through the window. "He hated the dementia. It terrified him."

A massive stroke took him three weeks after Poet was released from the hospital. Mal and Poet had stayed in the mansion the entire time. His mother doted on Poet, and he spent every morning with his father. They'd mended the damage that existed between them. Years of regrets still existed, at least for him.

"He told me the day before he died that he was so proud of you." She chuckled and shook her head. "Then he said you needed to shave that damn beard, or no one would take you seriously. Your father, ever the control freak."

"Surgeons tend to be that way," Poet said and patted his hand in a condescending fashion.

His mother chuckled again. "I'll miss him. He was my friend." Tears shimmered in her eyes. "We never had what you two have. That spark, the connection. Never let anything come between you two. Obligations, status, expectations of others, all of it is worthless drivel."

"What are you going to do now, Mother?"

"Oh, I'll continue living here. The Boswell fortune flows to you, but if you'll allow it, I'll keep the house here."

"I want you to have it. It's your home." He'd make damn sure it was maintained and guarded to keep her safe as she aged.

"Of course, someday, my grandchildren could visit me."

He cut a quick look at Poet who smiled and then laughed. "Catherine, I believe you're putting the cart before the horse."

"Oh?"

"We should probably get married before you plan grandchildren." Poet squeezed his hand at his comment.

"True." His mother turned her stare to him. "When can I expect that?"

"Mother," he warned, and she smiled impishly at him.

"I'll wait, but not for long." She turned and looked through the limo's window again.

Poet chuckled and dropped her head onto his shoulder. She'd physically recovered from the abduction. Her arm had three more weeks in the cast. Nightmares weren't frequent, but when she did have them, they were hard to shake after he woke her. He understood that, hell, after losing his team, he'd dealt with nightmares, too.

"Before we get to the house and I have to act as hostess, when will you be leaving?"

"I'm not sure, Mom. I'll need to settle the estate, and then I need to meet with my employers. I have to make several decisions. Why?"

"I've been thinking of taking a cruise. I want to

live here for the rest of my life, but the last few years have been hard. I thought a vacation may be in order."

"Will Richard accompany you?" The idea of his mother in the middle of the ocean alone bothered him. Not that Richard made him feel much better...

"No. I'm afraid Richard had the wrong idea about our relationship. He assumed I'd be moving in with him. No, I'm not marrying or sharing my home with anyone except grandchildren. I have a friend, Alexandria, you've met her before. Her family is in plastics. She recently lost her husband, and she's scheduled a trip. I'd like to go with her and take Lucinda. Sweet Lucinda wouldn't have much to do to look after me, but she's been so good to me, I thought the cruise would be a nice way to say thank you."

"It sounds like a wonderful time. By all means, go with Alexandria and Lucinda. We can stay in D.C."

"You wouldn't mind?"

He shook his head. As a matter of fact, he'd prefer it. "Not at all."

"Wonderful. We'd leave in ten days."

"I meet with Father's lawyers tomorrow. If Poet

is up to it, we can head to D.C. on the weekend, and we'll let you close up the house."

"I'm good with that. I need to say goodbye to Tillie, and I'll need to spend a day or two packing up my apartment."

Mal squeezed her hand. She'd been back to the apartment once since she'd been abducted. He leaned over and whispered, "We can have a moving company come in and pack you up."

She lifted her head and accepted the kiss he offered. "True, but I want to get a few things anyway."

"We'll make the trip, then." He was rewarded with a dazzling smile.

They drove up to the house and exited the car. A long string of vehicles crested the hill in a procession to the house. "Well, son, are you ready for this?" His mother stood on the steps and looked at the slow-moving vehicles heading their way.

He put his arm around Poet and held her close as he glanced at his mother. "None of us are ever ready for days like today, but we'll do the best we can."

He held his mother's elbow as the last couple left the porch where they'd put on the reception. "I'm exhausted."

He had no doubt. She'd been 'on,' ensuring the food and drink was perfect, that each guest was greeted, and smiled through countless stories of her late husband. Richard had paid his respects and left shortly after arriving. "I can imagine. Richard didn't stay long." He turned his mom toward the house, and they strolled together.

"Oh, he's in a snit. He'll get over it. He can be quite child-like if he doesn't get his way. Much like your father was when we first were married."

"Did you ever think Dad was your soulmate?" They entered the house and their footsteps echoed on the elaborate marquetry floor.

"No. We married because it was expected." She stopped and turned to him. "I rue the day your father hurt you, and then I was complicit with my silence, but sadly it did have one silver lining. Clarissa wasn't right for you."

"Ours was a shallow relationship, of course at the time, her lack of faith hurt."

"I'm sure it did. But now you have Poet. She's such a wonderful person."

"Would you have thought that ten years ago?"

His mother blushed and shook her head. "No, but I'm not who I was ten years ago."

"Nor am I."

"She's wonderful, and I can see the connection between you."

"We're happy together and hoping for a future." He was falling in love with the woman, of that he was certain. The future was still unfolding. They'd agreed to take it one day at a time, and it seemed that pace was where they needed to be.

"Hopefully that future will include marriage."

"One day, perhaps." He patted his mother's hand and started walking toward the stairs leading to her quarters.

"Have I mentioned I'd like grandchildren?"

"At least once a day since we've taken up residence."

His mother laughed, "Only once? I'll have to do better."

She stopped him at the bottom of the stairs and nodded to the guest wing where they'd been staying. "I can make it to my room. I'll have the chef send something up for dinner. You two spend some time together."

"We'll do that." He lowered and kissed his mother on the cheek. "Good night."

He watched her climb the stairs and then headed the other direction to the suite of rooms that overlooked the gardens.

Poet smiled at him when he walked in. With a careless shrug he lost his suit jacket and flopped it over the back of one of the sofas on his way to her. He tugged at his silk tie and loosened the knot before he unfastened the button at his throat. Straddling her legs on the chaise lounge, he crawled to her and kissed her before he landed on his side and moved her closer.

"It was a long day. I bet you're exhausted." She pushed his hair from his brow and then ran her fingers through his beard. Her fascination with his beard made him smile every time she combed through it.

She kissed him, and he lost himself for a moment. She moved away and placed her good hand on his chest. "How's your mom?"

"Tired. How are you?"

"Fine. I needed to take some anti-inflammatories and keep this elevated for a bit. The swelling is gone." She wiggled the fingers of her casted arm, tickling his stomach. "I'm sorry for leaving early."

"A half hour is not early. I'm sorry for my mother's comments... again."

Poet chuckled. "How about a compromise. You stop apologizing about *your* mother's comments, and I'll stop apologizing about *my* mother's. They are cut from the same fabric. I think they've already planned our wedding and named their grandchildren." She used her good hand to unbutton the rest of his shirt.

"Nothing like outside pressure." He removed his tie and unfastened his cufflinks, dropping them onto the table beside the chaise.

"They're harmless. We have so many other things we need to worry about." She leaned forward and kissed his throat.

"Like?" He pushed his hips into her.

"Like how long will it take us to get to the bed." She smiled up at him.

"That is definitely a worry. What else?" He rolled on top of her and kissed her collarbone, moving her silky top with his lips.

"Is Guardian going to accept my application? Where are we going to live? How many orgasms are you going to give me tonight? How many am I going to give you?"

He lifted her shirt and kissed the lace edge of her bra. "Guardian would be a fool not to accept you. We'll live together. The place is irrelevant." He nudged the fabric out of the way and swirled his tongue, teasing her nipple until it tightened. "What was the other concern?"

"Ahh... orgasms. Mine... yours." She ran her hand through his hair as he delved lower and dipped his tongue into her belly button. She giggled and curved up, dislodging him.

He stood and extended a hand to her. She took his hand, and he helped her to stand, then wrapped his arms around that small waist and walked her backward as they kissed. They bumped into an end table and something hit the floor with a thud. She attempted to pull away, but he kept walking her backward, kissing her until she wrapped her good arm around him. The closed bedroom door played backstop for several minutes. He managed to undo her slacks and drop them to the floor. She stepped from them and tilted her head back as he feasted on her long, slender neck.

Finally, he turned the knob on the door, and they almost fell when it swung open. Her laughter and his preceded them to the bed. He broke the kiss long enough to remove the rest of her clothing, careful not to catch her shirt on the cast. She squirmed to the middle of the bed as he shrugged out of his clothes and moved to cover her.

He entered her slowly and bare. They'd ditched the condoms after they'd agreed to a committed relationship. The definition for both of them was exclusive. Any other labels weren't welcome. The sexual chemistry flowed between them like molten lava, and from that current, the progression of their time together produced a fertile soil to nurture their relationship.

He held his weight over her, careful of the cast. They'd experimented, finding ways to stoke the heat between them. She wrapped one arm around his neck, but he didn't lower to her this time. Her flushed cheeks and kiss-swollen lips were the most beautiful things he'd ever seen.

"What?" She smiled up at him and arched her hips, seating him deeper inside of her.

"Is it too early to tell you that I'm in love with you?" He withdrew and moved forward slowly.

Her eyes fluttered shut, and she sighed. "I know."

He chuckled. "You know?"

"Mmmm... just like you know I love you." She opened her blue eyes and tugged at him again, wanting a kiss.

He lowered and spoke against her lips. "You're amazing."

A low sexy laugh rumbled through her. "We're amazing… together. Now shut up and give me an orgasm."

"Bossy." He nipped at her lips with his teeth, finally kissing her when she begged.

He held her as she shattered under him. His orgasm was stolen from him when her body gripped tightly around his shaft.

Poet rolled on her good arm and pressed against him, connecting flesh against flesh. "I'm looking forward to finding my future, with you."

He trailed his fingertips along her arm. "It won't be easy."

She sighed. "Nothing in life that is worthwhile is easy, but I promise to do the best I can to be your lover, and partner in life, each and every day."

He turned toward her and lifted her chin, echoing her words back to her. "I promise to do the best I can to be your lover, and partner in life, each and every day."

"Don't tell our moms, but I think we made a commitment." She kissed him and snuggled closer.

He sighed and closed his eyes. They had. It was a commitment, a promise, and a new way of looking at life. One he'd cherish and grow with each passing day.

EPILOGUE

Mal took a drink of his green tea. "The sentencing wasn't a surprise to anyone."

"I hate it. That bastard should be in jail, not a mental institution." Jason leaned back and took a long pull from his soda can.

"Poet called it. Giles and Watson were in this together. Finding all the recordings on Giles' computer put the murders on Watson. Same mask, same clothes, same size and the eyes when they are on film match Watson. That phone with the URLs on it had to have been dropped by Watson or Giles at the first death scene. As far as the computer files Jewell extracted, the originating IP address was the same each time. The same IP assigned to the computer equipment that was taken from the house. Watson killed those women and Giles had the films for each of the murders. I feel sorry for his half brother. The man was in the absolute wrong place at the wrong time."

"Why did his brother go to the house? I never understood the timing or the reason for that man showing up."

"Yeah, the half brother was the actual owner of the house. He was paying Watson for the house. It was a purchase agreement they'd finalized with a lawyer. Jewell tracked the money and the paperwork."

"I got that, but why *that* day?" Jason took off his glasses and rubbed the bridge of his nose.

"Believe it or not a water bill is why he went down to the house."

"A what?"

"His girlfriend said he got a water bill for the house that was over three hundred dollars. Since they'd only stayed at the house once they thought a pipe may have broken. He went to the house to check on it."

"What was Watson using so much water on?"

"He wasn't. The pipe from the road had broken. That's why it was so damn muddy when I was going through the woods."

"How did Watson think he could get away murdering his brother?"

"I don't know. When I stopped him in front of the house, he was trying to get Poet to his car. My gut is telling me he was going to finish what he started. He had a fall back plan, but I don't know if we'll ever find out what that was. He's not talking."

"The DNA on the mask had both Watson's and his half brother's markers on the inside." Jason shook his head. "He isn't mentally insane."

Mal shook his head. "I don't know. I saw him in that jail cell before they transferred him. He was having a conversation, but there was no one in the cell with him. Seemed like there was enough evidence to support a possible psychiatric diagnosis to me."

"I don't believe that act for a second, but the shrinks must. He's fucking smart and devious. He should be on death row." Jason growled. "But rehashing Watson isn't why you're here. Is it?"

"I'll trash that man every chance I get, but no. I was hoping for a final decision."

Jason reached for and opened a file on his desk and nodded. "We've approved your proposal. It'll be an uphill struggle. The areas they drop you into could be hostile." Jason tossed the folder across his desk.

Mal picked it up and fixated on the big red 'Approved' sticker on the outside of the cover. "Anything worthwhile always is a struggle, and I'm confident we'll be able to cover each other's six." He'd brought this proposal to Jason six months ago. After it had been reviewed by God and creation, Jason had finally signed off on his request to become a deployable medic. The prompt for the idea came after they'd lost several team members that might have made it if a medic could be deployed to reach the injured Guardian within the first twenty-four hours. It was what he trained in the Air Force to do, but now he was doing it as a doctor, *with* his assistant.

"Is she jump certified yet?"

"Hell, yeah. We both recertified. Accelerated Freefall Skydive Training. Poet aced her advanced EMT certification, and we've both made it through the physical skills challenge at The Rose."

Jason chuckled. "How did she take to staying above ground at the facility and being blindfolded on the drive?"

"Honestly, she fell asleep on the way there and back. Poet doesn't want to know anything about the place. She never suspected there was anything underground. She and Tempest spent time together when I wasn't around. Other than that, she studied and kicked ass on all her tests."

"How is Tempest?"

"He's... he's recovering. He's getting back into training. He's determined. He'll make it."

"It's been a long slow recovery."

"Physically, Ember could release him at any time. He's fit enough."

"Wheeler has a few more assessments to do."

"Agreed. One other thing. Poet and I are getting married. You're invited. My mom and hers are going crazy with the plans. Poet told them she was picking her dress and the rest of it was totally up to them. So, would you care to be one of the multitudes coming to the event?"

"Multitudes?"

"People we didn't even know we knew are coming. Six hundred guests so far."

"Holy hell. Do you need crowd control?"

"Don't offer it, I may take you up on it."

"I think I may decline. Taking the family into crowds takes extra teams for security."

"Sure, I get that, but you're giving up a chance to see Joseph in a tux."

Jason froze and blinked once before turning his head slowly back to him. "What?"

He smiled. "He's my best man."

"Does the rest of the family know?"

Mal smiled and stood up. "Nah, I thought I'd leave that pleasure to you."

"Holy fuck, Mal, you made my year." Jason stood and cuffed him on the shoulder with one of his meaty paws.

Mal caught himself before he stumbled forward. "And you made mine by approving this program. Poet and I will be an asset."

"I know it. Otherwise I wouldn't have authorized it." Jason gave him another pat on the back before he made his exit. Damn, that man did not know his own strength.

He made his way to the elevator and got in. As the door started to close a hand split the doors and they reopened. *Holy shit.*

Mal chuckled and extended his hand. "Damn, I didn't expect to see you here."

The man smiled and shook his hand. "I'm not really here, so..."

He knew John from his workings at The Rose. What he did to alter government documentation and personal histories was fucking amazing. He was rumored to have worked for several agencies at one time. It was also whispered that one of those agencies had tried to have him eliminated. Why he was in D.C. was beyond his limited comprehension. "I understand. How have you been?"

"I've been... existing." The man shrugged.

Mal wondered if his past haunted him, if the rumors were true and he was a hunted man. It wasn't his concern, but he liked the guy. "Sometimes that's all we can do."

"Indeed." He smiled briefly and spoke as the door opened. "My stop. Good day, Doctor Blue."

"Good day, Mr. Smith." Mal watched the man until the door shut. He glanced at the lighted display as the floors descended, and it occurred to him that the demons of past lives and deeds haunted most people. It appeared John Smith was no exception.

The End

ALSO BY KRIS MICHAELS

Hope City

HOPE CITY DUET - Brock and Sean

HOPE CITY - Brody- Book 3

Kings of the Guardian Series

Jacob: Kings of the Guardian Book 1

Joseph: Kings of the Guardian Book 2

Adam: Kings of the Guardian Book 3

Jason: Kings of the Guardian Book 4

Jared: Kings of the Guardian Book 5

Jasmine: Kings of the Guardian Book 6

Chief: The Kings of Guardian Book 7

Jewell: Kings of the Guardian Book 8

Jade: Kings of the Guardian Book 9

Justin: Kings of the Guardian Book 10

Christmas with the Kings The Kings of Guardian

Drake: Kings of the Guardian Book 11

Dixon: Kings of the Guardian Book 12

Passages: The Kings of Guardian Book 13

A Backwater Blessing: A Kings of Guardian and Heart's Desire Crossover Novella

Montana Guardian: A Kings of Guardian Novella

Guardian Defenders Series

Gabriel

Maliki

Guardian Security Shadow World

Anubis (Guardian Shadow World Book 1)

Asp (Guardian Shadow World Book 2)

Lycos (Guardian Shadow World Book 3)

Thanatos (Guardian Shadow World Book 4)

Everlight Series

An Evidence of Magic (Everlight Book 1)

An Incident of Magic (Everlight Book 2)

STAND ALONE NOVELS

SEAL Forever - Silver SEALs

A Heart's Desire - Stand Alone

Hot SEAL, Single Malt (SEALs in Paradise)

Hot SEAL, Savannah Nights (SEALs in Paradise)

ABOUT THE AUTHOR

USA Today and Amazon Bestselling Author, Kris Michaels is the alter ego of a happily married wife and mother. She writes romance, usually with characters from military and law enforcement backgrounds.

Made in the USA
Coppell, TX
11 March 2024